THE HUNGER OF THE WOLF

A NOVEL

Stephen Marche

Simon & Schuster
New York   London   Toronto   Sydney   New Delhi

Simon & Schuster
1230 Avenue of the Americas
New York, NY 10020

First Simon & Schuster hardcover edition February 2015

SIMON & SCHUSTER and colophon are registered trademarks of Simon & Schuster, Inc.

For information about special discounts for bulk purchases, please contact Simon & Schuster Special Sales at 1-866-506-1949 or business@simonandschuster.com.

The Simon & Schuster Speakers Bureau can bring authors to your live event. For more information or to book an event, contact the Simon & Schuster Speakers Bureau at 1-866-248-3049 or visit our website at www.simonspeakers.com.

Interior design by Jill Putorti

Manufactured in the United States of America

10   9   8   7   6   5   4   3   2   1

Library of Congress Cataloging-in-Publication Data is available.

ISBN 978-1-4767-3081-3
ISBN 978-1-4767-3083-7 (ebook)

In memory of Sunny Marche

"All money is a matter of belief."

—ADAM SMITH

THE
HUNGER
OF THE
WOLF

ONE

Hunters found his body naked in the snow. Peter and Samuel Seguin, Cree brothers who drove from Tamaskan to North Lake every February to shoot moose, stumbled on Ben Wylie in a small clearing of aspens at the end of an abandoned lumber road, his corpse encircled by curiously hesitant ravens. "We were all, like, pow, because he was naked and it was cold and he was just a man to us. We didn't know what it was that we were looking at," Samuel Seguin told the reporter from *Bloomberg*. Only after they had delivered up the body would the brothers learn that the man in the snow, far from being nobody, was the eighth-richest person in the world. Curled naked in the killing cold lay twenty-seven billion dollars.

The Seguins could never have recognized Ben Wylie. Through discipline and money, he had willed himself into irrelevance. By 2009, his photograph hadn't appeared in a newspaper for twenty-one years and business pages rarely feature stories about the Wylie companies despite their enormous size. Wealth of the Wylie magnitude, money on the scale of small governments fashioned from the profitable organization of hundreds of thousands of people, can grant itself the power of invisibility, fading into the fabric of everyday life. Capitalism can be good, proper, brutal fun, the biggest schoolyard game in the world. Some kids take all the candy and some kids lose eyes and other kids run home crying. But WylieCorp is too big to be fun. Even the death of the owner warranted, in the judgment of the world's capital-allotment, less than a half-point drop in its stock price.

The obituarists had to splay their quarter pages with Ben's grainy appearance at a shareholder's meeting in 1988—more like Bigfoot in the swamps than a human being. The picture has always been a favorite of newspaper editors, particularly the older, more showoffishly jaded ones, with Ben in well-worn budget sneakers and a suit seemingly borrowed from a middle-management uncle. The most famous photograph of Ben's grandfather, Dale Wylie, caught him stooping for a sixpence on Fleet Street the day he purchased *The Record of London* in 1964—at that time the largest media deal in history. Ben's father, George Wylie, appeared at a public offering of bonds on the NYSE with a four-stitch tear down the back seam of his jacket. Ben's 1988 picture fit the well-established pattern of the legendary penny-pinching Wylies; he looked exactly like the scion of the world's cheapest billionaires.

The hustled, deadlined world tells only the stories it has told before. Rather than the mystery of Ben's death, the magical scene in the snow, the frost-shrouded, fetally coiled symbol revealed in the openness of a primeval clearing, the reporters ran with drudgery, the family pattern, the inheritance of melodramatic restraint. He died "in a freak hunting accident," *Bloomberg* mentioned before reciting the list of companies he had owned—another broken family remarkable for their garland of zeroes. The 0.0000001 percent.

Money can turn into everything but we can only turn into ourselves.

I met Ben Wylie in the aftermath of the 2008 market crash, as the value of the world seemed to have lowered forever, and *crisis*, as a term, was beginning to lose its ancient meaning, smoothing into an ordinary condition. I met him once, although I had known him, or believed that I had known him, my entire life.

The Wylies own a cottage near North Lake, a town in northern Alberta brimming with quiet judgment and rude health and stuck economically between lumbering and resorts, as if it can't quite make up its mind whether to frolic in the wilderness or to hack it to smithereens. The Canadian government, in the final land bonanza of 1917, granted Dale Wylie and his brother, Max, a complete section along the Peace River, and in 1937, Dale assumed eight thousand acres on the north side of North Lake, land so scarred by clear-cutting for the lumber mill in Tamaskan that the locals branded Dale a rich American idiot for the outlay of twenty dollars. Now, regrown into a private wilderness, the Wylie property, encompassing three lakes, amounts to a province within a province.

The Wylie cottage itself lacks ambition, at least by the standards of the pleasure domes to weekend warriordom which the Kublai Khans of our moment tend to fantasize for themselves. No Sea-doos or bouncing water trampolines here. Just a small dock for the floatplane, and two canoes by the water, birch bark canoes handcrafted by a local tribe of Dene. A Gothic fireplace, imported in blocks from a German castle, dominates the cottage interior, but otherwise the place is an ordinary Canadian cottage—maybe cleaner than most since a family in the area served as caretakers, trimming the edges of their lawns in the summer and shoveling the Alpine roof of billowy snowdrifts in winter, then in the spring cracking the windows against the cozy atavism of rot. For these infrequent services the local family, the Cabots, earned several thousand dollars a year, even if, that year, the Wylies never bothered to open the place. It was a good deal for that family.

I should know because that family was mine. North Lake was my home. My name is Jamie Cabot. It remains Jamie no matter what I do. I have tried to turn myself into James twice, first when I went away to university, and again when I went away to New York. Though I asserted my Jamesness both times, I inevitably drifted back to Jamie. Now I am resigned. Maybe when I'm sixty, it will change itself to Jim. My grandfather was a Jim Cabot, and one sweltering Depression day, he helped lay the foundation of the Wylies' cottage between snorts of homemade rum and pineapple juice. Later my mother straightened the doilies on the arms of their sofas. During my childhood, the Wylie family had a vague other-worldliness. I recall, as one of my earliest memories, their floater plane circling overhead in a delicate maple-seed half helix and then skimming, skipping like a stone over the drab lake water. Even as a child, four or five years old, that machine—so like a radio-operated toy—bred in me a sense of my remoteness, my status on the periphery of the world. There are still unnamed lakes in Canada, places marked with numbers because no one cares enough to entitle them. North Lake was such a place, a few random cottages strewn among the boulders and pines. Looking up into the pure overbearing sky at the elegant descending curve of the Wylie biplane, I knew I came from the north, the nothingness, the irrelevant truth.

As an adolescent, when my allowance hinged on how neatly I mowed their lawn, the Wylies were a chore. Or sometimes a lark. I would break into the cottage with my high school friends to drink and screw and listen to the cheesy, lovable collection of antique country records, all neatly filed in red milk crates. Hank Williams. The Carter Family. Johnny Cash before he became interesting. It was either the Wylie place or the quarry, where the chilling howls of distant wolves would sour our jokes, sliver into our make-out sessions, collapse our attempts at nonchalance with that truest sound, the howl.

My mother may never have mentioned the Wylies by name. I only remember her calling them "the family," as in "the family are coming up so you'd better go over and trim those hedges" or "I never hear if the family are coming to stay until they come to stay." My father called them "the Americans." I thought of them as "the money." Only when I left North Lake—on a Greyhound bus rather than a floatplane—only when I ran as far from home as I could run, intellectually and geographically and morally, did I begin to fathom their prominence. Nothing is stranger to me than the idea that people I know, even casually, matter. I was raised to irrelevance the way Catholics are raised to the Church. I know in my bones that life must be happening elsewhere.

The Wylies, to me, are like the close ringing of a bright bell, like my mother's voice calling me home across winter fields. They are lords of money, separated by a chasm from the new breed of plutocrats rising to rule us without so much as a suppressed sigh of debate, the new money with their ridiculous yachts and their continuous plastic surgeries and their bought-and-sold SuperPAC politicians who jangle like the spare change in a pimp's front pocket. The Wylies are more, much more. The Wylies are rich because they have seen a truth.

Balzac said that behind every great fortune is a great crime. If so, then the Wylies' crime has been the most human: the desire for growth, the hunger for more. They have never, at any point, been involved in any morally suspect businesses, and not for lack of opportunity. When they were media moguls, they refused to trade favors with politicians. Though they were at the forefront of on-demand television and digital media, they never dabbled in pornography. They have never bought a company to raid its pension fund. If they buy a business, they mean it; they attempt to grow it.

They disdain power and charity, both. When Bill Gates asked the world's billionaires to promise half their wealth away, the Wylies were never asked and never offered. In an interview for Scottish television in 1963, Dale said straight out, "I am not a giving man. I believe that charity doesn't help anybody." His son George, twenty years later, was shocked when a friend who ran a well-digging charity in Africa sent back a check for a hundred dollars. Wasn't a hundred dollars a hundred dollars? Ben, who in his decade controlling the fortune gave away more every year than his father and grandfather during their combined lifetimes, resented every request.

But the Wylies' lack of charity isn't a meanness of spirit, as most outsiders assume. All three Wylie men share the same view of money. They believe in growth; they believe in a fair deal. Charity is a gift, and a gift is the flip side of theft. Given the violence nestled within them, the shame all three men swallowed down the long throat of their lives, their ethical scrupulence was doubly polished, extreme even. No wealthy family in the world has a cleaner conscience. No one's desperation is quieter. They give so little, they leave so little trace of themselves, not out of humility but out of a kind of intergalactic pride. They are wild men and, like all wild things, even their everyday struggles, the most ordinary movement from moment to moment, for food, for sex, for protection, for comfort, for rest, hunger in all its inarticulate variety, rises as an inevitably failed testament against nothingness. Their fortune exposes the size of their terror, their vitality.

Many rich families, once they scrape their fortunes from the hinterland of the great American middle, drift to the coastal metropolises. The idle and indulged children wander to Los Angeles. New York swallows the ambitious. The well-maintained antique women, displaced by trophy wives or sailboats, redecorate flats in London cyclically. The Wylies have always stayed in a somewhat decrepit mansion in Champlain, Pennsylvania, now a suburb of Pittsburgh, or the cottage in North Lake. Rust or Alberta.

The meaning of the Wylies grew and shifted the farther I wandered from North Lake. Struggling in New York, staring through the various windows of the world, half broken by my envy for all that I couldn't have, I would look at all the people I could never be and think, "You're not as rich as the Wylies, are you?" I was proud, if you can imagine such stupidity, of their wealth—the crookedness of our local lives is limitless. Why had they come to North Lake? That question never occurred to me. Why American billionaires, from Pennsylvania, would cross the continent and the border for a summer home somehow seemed to require no explanation.

Like the brothers who stumbled on his naked corpse at the end of the abandoned road, I failed to recognize Ben Wylie when we met six months before his death, despite my clandestine fascination. We met shortly after I had been fired from *The New York Standard*, a conservative paper read by about fifty thousand nostalgics lurking somewhere in the dry corners of the sweating city. My firing had a measure of grace I came to cherish later. Mort Wilner, the *Standard*'s publisher, a robust old-timer with a bow tie, a Tom Selleck moustache, and a moral code, held up a graph across his desk. I squinted to read that ad sales had fallen forty-five percent in a month. "These are the times you've been given to live in," Mort announced and shook my hand.

You can't argue with graphs. In the struggle between the humans and the graphs, the graphs won. As the escalator drearily lowered me from the heights where a few blessed ones still had employment, I remembered all my clambering to be where I was: covering sports for Toronto papers, attempting big features on restaurant trends and real estate, hustling small gigs, then landing the job at the *Standard*. Making it had always meant making it in New York. Far worse than losing my job was the chance of losing the city. After the crash, my wife knew her Big Law starter position at Mainwire Price was fragile, and then Torys in Toronto offered her associate partnership. Toronto was then the only major city in the world that had managed to escape the financial calamity (mainly through ingrained caution and a tremendous capacity to endure boredom). For my wife, the deal was clear enough. She believed that a good life in Manhattan could not be earned anymore. You had to own it already or you never would. In Toronto, we could build. We could have "a real life."

"Why does real life always have to be smaller?" I shouted, during our fourteenth or fifteenth fight on the subject. "Why does real life always mean moving to a shittier city?"

"Moving to Toronto is not the same as dying," she said. My silence conveyed that I was not quite convinced. "It is amazing to me that you consider having children and giving them a comfortable life in your own country to be small."

She was right, right about everything, but as I stepped onto the buzzing stream of noon-hour Fifty-fourth Street, I came to the surest decision of my life. No matter what I had to endure or destroy or abandon, I would never leave New York. You know that scene before the intermission in *Gone with the Wind*, the one where Scarlett O'Hara is standing against the dawn, shoving parsnips into her mouth, shouting, "As God is my witness, I'll never go hungry again"? It was sort of like that, except I wasn't hungry. No economic crisis or emerging trend would swallow me up.

Maybe my blazing defiance would have cooled, maybe I would have returned to sensible passivity, to making good Canadian decisions, if I hadn't seen Jorn Pelledeau walking on the other side of the street. Until that moment, he meant nothing to me. He was just another hustling Canadian lost in New York, whom I know vaguely from home. He was an editor at *Vice* magazine, mostly of bits like "A Russian Whore's Guide to Anal" or "How to Date Girls Who Are Much Richer than You," a master of the fusion of exaltation and degradation which they sell as youth. Thirty-eight dressed as twenty-three, with rolled-up jeans and fluorescent blue sneakers, and a Paul Smith shirt worn loose, he looked like he was winning. I couldn't stand it. Jorn Pelledeau could not win. I refused to let him. I would not exist in a universe where that man could live in New York and I couldn't. I would remain in the city no matter what.

And so I am forced to contemplate the possibility that if I had not seen Jorn Pelledeau that day, I would still be married and living in Toronto, probably with children. I let that man shape the destiny of my genetic code. Perhaps Jorn was only an excuse. The geographical differences between my wife and me were pretexts, I've come to see. The truth is, like so many marriages, ours was a product of inertia. In the supposedly free-loving cities of Europe and the wealthy Americas, convenience arranges more marriages than Indian aunties. When we were kids, the sex was convenient. When we graduated, moving in together to save rent was convenient. Getting married, to move to America, was highly convenient. But when we were no longer convenient, we no longer were.

Canada was just a name to me by then. My home was among the freelancers, that reluctant tribe found in every city, gathered in semi-public rooms, illuminated by the anxious coziness of Mac glow, drinking four-dollar coffees under the shade of cherry trees. The boys worry about whether their pornography is too weird and the girls worry about their Adderall supply. The more ambitious try to figure out which genre the publishers won't hate two years from now, and the less ambitious work on screenplays. I found myself in a fairly typical position: I was fighting with all the fury my body and soul could muster to belong to cliques I despised. There were the preprogrammed, utterly predictable Ivy Leaguers who approached every conversation as if they were trying to impress an invisible professor in a seminar they had never left. There were liberal arts college grads who had read *The Second Sex,* Susan Sontag on camp, and Roland Barthes on photography, and who had listened to The Smiths in high school, and watched a lot of reality television. There were the people who insisted that if you hadn't tried Molly you hadn't lived in your own time. There were the people who were in the middle of founding a sort of online version of the *Partisan Review* and who loathed the people who had founded other online versions of the *Partisan Review,* and who lived off instant noodles in their closet apartments but could taste the difference between ice cream whipped from local cherry blossoms and ice cream whipped from imported cherry blossoms. There were the children of writers and artists who had attended St. Ann's in Brooklyn Heights and would do whatever it took to send their kids there, too. And then there were the guys like me, from the sticks. The guys from the sticks usually warmed their suburban hands on the coals of the world's center for a few years and then slunk back to Omaha or Miami or one of the Portlands with just enough information to assuage their need for superiority over their neighbors. But a few stay and rise. Graydon Carter is a boy from the sticks, from Ottawa. André Leon Talley one day took a bus from Durham, North Carolina.

The day after my wife moved home to Toronto, I used up my last chance for luxury and flew to Berlin to bandage my shocked pain, to mull over my catastrophes. Berlin is a great city for personal crises. Whatever your problems, the problems of Berlin are so much greater. It's history's high roller table; everyone wants to play for the highest stakes there are. I stayed at a youth hostel and wept with suppressed sobs in the shared bathtub. I ate curried sausages. At Checkpoint Charlie, I watched Chinese tourists photographing each other with dress-up American and Russian sentries—the new empire coming to witness the fresh ruins of the old. Even Chinese tourists made me think of the Wylies. They had somehow predicted the improbable handover of power, investing in Chinese manufacturing companies as early as 1986, being fully connected with the Red nobility who had straddled Communism and global markets with such improbable ease.

On my return, I understood my predicament clearly for the first time. New York was filling up with overeducated drifters and overweight homeless, and all my efforts would have to go into staying the former, not becoming the latter. Hanging on by the thinnest of margins, I rustled up some stringer sports and restaurant writing—the energy drink habits of the latest Yankee purchase, where to find real grits in Brooklyn, the quietest coffee shops on the planet—and rented a basement in Washington Heights from a shouty Portuguese couple. I wrote a lot of corporate prospectuses, for coffee chains and oil refineries and macadamia nut farm collectives and sex toy manufacturers. They all paid but I was in that state of unwilling, pleasureless gamble known as "without benefits." I couldn't afford for a single thing to go wrong. And I was in my mid-thirties, that time of life when you realize that the one thing life inevitably does is go wrong.

New York was the same at least, even if my role in its drama had shifted: It still had the little black girls at Greek corner diners poring through their pockets for nickels to see what size fries would be dinner that night. It had stores that sold three-thousand-dollar scarves made from the hair of Himalayan goat fetuses. It had the subway and Central Park: meeting places and the means to get to them. It had the best dive bars, the purest obsession with the next, next thing, and the frankest conversations. The greatest gift of New York is that it requires no justification to live there. It's New York. But slowly I was drifting into that shadowy category of New Yorkers who live in the city because living in New York is something and they have nothing else.

In this state of being, I met Ben Wylie at the fourth-birthday party of Sigma, the daughter of Leo and Kate Stathapolous. Leo and Kate are my rich friends. They own a Miró and a Paul Klee but are otherwise unostentatious, residing in a voluptuous, eccentric, sandstone four-story in SoHo, which they've filled with blond children and brown servants, both of whom they are continually trying to stop from crying. Sigma must have had fifty friends at her birthday. My ex-wife had always hated Kate and Leo. At first, I thought her contempt was mangled envy at Kate's clothing budget. Later I came to understand that my wife was prejudiced against people who seem to do nothing, particularly women who seem to do nothing—a natural enough point of view for a woman whose quest for partner consumed between eighty and a hundred hours a week.

A caterer took my coat before I was carried away on a floe of sports commissioners' second wives and art dealers with trust funds and investors in online payday loan sites. I admit I like to watch these people. The men always look like they're waiting to see what they can get away with, the women have excluded from their lives anything a credit card won't solve. Kate's house was almost a gallery, or not a gallery so much as a freewheeling repertory of beauty where everything was available for purchase. Kate's job—an ancient profession in New York—was bringing together those who are interesting in themselves with those who are interesting because they have money.

On the other side of the room Leo glanced at me over a cynical shoulder with relief. Leo, like me, was not born into money. He had knocked up Kate after they had been dating for a month and their wedding invitations had shotguns printed on them as a half joke. I had met him when he was an editor of the real estate section of the *New York Observer*. His father sold appliances for a Greek outlet store in Long Island City, and Leo used me to maintain a fresh grip on the old realities. He needed me to look like I thought that ten thousand dollars was an absurd amount to spend on a child's birthday party without *saying* that I thought ten thousand dollars was an absurd amount to spend on a child's birthday party. I obliged.

Behind a Bertoia bird chair, fortified, I could reach the elk sliders and a glass of blaufränkisch from the circulating waiters, and watch the animals, too. Kate had hired one of those mobile zoos for the party. Not that any of the children were old enough to appreciate life's purchased variety. The lizards frightened them. The rabbits bored them. Only the chinchilla held their attention, its vivid fluff pleasing the investigations of their puffy careless fingers. Fading to the emptiest room in the house, the study, I stumbled on a beast of another sort—a tall, bedraggled, hungry-looking dad in his mid-fifties who had similarly tucked himself away. He was crooked at an angle, crackling with looming tension though his body stood slack, intently studying the small Klee over Leo's desk.

"What do you think of this?" he asked me, gesturing with a half hand at the painting.

"I think it's a Klee," I said. I have since realized that we lost each other in our incomprehension. I couldn't believe that I was in a house with a real Paul Klee, and he thought I was reducing the painting to its signature, to its market price.

"It's from 1938. It's called *The Wolf*," he said. The painting itself was a composition of red and deep red and scarlet squares fringed by what looked at first like finely circled roofs. "He did no other drawings called 'The Wolf.' He drew angels. He drew foxes. He drew men and women and houses. Why would he call this 'The Wolf'?"

"It's red," I said.

"That's stupid. Wolves are all colors. Brown, gray, but not red. Except for the nearly extinct red wolves of North Carolina. Foxes are red."

"No, I meant the color of blood. The color of killing. It's 1938. The streets are running with blood."

"So the city is the wolf," he said, before we were interrupted by a kerfuffle from the direction of the children. His son Max had started a squabble with Sigma over one of the rented creatures, and he had to go tear the kids apart, scold, comfort. That little boy, Ben's son with his wife Anna Savarin, would, after his father's death, come into the possession of 28 billion dollars at the age of six.

So ended my sole encounter with Ben Wylie, the man who now crouches like an icon, frozen and naked, in one or another of the chambers of my heart. Ben looked nothing like his photograph, much slimmer, more elegant; his eyes were more tired, more intelligent. No distinction of body hinted that I was discussing the meaning of Paul Klee with the eighth-richest man in the world. At the time, I imagined he was an outsider like myself, not yet attuned to the vibrations of the internationalized parochial urbanized elite and their code, which must be intuited by perpetual fiddling, like a radio station just out of range. If personality is dancing to music that nobody else may hear, then his jerky sudden gestures hinted at a rolling shuffle, a pastiche of florid, zany melodies, or perhaps silence, no music at all. Perhaps he did his dance over nothing.

Leo rumbled over after the party began to wind down. "An argument over an animal," he explained with sheepish pride. "Sigma and little Max had a fight over a blue-tongued skink."

"Everybody survive?" I asked.

"Even the blue-tongued skink. Though I suppose there are better practices for my daughter than spitting on the heir to the Wylie fortune."

"That was Ben Wylie?" I asked, amazed as much by my failure to recognize him as by his attendance. I had never seen Ben before, but I could recall with ludicrous precision the one time I had encountered his more famous sister Poppy. I must have been eight, a boy in late summer, playing on the rusty swing set on our front lawn. Her limousine had pulled up beside our house. The window rolled down and a woman looked out, a great beauty—a great *indifference* would be a more precise term. I did not know then about her time on all the covers of the magazines, her celebrity, her reputed string of lovers, Lou Reed and Ayrton Senna and the others, but I knew, even before then, that she was the real world of which my own experience was only a dappled, incomplete reflection.

"I hope you have good lawyers," I said.

Leo's hand imbued my shoulder with mock gravitas. "At least the kid is meeting the right sort of people." He needed my approval again. Leo was always in need of something. In need of a cigarette to smoke or a golf club to swing. In need of a helping hand. Probably in need of a good talking-to. Possibly in need of money. Just generally in need, though the man had everything that a reasonable person could desire.

Kate joined us, miming exhaustion with a droop of her shoulders, hugging Leo loosely around the belly. "Sigma's napping," she said dreamily.

"We all should be so lucky," Leo said, kissing the part in her hair with the tenderness of a salesman before a negotiation.

Kate's good fortune radiated. The handsome husband. The beautiful daughter. The house in SoHo. The wealthy friends (Ben Wylie) and the interesting friends (me). Now I can see, looking back on my sole encounter at Leo and Kate's house, that one of the reasons I didn't recognize Ben was my incredulity that a Wylie would be out eating Moshi Monster birthday cake, looking at paintings, scolding children. In the recesses of my imagination, the Wylies dwell far, far from children's birthday parties in the shivering wasteland of their utterly banal mystery.

It took my father's death to bring me back to Alberta. A pulmonary embolism blew his brains out in the breakfast cereal aisle at the local Safeway. He died at the age of sixty-one, before he had a chance to grow old. A guy I went to high school with, a Mountie, informed me over the phone while I was on the Q train returning from Coney Island. Three Russian women inspected my pain with a reserved fatalistic air I appreciated as I began openly sobbing.

I hadn't seen North Lake in ten years. My parents had always visited me, traveling to wherever I happened to be. The funeral for my father was in the school gym where I had received my high school diploma and accidentally cut Jimmy Prescott's eye playing ball hockey in the third grade, and where I had, one glorious April morning, skipping biology, fingerfucked curious, fervid Mellissa Leung in the darkest corner we could find. Everyone in town came for Dad. The managers from the pulp and paper mill where he had worked as an accountant, the farmers and ranchers, the townies who worked the resorts. My father had helped them all with money. He had been that guy. He had explained the difference between appreciating and depreciating assets, the connections between retirement savings and the tax code, the power of compound interest. All those rough men who wanted to shake my soft hand, all their wives who pressed against my too-crisp suit, their mourning was genuine, not sentimental. The world had lost a useful man. Are you useful? Am I? I tried to be that afternoon. I held my mother's hand as a half dozen North Lakers spoke halting words over his manicured corpse.

After the funeral, while my mother napped, I stared numbly out the front window; the Wylies' lawn was ragged. So I found myself at the age of thirty-five mowing Ben Wylie's grass. Then I found myself slipping inside the old cottage to smell the disintegrating country album smell, to stare upon the ridiculous paintings on nautical themes crowding the walls, to inhale the residue of my teenage naïveté, my teenage longing. To remember life before my firing, before my separation, before my father's death. The slightly sweating walls were still sweating slightly. The thick white shag carpeting that my mother hated because it was so hard to vacuum remained thick and white. I lay down in the stale regret I was indulging so thoroughly that year. There seemed to be no end to the end of innocence.

In a nook off the living room, a small well-lit space with a desk overlooking the lake, the painting surprised me. Sitting on a pile of books, leaning against the cracked wall, *The Wolf* by Paul Klee. I picked the canvas up to assure myself that it was no reproduction. He must have bought it from Leo and Kate. My wonder infused with doom: The painting must have taken the same ridiculous flight as myself, the same five-hour car ride. I was holding a concatenation of paint and canvas worth several million dollars.

An envelope peeked out from a large leather folio of Audubon's *Birds of America*. It was the letter George wrote to Ben in the eighties about his struggle to uncover their origins. All the personal papers, the private history of the Wylies, the record they kept to help each other through their inherited sickness—I found them tucked inside other books, in furniture crevices, inside a blue trunk that served as an ersatz coffee table. I had fled my hometown to gain an education in the world, but the education I sought, a glance into the hidden workings of the machinery, had been there all along. I discovered the basement too, its dirt floors scarred with claws and a large cage fitted with chain leashes.

I left the painting in North Lake. I took everything else, every paper I could suss from the nooks and crannies of the Wylie cottage, back to New York in their blue trunk. Sneaking out the material without my mother noticing was embarrassingly adolescent, but adolescently delicious as well; forbidden cigarettes and forbidden knowledge are always the best kind.

The miniature Wylie archive I had purloined filled the shouty Portuguese basement. In the morning I would spread out the diaries and the letters and the photographs and the newspaper clippings that I arranged into a vast map to a subterranean geography, and in the evening I would fold up their secrets like a tablecloth, delicately fearful that a crumb of significance might tumble off. The presence of Wylies gave my subterranean life the thrill of a secret, the secret history of how money became everything. Stealing up to the street to eat, or to fulfill the conditions of some gig, I could anchor my drifting self to the blue trunk. I only wanted to be back with them, in my dark room. The Wylies had always been my unspoken fascination. The job of a writer is to monetize fascination. I was broke and alone but I had them.

If I could uncover their story, I could sell their story, and if I could sell their story, I might have something like a future in New York. Every story is a little miracle. You make it out of nothing and you sell it for money.

The Mounties declared Ben's death a hunting accident. His nakedness was easy to explain, at least to the professionals. In the final stages of hypothermia, the body often senses warmth as the blood ebbs into the core. Many hypothermic deaths end with naked corpses. Coyotes or a bear may have dragged off his clothes, or wolves, who would have buried the clothes. Even if Ben Wylie had been murdered, if somebody had wanted to kill him, that somebody was far away. The official cause was death by exposure. Everyone seemed to agree, without bothering to look too closely, that the wilderness had killed him.

The mills of Champlain, Pennsylvania, now lie crumpled beside the brown sludge of the Monongahela River but for a hundred years they spat hot prosperity, rolling in iron and coke and manganese to be turned by the brawn of thick-tongued men on twelve-hour shifts six days a week into steel. Carnegie and Frick sold Champlain's rolled steel for a penny a foot. In the middle of this grubby miracle, somewhere around the beginning of the twentieth century, the grandfather of the dead man in the snow was a boy.

Dale Wylie stood in the brickworks baseball diamond and watched his brother, Max, sprint around the corner and across the crushed red field. Dale had no time for rising excitement; his brother was there so quickly. Max panted his urgent message: "I found a dead dog."

A line drive cracked by, to the howled outrage of Dale's teammates. Like Dale cared about the other boys when there was a dead dog waiting. His brother led him by the hand through the quiet streets of small but respectable houses, down to the intersection of the ravine and the train tracks. Under a mantle of pine branches lay a dead husky, its eyes already consumed to squandered holes by the tenderness of maggots.

"You want to bring the boys down to see?" Dale asked.

"Nah. They'll just poke it. That's why I brought you."

"We have to bury it." No justification between the brothers was needed. Boyhood has its codes.

"I know a place out of town. We could be home by supper."

By nightfall they had only reached the junction of the train tracks across the river, and the grandeur of the sunset meeting the water was no more vivid or apocalyptic than the punishment waiting for them at home. On the weedy banks beside the bridge, Max lay down the dead husky he had been carrying so he could rest, so they could contemplate the border they were about to cross. If they followed the river through the stubbly fields, they would eventually reach a place of no human habitation. If they turned back, home.

"Maxie, do you think he belonged to anybody?"

Max sniffed. "No collar. No signs up asking for him."

"Maybe he belonged to a drifter who was passing through or something."

Max stared at the husky corpse for a moment, weighing.

"If he belonged to anybody, would we be out here burying him?"

They pressed on. Night pressed down. They found a stand of black pine forest, a zone of abandonment between two settlements which would have to do, smoothed out a patch naked from the needles, and dug, their cold fingers clawing at the earth, scraping the stony soil.

They laid the dog's body down in the hole, blanketed the corpse with earth, and smoothed the ground with leaves. No prayers, no condolences. Their hustle was their ceremony as they tore back home, lit only by the moon. They knew they had done the right thing. Nothing would shake their conviction, not the irritated policeman lounging in the kitchen, not the boys' resigned, disgraced father, not their weeping mother. Neither did the salty cutting lashes from their dad's belt. The beast needed to be buried in the wild. They had buried the beast in the wild.

When their friends asked about the brothers' limping tenderness the next day at school, Dale made up a fib about a broken family teacup smashed by a mistimed ball. The Wylie boys kept their profane pilgrimage to themselves. Their parents had beat a lesson into them, though maybe not the intended one. Max and Dale learned that everything, even sacred journeys, even mysteries as profound as the moon and the stars, every last thing in this world has a cost.

If we could scrape away what time does to men, we would love every boy. If we could wash away the grime of the last century, the boy would be waiting at the beginning, his greed indistinguishable from hope. Every morning, six in the morning, at the whistle that called out the turn of the Champlain Steel Company shift, Dale Wylie woke up hungry for bacon. His mother had to feed every needy body, boarders as well as the family, as cheaply as possible, so her sons always woke to the slop of oatmeal, never the sizzle of bacon. Dale woke up every morning in a mortgaged house with his mouth watering from dreams.

No house was ever as mortgaged as the Wylie house on 17 Flora Avenue. The mortgage was a state of being, like living in three dimensions. Every little thing, whether new trousers or a better brand of tea or dentistry, had to be weighed in the balance of whether the cash might better serve the almighty debt which was in the hands of their aunt Millie. When the classroom chalkboard grew to be an indecipherable smear, Dale's mother and father told him to try sitting at the front of the classroom. Dale was eventually fitted with Coke-bottle glasses at the teacher's insistence.

The boy was a living thing. The world frowned on the liveliness within him. The whole world wanted him to live less, to live quieter, more controlled, civilized. Everybody except his brother, Max, compatriot exile from the country of the dreamy and mischievous. Max was dark and rough and liked a good scrap, liked to fan open a grim, cheerful smile when the bigger boys wanted a punch-up, happy to oblige. He was a natural, a force of nature. And under the nobility of Max's eager strength, Dale had a pocket for abstract thought within the street-level realpolitik of Irish and Pollack and German children over which his brother was the ragged raja.

Number 17 was swept every day, painted every spring—the property a crack on the cliff face of respectable life that the family gripped with all its strength and stoicism. The biggest accomplishment for the Wylies, a purchase second in importance only to the house itself, was a brand-new twentieth-century American upright piano—the status symbol of the day. For the boys, playing the instrument was the same as any other chore. Chopin and Mozart and Bach were pieceworks of drudgery. The house was large for the neighborhood, a stately pile built by an antique company owner before the surrounding lands were bought up for the squat serviceable brick houses that the steelowner-run banks mortgaged to their workers. There were ten rooms in 17 Flora. The Wylies let to twelve girls. The lone surviving picture of Marie Wylie shows her with a smile as bland as potato water, leaning against a wall and staring into the middle future, fraught with the anxiety of a poor Scottish immigrant paying off a boarding house on laundry and a barber's salary, a life devoid of any luxury, even rest—a disciple of that most demanding of creeds, the belief that one must always find a way to get along.

The trouble of money blew in from all directions. How much was each girl bringing in for the rent? How much were they eating at breakfast? How fast were the boys running down the street and how soon would they need new shoes? How much of his tips was her husband keeping for himself? How much could she put on the mortgage this year?

Sentimentality was for Jews and violin players. Champlain was a furnace, ringed by bodies that fed it. The Wylies came from the tumult of a steel town, the sweltering grind of factories and new houses and slabs of beef with heaps of potato mash and babies every year and death by accident in the spark ore furnaces. When Dale's father, Bob Wylie, fresh from the mediocre town of Abermarley in the ugliest corner of Scotland, had married Marie Simpson in 1894—they met and courted perfunctorily at a Methodist church on Isabella Avenue—her aunt Millicent provided them with a mortgage because no bank would. Aunt Millie ruled the material world, in all its hard edges and bland rules, from her verandah in the middle of High Castle Road, the street immediately west of Flora. She owned the property. So when Dale, aged four, corrected his mother's play at a hand of bridge, Aunt Millie slapped him hot roses across the face and told him that children should be seen and not heard and everyone considered it her right to do so. When Max ran away from home at the age of seven, turning up at a dairy farm three towns over, Aunt Millie called Bob Wylie to an audience in her velveteen parlor, and the man showed with his hat brim twisting in his fingertips.

"You are raising wild children," she said.

"I know, Auntie, but he will be punished."

"Absolutely not." The announcement lifted her off the throne of the settee ever so slightly.

"But he ran away, Aunt Millie."

"All children are wild. So put away your belt, or I will have something to say about it. The boy is going to be rich. He has spunk. We need men with spunk."

Bob Wylie listened, because he had no spunk. He arrived from Scotland for work at the mill on the promise of a cousin and took a swung beam to the shin his third day. No one had any use for a limper in the world of men who stand up. He cut hair at The American Hotel on Davis Street, keeping the barbershop open from eight to eight Monday to Thursday and eight to midnight Friday and Saturday. Marie took in laundry at first and then lodgers—always young, always female.

In the busy afternoons after school, the Wylie boys wafted down to their father's barbershop to help out. The burgundy leather of the everyman's throne, the mingled odor of manly cleanliness, bitter herbal elixirs, delicate powders, musk, the lugubrious ache of working men at rest. The place ran with the tableside chatter of the nobility of Champlain, the steelworkers who don't have to say anything because they know they are making the world. Max and Dale sopped it up with bread-butt ears. And to everyone, whether an awkward teenage mustache or a factory-magnate muttonchop, Bob Wylie smiled mildly, servile and polite, a functionary who spoke or not at the whim of the customer. The boys swept the gray-brown pile of clippings into the corner and learned the lessons that only children can learn. They learned what money is: Who shaves. Who is shaved.

And if ever a shiny nickel were to drop gratuitously into the dazzled palm of Max or Dale, the tip traveled straight to Bob, and from Bob to Marie, and from Marie to Aunt Millie—the large, round blackness swallowing all joy that passed into her orbit. She was the living symbol of how much of life is owing. Bob Wylie stumbled home from his twelve-hour days over the grim and gray Monongahela River into a house of women, clomping down the back stairs into what he craved most: furious basement drinking, the ultimate privacy of oblivion. Marie and the boys would grant him his unspoken wish—they pretended he wasn't there. The basement may as well have been a grave. This too was another inarticulate childhood lesson. If you worked a full day, the women would let you go down alone.

The Wylie brothers' sickness revealed itself on April 19, 1905, the day after Champlain's Great Fire. From the roof of 17 Flora, Max and Dale observed the blaze beginning to swallow the city, the fire invigorated by shoddy building materials, roused by a freak gale on the evening of the eighteenth that pitched the fire to an omnivorous crackle. Crowds flooded down Flora Avenue, and when the gale started, fear washed back up the city in running stragglers. New firemen, with ever-louder alarms, arrived on the half hour, from Homestead, from Pittsburgh. All night, dread and excitement kept the boys on the roof, and in the morning, after a heavy rain had smoothed down the danger, the boys slipped to street level to explore the burnt wreckage as if it were a kind of black-boned ancient ruin designed for their personal pleasure.

"You know what would be a cracker?" Max asked.

"Something to shock the boys."

"Exactly. Some old man's dentures."

"Or a charred Bible."

"A burnt baby shoe."

"The hacked-off hand of a Chinaman."

That night, exhausted from anxious fun and morbid fascination, they fell into a sleep more profound than any sleep they had ever known. And out of this total darkness, Dale woke to find his brother screaming in agony. Max had bristles prodding through his skin and new teeth slivering their way through his gums. His face had petrified in a half scream, a half beg, fear and pain and confusion, flailing, raring on the bed, ripping the covers with fresh claws. Terror poured over Dale's head like ice water. Father and mother rushed into the room. Bob grabbed the wolf-Max and Dale both by the scruffs of their necks, dragging them down to the basement. A leash chained to the wall had already been prepared.

Marie held Dale gently by the hand while his father beat his wolf-brother with a bundle of willow branches. Then Bob shaved off Max's fur, stripe by stripe, leaving a naked wolf cowering and whimpering, civilized on the dirt floor. His mother held Dale's hand but said nothing. No one explained the magical transformation to Dale or Max: Their parents knew how to bear beastliness, and they would share that knowledge with their children, but as for its origin or its purpose, they could no more comprehend the wolf than they could comprehend other everyday miracles like the birth of children or the existence of stars. Their humility kept them stupidly wise; they could instruct their children in endurance. Dale took instruction from his mother's ancient eyes, which stared past the suffering of her sons, into some private, unspeakable knowledge. He learned from the steadiness of his father, who held down Max the way he held down the beast within himself. They were never more of a family than at that moment, wordlessly sharing the truth of their nature, some howling, some moaning, some unspeaking.

The boy stood in the basement with his secret, a mysterious ancient recognition. In all the agony and loneliness and magic, his whole being craved to be out again in that small patch of trees and grasses beyond the edge of town, down the tracks, down the river, where they had buried the dog. A broom leaned in the corner, the same as the one at the barbershop. Dad must have bought two for one.

Dale picked up the broom and swept the clippings from the floor before returning to bed alone.

They were monsters. It didn't seem to matter much. Their new natures followed the old routines. For three days a month, they had to skive off school, handing explanatory letters from their mother to the principal's office and making up stories for their friends about work in neighboring towns. On a blood-warm June day that defied all classrooms and lessons, the boys finally egged each other to drop out together at the end of tenth grade—Max having failed the ninth twice. They could no longer stand the imprisonment. The only problem was that they would have to tell their mother. Dale was declared ambassador by eenie-meenie.

Marie Wylie was scraping the street's grimy laundry into hand-scalding water when he made his presentation.

"You don't go to school, you go to work," she said without looking up from the gray sudsy mist.

"That was our plan, Ma."

"You put money on the mortgage same as everybody else."

"When we have jobs."

"Don't give me when. Five dollars a month or you're back in school."

The Wylie boys had struck their first bargain. Freedom for five dollars a month. It seemed fair. As their mother turned back to the mass of laundry, the boys' hearts fluttered with the moment's terrible significance. In the morning they had been boys. In the evening, men. Dale and Max would receive no first communion, no bar mitzvah, no spirit quest. They received a much more powerful injunction: Get a job.

Max launched himself into the streets, a glutton for labor and for everything else, hauling impossible loads of garbage to the city dump, roofing entire apartment buildings by himself, alone with the fumes of tar and the high winds, delivering bottles of rye to restaurants that should not have been receiving bottles of rye. Risks of legal or spiritual or physical harm were strictly points for negotiation with him. After tumbling six stories to a stretched awning and bouncing into the street on a painting job, he walked away with nothing more than pretty plum bruises and the neighborhood nickname "Blessed Maximus." He chased down errands—skidding messages across town or moving houses on crews or de-thistling yards—in between floury bakery shifts that stretched from four in the morning until eight and continued stretching from eight in the evening until midnight.

Max gambled as soon as he had money to gamble with. He once bet a neighbor a month of bread on whose lawn would sprout crocuses first in the spring. He won, and then realized that he didn't need any bread because he worked at a bakery. With that same neighbor, he wagered a week's wages on which of their glasses of beer a fly would fall into first. All winter the glasses sat outside, filling and emptying with snow like unresolvable questions. "Blessed Maximus" eventually won when a mayfly obligingly offed itself in the scum of the remainder.

He had the grace of those who live inconsequentially. The others in Champlain gave him the same place set apart for saints and idiots and wild animals. Max never worked in the mill, even though the steelworkers were the aristocracy of Champlain's laborers. "Too hot," he said to a mill man who had heard about an opening. "There's time enough to burn later."

Dale wanted a desk. His father never had a desk. His father shaved the cheeks of the men who worked at desks. In his starchiest high collar, a razor ring around his babyfattish neck, Dale presented himself at Mac-Cormack and Sons, the general trading company on the corner of Main and Jarvis, whose owner, John MacCormack, had known the Wylie family in Abermarley. The windowless back room behind the storage was a claustrophobic schoolhouse of calculation and grind, an academy of pinching. MacCormack himself, with his curled white eyebrows and up-swirled hair, resembled a Scottish prophet dispatched by the god of gains and losses to ensure that the terrified clerks kept accurate reckonings of all matters local and terrestrial.

The old man was excoriating one of his clerks as Dale timidly ducked his head inside, his presence disturbing the rhythmic humiliation that the old man was spelling out. Still stooped and without turning, MacCormack barked, "Who are you, then?"

"Dale Wylie, sir."

"The Wylie boy?"

"Yes, sir."

"Can you count?"

"Yes, sir."

"Can you read?"

"Yes, sir."

"Do you lie?"

"No, sir."

"Do you want to be useful?"

"I do, sir."

MacCormack paused to allow the air to tingle with the electricity of his judgment. "I suppose we'll see." His sorcerer's fingers conjured a stool at the clerk's booth. A job. A real job. The realest gift one person can give to another.

Dale received his business education on MacCormack's carts from the salesmen deployed to homes and construction sites peddling everything from twine to two-by-fours to encyclopedias to Easter baskets. He learned that you sell hard to a house on a corner because you can go in three different directions and say to each neighbor that you've had an order from the last house. If you want to sell scissors for 25 cents you divide your scissors into two lots and sell one for 20 cents and the other for 50 cents. Collect overdue bills by sitting in the debtor's house, smiling and ticking away paperwork, until the debt is paid.

MacCormack's mobile army roamed Champlain, struggling every day against the swift-flowing current of the steelworkers' ingrained hatred of spending money. The salesmen admired, at least among themselves, panache. Their boldness, their camaraderie, their indefatigable toughness appealed to Dale's antic heart. Like him, the salesmen were fortune-dreamers. Not like Dad, who cut hair and swept the clippings and culled the tips to buy whisky so he could slink to the basement and never look his wife in the eye. In the dusty courtyards of immigrants, the salesmen prospected enough desire for belonging to tease out the price of a magazine subscription. They cheerfully pretended to undercut one another on staples. They spoke to the wealthy as if they were poor, and spoke to the poor as if they were wealthy, and to everyone with the most perfect manners, their politeness and affability honed by the purifying worship of self-interest. Dale was an eager baptism to its witness.

Every salesman in the pack was an object lesson, a comitragedy kernelled in a nickname. There was Jimmy "The Jew" Cartwright, who haggled with prostitutes, and there was Freddy "Freckles" McElvie, whose redheadedness faded and wrinkled so even in his fifties he looked like a dissolute boy. There was Marvin "The Moth" Carruthers, who suffered a broken engagement to a high-society lady in Philadelphia. There was Marty "The Temper" Shragge, a gentle soul who one time slapped a customer for reneging on a magazine subscription, and Peter Shore, whom they called "Roses" because he always wore a carnation in his buttonhole, and Bob "The Slob" Daggett, the sharpest dresser in town. There was Albert "Lodgepole" Pine and Don "Bushes" Dogwood and Sammy "Honeysuckle" Rose (to distinguish him from "Roses"). There was John "The Pleader" Coleman, who would resort to begging when his customers refused to buy, and John "The Hobo" Campbell, who rode the rails into Champlain from San Francisco when he was a kid, and David "The Closer" Klein, whose name either glowed with an aura of easy success or crackled with irony depending on which way he was streaky. And there was Lou "Three Strikes" Himmel, Dale's mentor, his instructor in the mysteries.

They called Lou Himmel "Three Strikes" because he had been married three times. Having to support three families in three houses meant that Himmel was constantly working, easily the best salesman in the city, and yet he could hardly afford the gray flannel suits he wore to rumpled disintegration. Dale ate lunch with Himmel whenever he could to pick at whatever scraps of his knowledge Himmel brushed away. On the job Himmel was as chipper as a cigarette girl; on his own time, dead eyes slouched over greasy eggs and metallic beans or thin, flat beer. His wisdom had to be reamed from the pulp of his exhaustion; he couldn't even appreciate the charm of having a young disciple. His taste for such comforts had been burned away, like a tongue frazzled and scarred by hard liquor. But if Dale was willing to pay for a sandwich . . .

"Why are you always hanging around 'Three Strikes'?" one of the other salesmen asked Dale.

"I'm sick of being around the rest of you guys, I guess."

"And what's so great about Lou?"

"The rest of us are just winners and losers. That man will never be either."

What he learned from "Three Strikes" Himmel was one lesson, repeated a thousand ways: Just keep going. No matter what the customer says, just keep going. No matter what you feel or think, just keep going. No matter the state of the market, no matter the state of your heart, no matter the state of the universe, just keep going. Just keep going, no matter what.

Hanging around the boozy night sessions or the diner lunches, Dale initiated himself in the folklore of the salesman—a tribe with its foundational mythologies like any other, stories that belonged to no one and to everyone. One hawker was famous for telling a new joke every day without repeating himself, a joke like "What's a fit punishment for bigamy?" "Two mothers-in-law." Customers flocked to whatever he was selling. The moral: You sell yourself, not things. Two salesmen were sent to Africa to sell shoes. One telegrammed to his employer: "Returning. No market. Nobody wears shoes." The other telegrammed: "Staying.

Market limitless. Nobody wears shoes." The moral: Perspective is everything. He learned that you cannot sell to men in crowds. They must be alone.

After an August rainstorm that had flooded MacCormack's warehouse through a busted shingle, Dale convinced the insurance company to cover the value of the goods at nearly three-quarters of their purchase price, news which he proudly brought to his employer. MacCormack sent him back; "The damage was only about a quarter that," he said. The Scot's honesty cost a sixth the value of his stock, Dale calculated, and no one was shrewder than MacCormack. If he was paying that price, his honesty was worth that much. Another lesson: Cynicism is not the same as worldliness.

Other lessons were vaguer; they had to be breathed in like mist. Champlain suffused itself in millworking pride, the American pride, each Moldovan or German or Italian or Scot a miniature Lucifer, overthrowing through the heft of his life the whole of the old world, the brilliantine palaces, the ancient churches, the established orders, for the self-invented squalor of the factories beside a sluggish brown river. The whole town was suffused with the exhaustion of their pride. The men were either coming or leaving, laughing or limp, dry or slick, at morning six or at evening six, into or out of the hellish furnace that fed the boundless continental appetite for steel. Not the salesmen. The salesmen belonged to no one and therefore they could not afford pride. This was their pride.

Dale was checking accounts in the MacCormack back room on a Sunday morning when he achieved a kind of secular enlightenment. This was after his twenty-fifth lunch with "Three Strikes," his eight hundred and thirteen exhausted accounting evening, his seven thousand and sixth rejection at the doorstep trying some pitch that never could have closed. He saw beyond the foolishness of his young dreams, which is as close as anyone can come to wisdom. He realized that hard work and perseverance aren't worth anything. Owning is everything. People work for owners. Respectability is ownership, not labor.

How could he have been so stupid as to believe what they had told him? Aunt Millie was respectable, not his mother and certainly not his father.

Over a beer with his brother, out with the boys, the fellow clerks, on a brief lam in a sordid bar, Dale wondered what would happen if he told them about the wolf. If he were to let it slip. Probably nothing. Probably an embarrassed silence. Everybody has a secret life. Don't tell me yours so I don't have to tell you mine. Better to share in the laugh and suck the bitterness down with angry beer and raw eggs. He was a man like other men.

At the cottage in North Lake, two newspaper clippings have survived, both from *The Champlain Dominion*.

May 14, 1913—Yesterday afternoon, several reports of wolves spotted near the confluence of Blanchard Street and Twelfth Avenue arrived at the offices of Precinct 10. They were thought by police to be a pair of large coyotes, as coyotes have been spotted in many places near the water.

SHOTS FIRED AT WOLF IN CITY

June 12, 1914—The city's growing refuse problem, shunted off by nearsighted officials, has begun attracting wolves to the neighborhood of Blanchard Street.

Since May, when the first reports of the beasts arrived, the fearsome predators have been stalking the piles of refuse that the city's builders have dumped without ceremony on the corners of the disused Extension. The wolves have been sighted both by constables and officers of the Office of Pest Extermination.

Finally the problem of rats, which have infested the city's Irish section, has blossomed into a full-blown wolf problem. What is next, the citizens of the city are free to ask: dragons?

Only the moon brought the Wylie men together. Max was always the last to appear for the caging. As the moon crept to its violent ripeness, Dale would wait naked in the cage with his father while his mother stood, fidgeting at the cage door with contained outrage over her son's lateness. The moment he came he would have to be whisked in clothed, followed by his mother's hard gaze of judgment: How had she managed to raise such inconsiderate children? Max resented the lost time more than anything, itching to be over with the transformation so he could run out again for a score or a joke or to place bets he couldn't afford on horses that stirred loose impressions in him. For Bob Wylie, the beast was one more aspect of the universe that had to be endured. Dale hid his fear. The agony always astonished him, his self ripped to rags, hair bristling up through the skin, teeth severing down, his eyes on flame. He never remembered anything. He would wake up three days later in a naked heap with his brother and father. They would unlock the cage, clothe themselves, sweep up their feces, gulp down another drink of water—the afterthirst was fierce—and then resume the ordinary commerce of their lives. Like everybody else.

Dale knew at least that he was not alone in his beastliness. With the salesmen railing through cagey streets or out drinking themselves to an approximation of joy in the back alley sawdust saloons, he needed no proof of the wildness in the hearts of polite men.

He woke up alone after the oblivion only one time. It was strange, the solitude. His mother hadn't left clothes out for him either. He called to the upstairs. Something was wrong. Something was not where it should be. He had never had to leave the basement alone. The silence began to shiver. Dale decided to chance it, unlocked himself, and remembered that Sunday morning in June meant the boarders were all at church. After a naked dash across the kitchen into the bedroom, he found Max, like a curled statue, head between his knees.

"You didn't hear me call," Dale said, as he hurried to find underwear and a shirt. "I had to run through the house naked. Anyone could have seen me."

Max stammered. "I didn't . . . I didn't . . ." His ineloquence stung Dale, his brother's standard fluidity cracked and shuffled. "I swear I didn't know it was that late."

"What are you talking about?"

"It was nothing. I shouldn't say that. We had something. We used to spoon over by Bottleglass Hill, over on the other side of town. I was there. I was supposed to be here." He mumbled down into insignificance.

"Where's Mom?"

"Buying lime in Boulder Falls. Lester Williamson lent her the truck."

"Boulder Falls?"

Max nodded. "Nobody knows us there."

"Max, I have no idea what you're talking about."

Max's eyes bubbled over. A long tear splashed the length of his cheek. His hand took Dale's hand like a boy's, like when they buried the husky. He led Dale out of the empty house, across the yard, to the garden shed. In the dark, thin bars of light patterned the grimy blackness and a mound on the floor among rusty shovels and busted flower pots. Under a pile of blankets, teased back like crepe paper, the mangled corpse of a black girl was a piece of judgmental meat. Her ripped-out throat had pooled blood to the sides of her face, all the way to her ears. The bugs were on her, her glassy eyes sinking back ecstatically. She was already an ecology. Claw and fang had scraped the dangling life out of her.

"She's young," Dale surprised himself by saying. She would be young forever.

The sudden entrance of their mother scalded the boys back from the body, which she quickly covered with the blankets. She turned on Dale with the ferocity of a glacier. "You didn't see a thing," she said.

"No, Mother."

"At this moment you don't exist."

"I do not."

Max and Dale went back to work as if nothing had happened. They woke. They had oatmeal. They worked. But every night, no matter the hustle or the grind, Max and Dale returned to 17 Flora Avenue to steam themselves in the calm of their mother's boiled beef and potatoes. Marie Wylie, exhausted by rounds of sewing or fluffing or sweeping or peeling or stewing, oversaw the flurry of feminine lodgers and her sons' increasing interest in the flurry with her poor woman's wariness. By 1913, Dale could say that he was assistant manger at MacCormack and Sons, while Max was about to start his own business.

"It's moving pianos," Max announced to the table. "I'm going to find two other hefty lads and we're going to call it 'Blessed Piano Movers.'"

"They'll think you're Catholic," Dale said, his mouth full of rubbery beef.

"So what? I'm happy to move an Irish piano for money."

One of the boarders suggested that Protestants never minded hiring Catholic labor. Dale agreed. "But think about the Jews, they all have pianos."

"Everybody in town with any money has a piano," Max said. "That's why it's a good idea."

"All I can say," Marie Wylie added, "is that I'm amazed we've discovered a way to make you touch a musical instrument of your own free will."

At the dinner table, Max and Dale could only fool the girls or each other or themselves so far. And if they ever needed reminding of their humble status, they needed only to look at their mother, who loomed over the head of the table, carving beef, like the grand goddess of no foolishness. The girls chattered from the edges and the boys joined in as the platters of food circled, but Marie was at the head, a reminder that life grinds bodies and souls, that music goes silent, that every luxury is somebody's loss. She fed them. After dinner, Max and Dale fled Flora to roar in the streets again. One of the advantages of industry is that it keeps you out of the house.

Into the turgid climate of 17 Flora Avenue, swirling with suppressed terror and boredom, stepped the unsettling stillness of Kitty Donclaire.

Kitty worked as an office girl at the brick factory, making tea and typing memos and submitting to the leers and straying palms of the company bosses. She had drifted into Champlain from a narrow, rural Kentucky schoolroom. At first, only the depth of her eyes distinguished her from the other tenants at 17 Flora. Amid the happy chatter, the whispered gossip, the innocent flirtations around the dinner table, she said nothing. Kitty brought silence, a swelling luxurious silence. And perhaps for this silence, Marie Wylie loved Kitty Donclaire. For the first time in their lives, Max and Dale saw the dawning of a smile on their mother's ravaged face whenever Kitty descended the stairs in her mysterious splendor, whenever she sat at the table or returned from the factory. The boys would find their mother combing Kitty's long black tresses in the parlor. The women could be heard together, lifted in clouds of laughter behind closed doors.

Dale and Kitty were always seated next to each other over the steaming Sunday roast; Dale would be called to fix a broken rail in the backyard fence when Kitty had stepped from her bath to spread her luscious, impenetrably opaque hair on a blanket to dry. Performances of English folk songs and Mozart duets became expected every Sunday afternoon in the parlor.

The only way for Dale to assuage the uneasiness the girl provoked was long sessions of midnight masturbation—tricky when the bed's shared with a brother, his mass of flesh snoring then wheezing, farting, calling mangled monologues in slurry tempos, then panting and curling away. Wet dreams, loaded with bunches of collapsing black hair with bright black eyes, and her bent animal body, relieved him, anxiety finding its own way out of the labyrinth.

On April 3, 1917, Max careened into the offices of MacCormack and Sons with the happiest news any young man could imagine: A public and acceptable killing was about to begin. The war was to be the great chance of their lives, the effort of a generation, the American boys setting off to solve Europe's stupid problems once and for all. Dale and Max skipped work to sign up along with the other clerks at MacCormack and Sons. The authorities snatched Dale out of the queue even though he had removed his glasses. His astigmatism was so marked that no examination was necessary. They refused Max for "a murmur in the heart" after a series of short, gassy doctors prevaricated into their beards.

Max wept in his brother's arms like a jilted bride.

"We'll find something else, Maxie," Dale said.

"All right for you, right? Everybody knows about your eyes, but I can see. I can see."

"We'll find another way to do our bit."

"That's what the fellows who can't serve say," Max said.

The Wylie boys never left Flora Avenue without their ATTEMPTED AND REJECTED badges, which deflected shame but not the anguish of irrelevance. The war had welcomed the other young men out of the light of the ordinary world into the deathly cool halls of history, where the names are inscribed forever on walls nobody reads. Even with the AR badges blazing, every gesture of the Wylies' lives, lifting a forkful of boiled beef or steeping tea or planning businesses or chatting with a fellow clerk about the latest speakeasy, wasted to insignificance.

The other men, the men who mattered, paraded down Main Street on their way to Cantigny and Belleau Wood and the Marne—their shoulders scattered with flowers from children and kisses from women and tearful gazes of old men—while Max and Dale roared in their useless privacy. Max moved pianos. Dale kept books.

More than money, more than the beast, irrelevance provoked the Wylie brothers to the wildest decision of their lives. They moved to Alberta.

The Canadian province had only possessed a name for a dozen years when the Wylie brothers set out to stake a farm in the country around the Peace River. Alberta had no shadows of any kind—a landscape free from the codes with which human beings spin a false, self-sustaining dream to blur the hard lines of hunger and death. Marie Wylie begged her sons to stay. She had been grateful that all the masculine silliness of the war had miraculously washed out, and now her sons were going to throw away their good fortune on a lark.

"You have solid jobs and good prospects," she said, sucking in her tears in the parlor as they made their announcement.

"They're giving away land, Ma," Dale explained.

"And they're not making land anymore," Max added.

"Bob, tell these boys. Tell them how likely it is they're going to get rich off farming."

Bob peered up with his sad eyes, somewhat shocked that he had been asked to speak, then shrugged. "Land is land," he said. It was as close to meaning nothing as he could manage while speaking.

"See, Ma. If we crap out, we'll still have the land."

"What kind of language is that? Already you're talking like gamblers. You'll have nothing. You'll have nothing." She tossed her handkerchief on the floor and fell back in her chair, defeated. She had worked so hard for boys who were going to throw over their futures for a patch of wilderness in a foreign country. The waste was only slightly less impious than suicide.

I found Dale's explanation of Alberta in the blue trunk at the cottage, right on top of all the other papers. It was a letter sent to George when he assumed control over the North American operations.

June 23, 1961

Dear George,

Now that you're the big man I should probably tell you about
the disaster. I should tell you about Alberta. It was more Max than
me, even if that does sound like an excuse. The pamphlet from the
Canadian government drifted down to him from the hand of one
German girl's daddy or another. A lot of them drifted down from
the north. Pamphlets and Germans. He just couldn't stand to live in
Champlain much longer and there wasn't any more work for him to
do. MacCormack refused to let me into the business, so we needed
something more, both of us. We just had no idea how much more
there was.

We left in what we thought was the spring, with what we thought
were the necessary tools and kit, which I had horsetraded down to
a pittance with old Johnny Mac. The deal itself was pretty sweet.
The Canadians were giving away, to anyone who asked, a quarter-
section of land, with the agreement that ten acres a year for three
years must be cleared or it reverted to the government. They had to
fill up that nowhere and why not with us?

A quarter-section of land is property enough, but I Englished the
ball a bit, so that I got a quarter-section, then Max got a quarter-
section, then Ma, then Pa, and I traded it around till they were all
neighbors, and the Wylies owned title on a full section of land for
nothing. I pray you never have to know this but a full section of land
is a kingdom. And I'm not just saying that. There are kingdoms in
Europe smaller than a full section, so I had finagled us a kingdom
for free, that's what I figured.

We should have known, from the train ride out, that we were
headed nowhere. Every berth filled up with Ukes. Ukrainians. Peo-

ple who had been farming for ten thousand years. If you opened their veins, grain poured out. The distances that boggled us didn't seem to bother them much. If you told those folks there was a free quarter-section on the far side of Uranus, they'd find a way to get there. We had heard it was a seven-day ride to Edmonton, and I don't know why we didn't believe it. It's like when the doctors tell you how childbirth works, and you figure, "They must be exaggerating. It can't be like that or we'd all be dead." But there it is, although that's for another letter, I guess.

They're not so much cities up there as depots that have sprawled. That entire place could be folded into a briefcase and carried away. It's funny to write down but we really did think we were going to make a fortune from farming. We rode out to the end of the tracks and then by truck the rest of the way to Grande Prairie, where they gave us our title, and we had our goods and chattels—saws and files, and spikes and baskets, and two stoves and two tents, and knives and hammers and chisels—and off we went. And we bought a couple of dray horses and a man came, ragged as a pony man, and asked, "How many axes you got?" And I said, "We got all our supplies," and he said, "You oughta have four axes, in case one breaks and another's lost. You're nothing without an axe." And so I did buy a couple more axes, and the fellow was right. A man out there is his axe and no more.

As we drove up to our little number on the map we were smiling. We sat out on our desolate strip of land, a huge piece of hugeness between four iron posts, and we were pleased as a dog on a meat truck. Look how much we own, we thought. Look at it all. But what is it that you own? That's what you have to ask yourself. Always. What do you own? We owned dragging ourselves off the ground because we didn't own a bed. We owned the soil. We owned the weather. We owned the risk.

It snows every month but August in that country. To raise a crop of wheat you have to be lucky, but we were in our twenties, we knew we were lucky. Max said, "You're the ideas man," and I said, "You're the brawn man," and we set about a sod cabin, our one-room subterranean home. You start with a basement and build up. The joke was "Nobody needs to dig a grave in Grande Prairie, everyone's living in one already." And that was half a joke because a couple of our neighbors did hang themselves in the winter and weren't found till spring.

I did the cooking on the cast-iron stove that nearly broke my back from stooping. Max couldn't parboil shit for a tramp. He chopped the kindling. On the plus side, there was a magnificent whorehouse in town. Just a small family place. The thing I remember most about Madame Helene's was the chess. Helene had brought all these fancy girls out of Montreal, and the rooms were only half full, but whenever you came into the foyer, Madame Helene was always playing chess with the customers and she always won. Always. I realized after a while that most of the men were visiting Madam Helene for the chess games. I would wager on it. Chess was the cure for the loneliness. The other stuff was more like sneezing. She sold the boys a confab over a game of chess with maybe a screw thrown in for good measure. No one is more polite than a prairie madam. Wouldn't say shit if her mouth was full of it. She figured me out, too, and whenever she came in from Edmonton brought all the papers for me, which she marked up about four hundred percent. Those were our happiest days along the Peace River, the days we drove back from Madame Helene's. The horses knew where they were headed and I could let 'em drift back, Max sleeping and me catching up on week-old news.

Even that pleasant journey nearly broke us. I remember once, drifting back home from our Sunday, we got caught in the worst hailstorm I've ever heard of. Biblical. We had to tuck the horses' heads with us under the wagon for a bit. Sure enough, when we stood up out of it, the first farm we crossed was fifty dead cows— beaten to death by the sky. And we passed another Englishman's farm where three little girls in floral-print dresses were frolicking through the fields and gathering up hail into glasses for iced cordial. They didn't own cows, I guess.

From sunup to sundown, we hacked away at our land. We scraped away the sod, slabbed the stuff. There was a part of the section treed but we took a whack and left it. The worst was the bouldering, and that was for Max. There is work that isn't fit for a white man, and that's it. I did the cooking, like I said.

Then the first full moon came. I woke up three days later on the side of the field, smeared in blood, with Max by my side. How? I don't know. I knew nothing. Blackout. You know, son, Max and I were always asking ourselves when we come back, what was the exact moment we knew we were never going to amount to farmers. I always maintained it was the very first day, the day cutting sod to build a house. Max believed it was the first moon.

At the time, you understand, we never discussed how we were only hacking at the earth because we needed something to do for a year so we wouldn't be too ashamed when we returned to Aunt Millie. We never discussed anything, as far as I remember. So maybe Max never recognized that we failed. He threw himself at the country. I knew soon enough, anyone could know, that the boy was throwing himself against nothing. The more he threw himself at the nothing, the smaller his efforts seemed.

We heard the wolves howling one night in June. I'll remember Max's face the rest of my life, that moment. The look of recognition.

Three days later we saw them, a pack roiling through a far stand of aspens, with their eyes low. We did not interest them yet. We weren't easy meat or imminent threat. So they slunk back behind the aspens.

"What do you think they want?" I asked Max, who was standing mid-roll with a boulder the size of a dead body that he was clearing off the territory.

"What do *you* think they want?" he asked back.

"I think they want us off their land."

We stayed because according to a fiction in a government office in Grande Prairie, those fields belonged to us.

The wolves didn't reappear until the winter. The winter came soon, though. That first blizzard surprised everybody, surprised the wolves, too. Covered the whole sod cabin. Took us two hours working the door to open it after. First a crack. Up and down, up and down, like a whore's shorts on payday. Eventually, we worked enough to stick a cup in the space and scrape it out and heat the water and throw it out. When we finally worked the door open we wondered why we'd bothered. Where were we going to go?

You know an odd fact about the prairies? In the Second World War, the Canadian navy discovered that the best submariners came from Saskatchewan. Know why? Because there's little difference between the prairies in winter and the bottom of the sea. We had splurged on a small pane of glass in our sod cabin, and we had built to all government plans, but the smoke from our fires was sooty and blurred the window and ourselves. We had firewood but had to use buffalo chips when it ran out. Burning frozen shit is about as fun as it sounds and the fire didn't matter anyway. The cold was permanent. In the morning the floor was a mess of snow and the wool blankets were frozen stiff. We were only doing a mite better than if we'd been laying up on the naked ground, but it was exactly the difference between living and dying. You have no idea how much a man craves a newspaper when he's so alone.

We had no newspapers so we played cribbage. What else? No hunting. Max tried, but anything that could survive that cold could survive Max. It is the stillness up there that stuns you. The way the snow stays in clouds along the branches of the evergreens with not so much as a raven daring to kick its defiant lightness. The snow amounts to a sneer. Everything is much too simple. Then the wolves came again. We reckoned they had come up against a herd of bison. One day we heard the howl, in the middle of the day. We could tell it was the middle of the day because the window was greasy yellow rather than greasy gray. Max ran out into the sound, without a coat, returned a freezing hour later next to death.

He said there were seven of them. I said it didn't really matter if there were seven or seven hundred, he wasn't going out there again. I needed him for cards. He said we ought to invite them in.

My boy, we were awfully far from Flora Avenue. Fucked and far from home, as Max liked to say. I tell you I would happily have cuddled Aunt Millie.

Then one night the moon lifted and Max vanished. Lord, I was furious. I even snapped on my snowshoes and followed him, followed the tracks of the wolves, but hunting wolves is like trying to catch fish in the ocean with your bare hands. If you're hunting wolf, you need a cheap trick, like a tied-up goat or something, and I was all out of cheap tricks. I managed to snag a moose kid, though, which I took to be a triumph until I carted the carcass home and tried to eat the thing. Alberta winter is so sparse the flesh of its animals is musky to the point of poison. It's leather all the way down. Not that I didn't eat every scrap of that moose. I ate that disgusting moose and played solitaire for about a month.

Then the moon came again, and Max returned with the brood, and I returned with him and with them.

We were wolves that winter. We ran with a pack of nine. The cold was our home. Hunger was our home. There were days when we ate and days when we did not eat. We wanted buffalo or moose. Ripping apart a rabbit or a fox was just practice, playing with killing and squabbling over the bloody snow. Then when the wind rose up, we hid together under the blankets of low pines where we could find them, or burrowed under the mossy stink of aspen leaves, our breaths heaving together. The first scent in the morning was a taste of life or death. It was pure. Our hunger began in the dark. We searched for a trace of weakness, any weakness, a whimper in the middle of silence.

We always ate until our guts sagged. Then we slept dimly under a pine tree, the nine of us, in the fullness of our bellies. And that was happiness.

We almost died several times that winter. We almost ate each other. Mostly we survived on the corpses of buffalo calves that had frozen, and we ran into a herd and that kept us through the worst of January and February. We ate disguised ptarmigan, we ate dangerous bobcat. We ate voles by the hundreds. We ate what we could

eat. We ran together until the spring, when we cracked up like everything in that country cracks up in the spring, when the faint new
warmth is the world trying on mercy for a lark.

The winter cored the Wylie brothers. Alberta hollowed them out. At
the end of all their agonies, their stake was wilderness. They left their
claim for Grande Prairie, where the sale of the tools paid for the train
that carried them back to the station in Champlain where they had initially applied for the grant, which brought the business back to where it
started, a neat round zero.

Stepping onto the platform, dragging their worn bodies back home,
Dale and Max peered at once-familiar scenes, store owners fondling
easy fruit on their counters, schoolgirls sharing lemon sherbets, old-
timers rattling uselessly to one another on the street, all as if through a
green-glass aquarium. If you forget, even for a moment, why people do
what they do, it can be hard to remember. On Flora Avenue, the boarders wouldn't allow them into the house, no matter who they claimed to
be, so for an afternoon, the boys sat on the blue trunk while their old
friends and neighbors crossed them without a glimmer of recognition.
Even Marie Wylie, bundling loads of laundry into the house, had to
squint through the raggedy grime to identify her defeated sons.

She walked them to their old room and then, arm in arm, up to the
cemetery, to the small plot with its small slab where their father, who
had been a small man, lay dead and buried.

"Flu carried him away. He was one of the first. Sudden. That was
more than a small mercy."

She inspected the grave and its marker the way she might a bolt of
gray flannel brought home from the fabric merchant. Had she over-

paid? Had she received quality for money? Max and Dale squirmed in their frayed outfits. They weren't dressed right. Max in khakis. Dale in gunmetal gray. Neither with a scrap of black.

"What happened to the barbershop?" Dale asked.

"Sold it."

"What happened to the money?" Max asked.

"The mortgage."

That was all the eulogy Bob Wylie ever received.

Kitty Donclaire was very much alive. Her dark eyes were still peering from the dinner table, always by Marie's side. She no longer worked at the brick factory, though no one ever saw her working in the house. She would sit beside Marie at the laundry or over the pot scrubbing, and every now and then Marie might whisper into Kitty's ear. Nobody asked the reasons, the nature of their arrangement, least of all Max and Dale. They slunk from her gaze with a primitive unease.

Mother's law had not altered: If you stayed in the house, you helped on the mortgage. Dale needed his old job back. He had to stoop to enter the back room of MacCormack and Sons, that shrine where the Scottish prophet of fiduciary responsibility lorded over the huddled scrutineers of the ledgers, the holy books. John MacCormack was pleased. The return of Dale Wylie, prodigal businessman, justified his instinctive and acquired pessimism. As if it needed justification.

"Gentlemen, behold. Not the gods can turn back time."

"Mr. MacCormack . . ." Dale began.

"Gentlemen, we are presented with an example," MacCormack continued, ignoring him. "I will not say a warning. I will neither say a beacon. An example. The man who took a chance and failed. What are we to think? Are we to respect his courage or condemn his folly? By what calipers are we to measure a man? By the scope of his ambition or the size of his achievement?"

MacCormack gazed on Dale with a tender and bloody contempt.

"How would we judge the ancient Romans? By their achievement? They have achieved, ultimately, a pile of dusty old stones. Or are we instead to worship dreams of eternity, the visions of the Jews in their desert?"

He pulled open a chair behind a stall, and shooed its disgruntled inhabitant over a half-desk's width. "I do not need to inform you gentlemen that time goes but one way. Otherwise, it would be very difficult to rate the value of municipal bonds. Time leaves us, at least, with something to evaluate. Something to look at. So what are we looking at now, gentlemen? Are we looking at a pile of dust or the elusive remnant of a dream?"

Dale sat back in his old chair. Nobody needed to explain.

After Alberta, Champlain wasn't enough for Max Wylie's body. He roared onto the autumn harvesting crews in Indiana, and beyond to the lumbering in Idaho and Washington, returning to spend the winter and the money in Champlain. Max would materialize without warning, gathering crowds as he strolled like a lord down Flora Avenue, everyone wanting to breathe in a bit of the winds that coursed around his strength, because he brought the smell of the whole country with him, the grandeur of the wild man. The boardinghouse women adored his stories of men who rode single logs down a hundred miles of river, and bets with Chinamen about who could climb a mountain faster, and murders in distant towns that hinged indirectly on Indian curses. No need to boast anymore. He could speak softly. The girls would lean in.

Over dinner to celebrate his return one July evening in 1921, one of the frail office girls asked, "Mr. Wylie, what is the West like?"

He launched into a romance of the plain's grandeur, pausing on its homely churches, and the honey-storm music that seeped through the stained glass on a Sunday morning. When his mother had passed out of the room, he asked them quick, "You want the truth, girls?"

The boarders insisted they did, and Max rolled a thick slice of bread into a ball, popped it in his mouth, and whispered, "The West smells like pussy."

Max meant that the West smelled like money, Dale knew. The West smelled like having a piece, not having to account for every nickel in your pocket to Mother, to MacCormack. Freedom and spending. Free-spending. Dale found out about the smell of the West soon enough. In the 1920s, MacCormack and Sons, expanding beyond Pennsylvania, promoted Dale to "director of the sales force," a grand title for a hardship post in the timber and mining counties selling axe heads and rope, engine grease and bulk seeds, biscuits and blue jeans, selling whatever he could figure out that people wanted to buy.

In 1923, Dale arrived for the first time in Atkinson, a mining town on the Minnesota–Dakota border. The founding myth of the town of Atkinson is an appropriately bleak fairy tale. The town sits on the site of a chicken farm where the original owner, over a supper of cockerel's gizzards, sunk his teeth into soft metal. The bit was solid gold. Immediately, he slaughtered all his chickens and rummaged through their guts for more.

Atkinson fit its foundational myth well, a bloody mess made in the quest for a little money. The minor gold rush of the twenties, thirties, and forties was all slapdash, shanties zanily sprouted along cracks of real and imagined subterranean wealth. Dale loved the action. Even the train buzzed with happening. Everyone was on the make or falling apart or both. As he stepped out for the first time, onto the muddy mush of the Atkinson roads, he breathed in the town's hilarity. A man in a bowler and a taut three-piece tweed suit, arm in arm with a drunken, flattering easy lay in an emerald dress, smiled nefariously while passing. Welcome to town, buddy. See what you can pull. In Atkinson, glamorous stories were everywhere: Irish who arrived with shovels and scratched out millions. Stakers who strained nugget gold out of their canteens by accident. Telegram boys palming five-dollar tips from gamblers. Greeks who turned single coffee stands into chains of dinettes. Men were achieving respectability all the time in Atkinson.

Dale hunted from call to call, from corner store to corner store, from hotel to hotel, from camp to camp, smiling at the frowning, bored men who either hated to buy things or wouldn't or couldn't, and then offering and insisting and failing and leaving. Rejection is the river in which the salesman swims. The river is shrewd and fierce and runs cold. The faces reflected on it blur into a single rush—dubious eyes and arched brows and stupid mouths and the cynical crook of a cigarette out of a cheek. People seethe and you must seethe with them. Even the boys looked up at him funny, like he was the pig about to be slaughtered. The whores shut their doors on him tenderly, pityingly. The bartenders added a fingernail to his finger of Scotch. The man who eats what he kills deserves respect and succor. After days of pure hustle, he would save on his quarters by heading straight to the train station where he could lean against the plinth on the platform, asleep, until the next morning's train. Why pay for a flophouse? The station had heat.

Dale stared through the grimy windows of train stations evaluating his slim chances while sucking back drab sodas and gray sandwiches, fending off despair with the stitchwork creed he inherited from his mother: Always find a way to get along. Atkinson was the opposite of Champlain. The money had mixed men up in their chances, their misery, and their furious gorgeous free women. Even the conservatives in the West are libertines. On the side of MacCormack's business, he took orders for himself. Hats from Pittsburgh. Books. An old Arab paid him a high price for Egyptian cotton. Potpourri for the brothel. To the Chinese he sold incense. But mostly it was door-to-door. Knives. Gramophones. Subscriptions to magazines. As much as he could. He went into the radio business for himself. He bought them wholesale in Pittsburgh, rented out a sufferance space under his own name to store them by the station, and hustled them wherever he could.

Luck is the by-product of effort. The effort was enduring other people, the maids who sneered and shook their heads from the sides of houses, the demented old-timers, the busy men of business pushing by, the drunks taking cracks from the barstool, reeking of pickling spice and vomit, the broken women and their adamant hate. He needed luck. That's the worst, needing luck. Dale's biggest stroke of luck was that old MacCormack never figured out how rich the territory was. MacCormack always received him back without comment, neither praise nor blame. Dale had no idea why the old man kept him on. Inertia? Or were his sales excellent? How were the others doing? The answers wouldn't have mattered anyhow. He just went out and sold.

A slow train from the men of Atkinson trundled him back to the
house at 17 Flora, to the women of Champlain. A long train ride to ask:
Who am I? What do I amount to?

In the mornings, 17 Flora floated up like a ship on a tide of girlish
laughter, anchored by stern Marie and silent Kitty, and, guided by
gentle Marie and silent Kitty, 17 Flora floated down to sleep on bil-
lows of sighs in the Champlain evenings. The boarding girls, wearing
their heavy ambitions lightly, miasmaed the house with a silly, soft,
delightful fuzz. Dale was either leaving, with the quickening scent of
desperation, or arriving with the smell of train furniture and too many
cigarettes on him like a cloak. He would never be a great salesman
because he couldn't forget quickly enough. The face of each housewife who brushed him out the door like a dead mouse stuck in him.
The dismissive eye of the shopkeeping Arab with his whoremaster's
odor of rosewater lingered slightly too long. The general mania of the
men laughing in pool halls, stuffing thick-skinned sausages into their
gapped faces, stuck just a little too much. At home, in Champlain,
on Flora Avenue, he relished the comforting somnambulance of the
rooms that hadn't changed much since his childhood.

One fine judgmental Sunday, at the hour he should have been returning from church, they were waiting for him in the parlor, the room
dusted every day to be used once a year. His mother beside Aunt Millie,
half her size, both in black.

"You know why we are here," Aunt Millie began. Dale perched himself on a chair designed for no one ever to sit on, and knew enough not
to speak. "We want you to become respectable."

"I am respectable," Dale answered.

"You have a job," Aunt Millie corrected him, upholding a bare finger. "That is something. That is not nothing. But it is not respectability."

Dale shuffled his feet. "What do I need to become respectable in your eyes?"

"A wife."

They were offering Kitty. The whorehouses that filled the gulleys of Atkinson as the sprawl sloped into the darkness—how many times had he slunk to and from their doors? The eyes of the women crooking their finger on the porches. Come here. Come.

"I don't have the money to marry."

"Get married and you will have to find the money." Aunt Millie stood up to leave. "That's how men become respectable. Marie, I said what I had to say. Now I will go."

Dale watched his propertied aunt waddle down the street. The neighborhood children rolled their play out of her path, warping around her black mass. His mother had disappeared into the housework. Why did he slink from Kitty like he slunk from the whorehouses? It was a fair offer. Kitty would stay with his mother while Dale sold in Atkinson. He would have two lives, one in Champlain and one in Atkinson. Which would be the reprieve? His time in the dark quiet parlors of women with their still and total judgment, or the knockabout rampage of men's business?

Dale slouched into the old recliner in the parlor the way a frog plops into the primordial succulence of mud. Exhausted, his mind configured and reconfigured with a welter of pluses and minuses, properties available, deals he was making and their odds. He plunged through darkness to his bedroom off the kitchen, and tumbled into bed, asleep instantly.

Sometime later, into his oblivion, Kitty wandered. She rose over him with her shipwreck eyes and the hot midsummer of her hair. Even the ecstasies were vague, smoothed over his body, then vanished. The next morning, the scraping of oatmeal out of the big pot woke him, and he let the impression settle at the bottom of himself. What had come into him?

Max would appear unpredictably—a vision of ragged liberty fresh from miracle or disaster—whether Dale was at home or at the MacCormack and Sons offices or on the path between. One evening he showed up after eight months' absence to take his brother to a touring burlesque, the Chins of Chinatown from the Curtains Up Theater, where nipples were revealed, reportedly, momentarily, around the middle of the second act. Dale had work to do but Max didn't care. A kid brother's refusal doesn't count.

"Some of us have real jobs, Max, and we have to work our way through the day. We make real money," Dale insisted.

Max was flush from six months in the northwest country. He pulled out a wad of bills. "This isn't real money?"

"That's wild money," Dale replied.

"Money's money."

"The idea that you think money's just money shows that you don't know the first thing about money. Like saying women are just women."

"You make my point for me, brother."

"There's won money, money you can't lose, money for jam, money for bread . . ."

"Enough."

"Borrowed money, earned money. Stolen money, money that's due soon, insurance money . . ."

"Why don't we go out and find out how many different kinds of women and money there are."

Dale was as helpless as anybody with Max. The man's body rolled with the strength of a boy who knows he's nothing but a boy. Dale threw an arm around the shoulder of the rollicking world and strolled into the night. He could enjoy the faces for one night, couldn't he? He could pretend to be one of them, laughing when they laughed, angering to their anger, galumphing along with the booze and the show they were all pretending to enjoy in the name of a kind of mischievous fellowship that was actually hiding in plain sight.

Following the next full moon, Dale woke sick in the cage as usual except that Kitty was staring back at him through the bars. She was silent. Her eyes were black. This was no dream.

"I'm pregnant," she said.

Life fell over Dale in delicate nets, nets by the thousands, secret nets, invisible nets. He let them fall. He had seen what escape meant. The mangled throats of colored girls. Blood pooling in the corners of their lovely ears like the blood on the dinner plate, her skin the shade of marzipan, the judgment of whatever justice the world could dream. No, no, much better to let the million nets descend like veils and hide from mirrors. Cage yourself so that you need not be caged. One final lesson: Everything that happens in life means you have to make more money.

He crept to the basement for a snort of the bad rum he kept in a wedge of the colliery, and found his brother, oddly anxious, already drinking the stuff out of a teacup with no handle. He ought to have been shocked but he wasn't. Naturally he wouldn't be granted even the moderate pleasure of rotten solitude to nurse his grievances. The bitterness would not allow him even to slink away.

"Look at us," Max said, grinning wide. "We're just like Dad. Anything but that, am I right?"

Dale took the dishandled cup from his brother like a morose chalice. "I wish we were like Dad."

"You want to be a barber?"

Dale drank the sick-at-heart rum. "He was a better man than you or me. He helped with a mortgage. He left a house half paid for. What are we going to leave? You're going to leave your raggedy-ass bones on some slab of forgotten prairie."

"Speak for yourself." Max took back the teacup.

"What have you got to say for yourself?"

"What have I got to say for myself?"

"That's what I asked."

Before Max could speak, overhead, the laughter of Kitty and Marie like a limping, outstretching siren healed back to silence. Max grinned stupidly, hurled back his head, and howled.

TWO

The party smelled of cocaine farts. Leo had to explain it to me: When the middle-aged rich kids gather to huff cocaine at a time in their lives when they are no longer restrained by thousand-dollar-a-night limits, their nascent paunches relax, their relaxed anuses open, their opened inhibitions dissipate, and their dissipated shame dissolves. The lamb with peapods and seaweed salad, the ironic caviar and blinis, the pork four ways, dandelion salad, and *terrine de lapin* with heritage parsnips, the deconstructed carrot cake with superchilled powdered walnuts and root vegetable purée, all drowned in white burgundies and sassicaia and delicate little sherries, rumble through their aging bellies and out into delicate poofs of cocaine farts. The smell of worldliness. The perfume of the time I've been given to live in.

Leo wore a $3,500 suit, a washed-out blue affair with an Orange Julius–colored shirt, Frenched with archaic pearl cufflinks. I wore the gray I was married in. We were stalking different animals. Leo had heard that Colin Farrell was showing up. I was there for Poppy Wylie.

Leo knew her in that distantly familial way rich people know each other and had promised to introduce us so I could try for an interview. I needed an interview, a high place in the realm of reality from which to overlook the family's monumental delusion. Poppy had the narrative advantage of being alive. To the breed of old-timer who still read print, her name would register. She had been adopted from China in the sixties, when foreign adoption was novel, ahead of the trends even in her origins. Her elegant shape mistily haunted the long-distance photographs of celebrity yachts in fashion spreads in the 1990s, when her beauty had been an overwhelming but removed force, like an aircraft carrier known to be patrolling the Persian Gulf. Her beauty now was as forlorn and ravaged as an aircraft carrier being carved up in a Third World naval yard.

My old boss Mort Wilner, mostly out of pity, had commissioned a four-thousand-word Sunday spread about her. I also put a call in to Jorn Pelledeau and pitched him a story about the "original poor little rich girl."

He texted back: Don't usually do history but WAS superhot.

I texted: She invented exultation through degradation.

Jorn texted a one-word contract: Xactly.

So I had options. My plan was to write the piece and try to sell it to *Vanity Fair* on spec, having Mort in one back pocket and Jorn in the other.

The rumors I had collected about Poppy resisted coagulating into any coherent story. She had dated a string of famous men in famous situations. Lou Reed was her lover just after *Berlin*. He wrote "Sick of You" for her, apparently. The Brazilian racecar driver Senna tried to call her the morning he died. She had an affair with the head of the IMF, too—"daddy issues." Poppy Wylie had been a minor celebrity, one of the world's vaguer apparitions. A celebrity is a party that is happening in the bigger house across the lake, the one you can't quite see from where you're living, and in the evening music and laughter thrill over the water, but the next morning there is silence, a still and crumpled silence that is somehow more intoxicating than the music or the laughter.

The party we were at was rich people waiting around for famous people. To me, the conversations of the peripatetic rich always have an unreal flavor, like the taste of paper clips. Their cosmopolitanism is shopping, and wherever they go, they encounter only their same smooth selves, whether it's in Scandinavian furniture or the hilarious foam of avant-garde restaurants or the newfound extremities of prostitutes in Saint Petersburg or Santiago, in the Maldives, or Milan. The true cosmopolitans, the world-embracers, are the servants who tidy up the wake of their parties and their wombs, the Senegalese women, the Polish men, the Filipinos, fleeing the antique brutalities en masse, microwaving the same meals in Saudi Arabian villas or in northern Ontario cottages for the vacuous riders of fortune who skim the world like petrels, and whose children are archipelagoes of physical reality in the ocean of their unconcern.

At least they were a break from myself and from the basement, that miserable repository where I pored over the unbelievable evidence, and filled the rest of the time garnering scraps of work to pay the rent, blowing delicately but furiously on the embers of the financial hope a big story might bring. The contrast maintained my wonder at New York at least. Thirty minutes by train from my squalid little room, the bar served free bourbon over roughly shaved ice and a jumbled double helix of or-

ange peel. Leo brought us a pair without asking what I wanted, fearful
that I might request beer in a bottle or a cosmopolitan or, much worse,
what I actually wanted, a rum and coke. "You going to kill the sister, too?"
he asked.

"Whose sister?" I mistakenly believed that he was speaking about
the one black woman in the room, the bronze-tinged Nigerian wife of
an IMF banker.

"Poppy Wylie. Ben died how long after he met you at Sigma's party?
If this one dies, we'll have to involve the police."

"The police didn't seem to care much about Ben," I said.

An unexpected gust of bitterness floated out of Leo's chest. "Those
are Canadian police. Besides, they're right not to care."

Leo shouldn't have come with me; my presence ramped up his latent
contempt and the cynicism could be exhausting. As if he were not so
perfectly fluid in the world of free stuff and debt, utterly of his time.
Waiting for rich and famous people to show up, we lapsed into a dubious silence, unclear whether its source was that we had known each
other forever or that we barely knew each other at all.

Leonidas Alexander Kaffavy Stathopolous. I am a fossil for him, a relic
from the time when he still dwelled among the people with mortgages,
the great middle tribe who look at restaurant bills before they pay them,
the hordes from which he is now as removed as I am from the 700 million subsistence-level farmers in Central Asia.

Leo shows me the folly of my virtues. Maybe that is why I love
him. All my struggles, all my preparations, my elaborately planned
and fulsome battles to escape North Lake, to blast beyond the gravity
horizon of the dying planet, the hometown—Leo makes me realize

that in all the ways that matter I remain the hick Canadian boy I have tried to erase. I believe in hard work and responsibility, even in duty, and he just rides the world on an easy entitlement that he has no right to expect. His first job after graduation was achieved through an epic schmooze. The best ad firm in the city had turned him down for an internship, so he booked a meeting with the vice president of something and just talked until the company created another job for him. His current gig, PR for British films, was the perfect sinecure. Since nobody expected British films to receive any publicity, he couldn't possibly fail. He needed to appear as though he were close to the possibility of publicity. He was literally paid to be seen at the right parties.

Leo finding and then marrying Kate was like a conquistador stumbling into the country of perpetual spring, because she was the kind of rich who could never become unrich. Descended from American revolutionary fathers, the owners of fundamental patents, the people who make money every time papers are stapled or snow is shoveled or buttons broken, she was a poor little rich girl of the classic type, with a distant, alcoholic, gigolo-prone mother and a father who died, aged seventy-nine, when she was three, leaving her a variety of trusts whose geometries neither she, nor the advisors, nor Leo, could pilot or wreck. She told good stories: drinking rosé in the Swiss Alps with African chiefs, drifting through Japan with rock bands, little embarrassments with lesser branches of the Dutch royal family in Macau. Through these screens and trapdoors, shallow glories and glittering horrors, she had tumbled and somersaulted, an unguided and blindfolded *saltimbanco*, unfurling at the end with a warm educated laugh. Money only counts for so much, even now. My mother would like Kate. She is kind and generous and real.

And Leo's luck was ridiculous enough that he knocked up a woman like Kate on their fifth date. Both of them had just turned thirty, and neither wanted to try the odds on having kids later. She even seemed to love him. She had taken on his ludicrous Greek name anyway. Poor Sigma had taken on his ludicrous Greek nose as well, no doubt to be scalpeled to propriety later.

I wish there were better fairy tales about envy. In fairy tales, envy is always confused with anger, with hate—the ugly sisters shredding Cinderella's dress, the Wicked Queen commanding the huntsman to carve out Snow White's heart, the concoction of poison apples. Fairy tales are usually so accurate, too, the wisdom deepened by the love of a million mothers over a thousand years. The search for love is like licking frogs; a father's abandonment has the taste of bread crumbs in the darkness of a forest; the world's towers must be climbed by pulling yourself up the hair of princesses. But the black hearts stewing in their blackness are so crude and unrealistic.

I could have used the insight of a fairy tale that night. Envy was everywhere. The glad rags had never seemed gladder, never sadder.

"Poppy knocked down half of Connecticut," Leo told me. "Did you hear about that?"

I hadn't. How had he?

"I should say she tried. She's just left half of Connecticut to rot. Bought three houses in the Golden Triangle and tried to knock them all down so she could live in the middle of a field."

"I thought they had North Lake for that," I said.

"She wanted a more convenient wilderness, I guess. It's not that unusual anyway. Bill Gates did the same thing on Lake Washington.

Bought out all his neighbors. Larry Ellison bought five houses along the beach in Malibu."

"Why?" I asked.

"The same reason they buy yachts that can cross oceans. So they can forget about the existence of other people. In the end, the only livable places will be the ones where nobody lives." His mind fluttered like an alert sparrow between winter-black magnolia branches. "What do you think she would be like in bed?"

"I've never met her."

"How would that matter?"

Leo began to explain how lovemaking—its techniques, it visual modality, its intensity, and its frequency—varies according to income level; from the garrulous mamacitas in their air-conditioned track-rattled ghetto bedrooms to the ultramontane upper-crust sodomites in Bora Bora executive suites. The lesson was interrupted by the heralded arrival of Colin Farrell, glistening with testosterone and greased-back hair and sunglasses—an attempt, I realized in the flesh, to look like an actorly version of Bono. When he removed the glasses, he had the scared look of a teenage boy who has wandered into a strip club. I remembered the period when he had haunted the stripper bars of Southern California in a wool watch cap and torn jeans. He was a historical figure in a way: The word *douche bag* would not have become nearly so widespread without him.

In the flurry of star arrival, Poppy was suddenly at our side—the woman herself. I couldn't tell: Was the delicate, hidden ravage of her face evidence of hard living, of ruin by luxury, or was she just suffused with my various memories, of the magazine spreads, the rolled-down window of the limousine in Alberta, my conversation with her brother over a Paul Klee painting? Leo leaned in and whispered an ingratiating welcome. She obviously had no idea who he was, which bothered him not at all.

"And this is James C. Cabot, my journalist friend who wants to meet you," he said, turning to me. She offered her hand. I touched a Wylie.

"Who do you work for?" Poppy asked, the way you might ask a plumber if he was certified and insured.

"I used to work for *The New York Standard*," I tried. The name of the *Standard* somehow displeased her.

"And now?"

"*Vice*," Leo answered for me.

"That's for young people, right?" she asked before I could correct Leo.

"It's for youth." The distinction seemed relevant, at least to me. Already Poppy was scanning the room for whomever was more interesting, more of the moment. I had to catch her. All I needed to do was make sure she would respond to an e-mail. "I remember I had a very interesting conversation about a Paul Klee painting with your brother once," I said. "It was called *The Wolf*." Her eyes hitched to mine, a reaction. "It was a small painting, red squares, set with scarlet squares."

"It doesn't sound much like a wolf," she said cautiously.

"No, but it feels like one."

The center of her eyes flickered in a spectral, indecipherable breeze. I had done what I needed to do. "You knew my brother?"

"I only met him once. It's Leo here who knew him."

"An interesting man," Leo added. "He had amazing taste."

"He did, didn't he? My brother"—her voice became flatter, more expansive, more removed, like she was describing a bathroom in a real estate tour—"possessed the most wonderful gift for finding masterpieces and buying them. He never knew how to display them. They were always stacked in a basement or in one of the houses on the floor." She snapped out of her reverie, smiled coldly, mildly embarrassed.

"He was good at buying and not so much at owning," Leo concluded.

"That's it precisely," she said.

"Owning is always harder than buying."

The moment of recognition, however paltry, however petty its surroundings, was real. I watched it blossom between the two of them with some unnameable black sap rising in my veins, some animal defense that I swallowed down.

"You seem to know me much better than I know you," Poppy said to me. "I used to know everyone in magazines."

"I remember your photo shoots."

"You do?"

"Everybody does." She seemed genuinely touched, so I pushed. "I was wondering if you might want to talk about it."

"About what? With whom?"

"With me. About your journey."

Leo could sense the disgust that threatened to overwhelm her and headed it off: "This boy's from your ancestral homeland."

"China?" she asked.

"That's typical Leo," I answered. "Not China. North Lake."

"North Lake," she said. Her eyes fizzed like soda dolloped into dark milk. "The Wylies all have such happy memories of North Lake. The water there is so clean and the air is so pure. Heaven can't be much cleaner or purer than that. A place like North Lake makes you wonder how much better the world would have been without us. I wanted to shoot a movie up there with Bobby"—there is a way of saying the name Bobby that instantly implies *De Niro*—"but it never happened."

"I have an uncle Bobby there," I said stupidly.

"Do you?"

Leo looked down at his five-hundred-dollar Prada shoes and at the shiftable ground.

"I just realized that I can't stand to be in North Lake one instant longer."

She wandered away. The abruptness of her abandonment made Leo laugh. "Surprisingly human, isn't she?"

"Surprisingly," I agreed.

"That stuff about her journey was inspired," he said with a sneer. "I think you nabbed her."

I had embarrassed myself but Poppy would talk to me, I was sure. She would respond to an e-mail. *The Wolf* was too shiny a lure. A trip to the mountaintop almost certainly awaited me: In a coffee shop or a restaurant or, if I was lucky, her apartment, I would have a chance to ask the remaining sister about Ben, about the body in the snow, about the frozen corpse whose meaning would answer all questions of my own and whose wealthy luridness would fit so neatly into the five-dollar-a-word story well of *Vanity Fair*. Why did the man who had everything strip himself naked in the middle of nowhere? How did all the money in the world fail him? Did his secret life overwhelm him? Meanwhile Leo was heading to a gun club on the Upper East Side, a luxurious cellar where you could fire an Uzi and knock back a Heineken at the same time. I passed. I wanted clean air. The rich kids were cloying my sense of the purpose of humanity. Soon I would have to go back to the basement, where I was running out of money, out of work, out of time, out of justifications for staying in New York. Even the journeyman fare of quarterly reports for corporations was drying up, going online, fading into nickel-a-word territory. The situation had deteriorated to the point where I was making coffee at home and writing in bed.

Poppy had joined Colin Farrell on the sectional and never looked again in my direction but I knew we were stretching to the same wilderness, the wilderness that will have to do for a home.

E verything that happens in life means that you need to make
more money. For Dale, in the winter of 1931, the expectation of
a child was like the presentation of a bill.

He married Kitty just as he was supposed to. The brief ceremony at
the desolate town hall; the wedding breakfast that followed, with orange
juice rather than champagne, at the second-least-expensive hotel in
Champlain; the stroll through town back to Flora Avenue instead of a
honeymoon—he saved as much as he could. The Depression had shattered all romantic expectations anyway. In faraway cities, the financiers
had conjured for themselves the great skyscraping towers so they could
leap to their deaths from the window ledges, and therefore the steelworkers in Champlain all had to be fired. The timing of the globally
logical conclusion couldn't have been worse for Dale's side businesses in
Atkinson, the auto parts, the radio sets, but the creeds he inherited had
been designed for plague and famine and whatever other catastrophes
his hardscrabble ancestors had reckoned with. Always find a way to get

along. No matter what, keep going. Foot-in-front-of-foot-in-front-of-foot rustles away any wonder at origins or destinations. We're all wind-up toys sent into the world, stumbling across the table until we fall off.

A fresh catastrophe was waiting for him one morning after his transformation. In the parlor, among the shimmering surface of clocks ticking on mantelpieces and leather-bound books beside silver-framed family photographs and side tables pooled by brandy snifters filled with odorless potpourri, a clipping from *The Dominion* rested like a fallen leaf on the doilied trunk of a comfortable armrest.

> January 21, 1931—Champlain's first murder of the year took place yesterday afternoon at the confluence of Church and Main Streets, in a dispute over a husky dog.
>
> According to horrified onlookers, the victim, one Myron Belluomini, was striking the animal forcibly with a broom handle, after the creature had leapt on his wife while in Miller's Hardware, the dry goods supplier. He continued to hit the animal after it had skulked into a corner.
>
> At this point the murderer, a large dark fellow in workman's clothes, arrived and remonstrated with the victim, who ignored him. Their subsequent argument escalated into blows, the killer landing a swift right to the temple which dispatched the unfortunate Mr. Belluomini instanter. Seeing his victim fallen, the murderer fled north along Church.
>
> The bystanders, coming to Mr. Belluomini's aid, failed to detain the suspect. No arrests have been made. The police are in the midst of enquiries and assure this reporter that they will soon have the suspect in custody, the man being a well-known criminal figure in the neighborhood.

*   *   *

Dale sat blankly listening to the silence of the women's mournful shame from the upper floor. They should have known. They all should have known after the black girl with her throat ripped out. No police would catch Max, but Dale knew he would never see his brother again. Who could be better at disappearing into the wilderness? He would miss knowing what happens next. Where was Max going? What was his fate? Max was gone. Dale was on his own. With a child on the way.

He needed money. Dale remembered that he had an appointment in Atkinson with Ron Ritchie, the owner of the Gasman Mechanics chain of garages in and around Atkinson, who owed him for nearly a year's worth of supplies. If Ritchie paid him, Dale might be able to finagle things. If Ritchie didn't pay him, he would go bankrupt. Whether his brother was a murderer or not, he just had time to race for the train.

The bar in the Late Spring Hotel in Atkinson was a mean, low room that smelled of mistakes. Dale liked to conduct business at the bar of the Late Spring because the booze was cheap and the only food on offer was pickled eggs for a nickel. If he was going to be bankrupted, it may as well be on the cheap.

Ritchie showed up late, while the radio behind the bar scratched out the latest disastrous agricultural news. He strolled in with a roly-poly air of unconcern that informed Dale, more than anything the fat man could ever say, that Ritchie was about to screw him.

"Looks like we're all going to the slaughterhouse together," Ritchie noted, nodding at the radio. "Last man out."

Dale mused over his beer. "Doesn't seem like much togetherness to me."

"You're right there." Even the way he tucked his belly under the rail was maddeningly indifferent.

"Seems like everybody's alone."

"Now, Dale, don't bring me down." Ritchie was restraining a grin, gauging within himself just how much of a bastard he was, which turned out to be quite a bastard, more of a bastard than he would have thought, more than his mother would have thought anyway.

Dale hiccupped and sighed at once. "All right, Ronnie, I won't bring you down but how about you don't bring me down either? How about we fight against all this destruction, all this collapse, and learn to be human beings to each other."

"That sounds good," Ritchie said warily.

"Now, don't get nervous. I'm not asking you for what you owe me."

"No?"

"I wouldn't expect that of you now, at this moment."

"That's good. Fine. Swell. What do you want then, Dale?"

"What I want is a debt guarantee, just a sheet of paper saying that you owe me, that you know you owe me, that I know that you know that you owe me, and that you plan to pay me." That would be something he could show to MacCormack when the heavenly books swung open.

Ritchie frowned solemnly as he took his first sip of beer. "Not really going to be able to do that."

"What part of what I said is untrue?"

Ritchie licked the luxurious foam from his primitive lips. "You want to be human beings about this?" he asked.

"That's what I said."

Ritchie's eyes glassed over, the sign of a man recusing his meaning from whatever he was about to say. "I can smell the death on you."

"What do you mean?"

"You'll be back, don't misunderstand. But even if I paid you all that debt, it would keep you alive for, what, six months? Another season in hell."

"So you're not going to pay what you're telling me you owe."

"What I'm saying to you is that I'm a businessman, and I know that if you go bankrupt, I'll only have to pay a fraction of the debt." Ritchie paused for a slug of beer. "That's what I meant when I said I can smell the death on you."

"So you're going to kill me," Dale said. A bored telegram boy was standing by Dale's side.

"No, nothing so grand. I'm telling you that you're already dead."

Dale fingered open the message from the telegram boy. Ritchie reached over the green-gray tub to finger-filch a five-cent egg from the reeky waters. The telegram read: SON BORN STOP.

Dale left Ritchie to pay for the drinks and walked to Atkinson Station, considering the fate of men. He was near middle age, had worked hard and smart for twenty years without pause, and now owed far more than he possessed. His child was born to an absent beggar, a drifter. He had nothing to show but two hundred Interceptor radios in a sufferance storage center on the outskirts of a two-bit gold-mining town. If he could sell the radios, he might be able to blanch over the auto parts losses to MacCormack. He might be able to keep his job. He couldn't go back to Champlain without a job.

He had to sell those radios. He had to. Dale Wylie started to make his fortune for the simplest reason there is: He had to.

*   *   *

The patter for radios in 1930 was elaborate, a full-fledged opera of a sale with enforced intermezzi between multiple acts. Approach was key. The houses of potential buyers had to be solid. Never bother walking up to a door if the lawn's not trimmed, if the steps aren't swept. Never bother with bachelors or the poor. Never bother with a busted roof. Dale mostly tried farms on the edge of town, which could at least sustain themselves, despite depressed food prices, with their own produce. Their remoteness, too, was an advantage. The radio was the latest cure for loneliness.

Never admit you're a salesman. To arrive at a farm in 1931 and to admit salesman status meant guaranteed rejection. Dale informed whoever answered, suspicious housewife or shirtsleeved proprietor rustled from his newspaper or dreamily uninterested teenager, that he was from a government office performing transmission tests in the area. Dale would then set up a radio transmitter in their parlor, or their dining room if they didn't have a parlor, completely free of charge, and return in a week to find out if they had received any signal.

In the salesman's fantasy, what played out a week later was a short scene. "So did you snag a signal?" The man of the house, bragging a bit, replied that he even managed some stations in Washington State, and then the salesman proposed, "Well, if you want to keep it, I can do a deal for you," and the man of the house replied, "Now, what would that cost?" and the salesman mused, "Well, seeing as you've done us such a big favor by allowing it to be installed for the test . . ."

The scenes we write for ourselves are the dramas that never get produced. The sparse territories around Atkinson huddled in a subcutaneous bowl of nickel, which screened out radio signals, so the installed receivers generated mostly a howling ruff of static. Even when Dale managed to slip through the suspicious door, set up the transmitter, pry his way out of pointed questions, and bait the sale, he received a curt "Get that bloody machine the hell out of my house" rather than "Where can I buy one?" when he returned.

After the tenth rejection, in the futility of February, Dale sat nursing a sudsy beer, tracing figure eights in the sawdust floor of the Late Spring Inn, ruminating on the day's nastiest sales calls, the dooming screech of the hectically oblivious static. How can you sell radio sets when there's no radio to pick up? He wondered: Why didn't Atkinson have its own station? It would give a radio salesman a chance. Then he wondered: Well? Why didn't Atkinson have a radio station?

Dale helped himself to the bar's phone and connected to a clerk at the Radio Commission in Minneapolis. The license for the town belonged to Atkinson Lumber, he was informed. They communicated with crews who were working outside the town line by radio. Or rather they used to, the clerk said. Why weren't they using them anymore? Dale enquired. Oh, new regulations. The camps had to be connected by telephone if they employed more than two hundred men.

The next morning, Dale admitted himself to the frantic offices of Rich Julian, owner of Atkinson Lumber. Drunk, lecherous, always in the middle of labor conflicts, mostly because he hated to pay men who did nothing more than work for a living, Rich Julian was permanently screaming into a phone or thinking about screaming into a phone. In the pause to light a cigarette, Dale piped up: Did Mr. Julian know that he was still paying property tax on the value of the radio license? Did Mr. Julian know that he could write off the sale as a depreciated asset with a simple transfer of ownership? Fine. Other fish to fry. What was the deal?

Dale paid one dollar for the radio license, with the understanding that if Atkinson Lumber requested the property back within one calendar year, Julian could pay back the dollar and have his license back. Rich Julian was in the lumber business. Not the radio business. Take the tax fix. For free? And get the little fellow in glasses out the door? Sure thing. He wrote off the loss and forgot that he had ever met Dale Wylie.

That single dollar was the outlay for the entire Wylie family fortune, the seed of billions.

Dale had a license. He needed a machine. He needed means of broadcasting. Over at the Atkinson High School, it so happened, he knew that a bright lad named Sidney Colman was halfway to being a solid radio mechanic. His family had bought one of the sixteen Interceptors he'd managed to fob off, and the boy had founded a radio club. Over a milk shake and a cheeseburger, Dale proposed a special project. He would pay for the parts if Sidney set up the transmitter. The fantasy of Sidney Colman's teenage years was to construct a functioning radio transmitter; here was a man willing to let him buy whatever parts he might need from the distributor in Minneapolis, on as much credit as was required. (And only Dale needed to know that the distributor was going bankrupt so he wouldn't have to pay. He could smell the death on them.) Sidney built his transmitter, and Dale wrote a letter to the principal of Atkinson High commending the boy, and a year later Sidney Colman was off to Oxford, the first Rhodes Scholar Atkinson ever produced, and Dale had a radio transmitter for the price of a cheeseburger and a milk shake.

Last and most definitely least, Dale needed something to put on. What do people listen to? Every media owner thinks of content as little as possible but Dale barely had to think. Preachers stopped him on the street. High school kids handed him well-formatted typewritten notes imploring him to let them volunteer as DJ. Any old man in town would have agreed to announce the high school hockey games for a mickey of rye. What did it matter? The Atkinsonians had nothing else to listen to. The bowl of nickel in which the town squatted had made selling radio sets halfway impossible. Owning a radio station was all gravy. He was literally the only show in town, and in a town with two of everything. Two gas stations. Two Chinese restaurants. Two grocery stores. They had to advertise or die, advertise or cede to their worst enemy in life, the owner of the other place.

A week after KCUV launched, he sold all the Interceptors, and then brought a thousand Victor sets and sold them to all the families that had just bought Interceptors. That's what you call progress.

Then, in the hallucinatory summer of 1932, the badlands encircling Atkinson hallelujahed with fresh gold seams. Dale needed more to get more, so he returned to Pittsburgh, to the Liberty Bell Bank, to ask for a loan. The jowly manager stared at Dale's single page of prospectus like a joke, his awe tinged with disbelief. The cost of Dale's business had been two dollars. That week, the profits had been four thousand dollars. How? Well, Dale explained cheerfully, one dollar on the license, and the transmission room was a building the owner couldn't rent out, so just to maintain the space in good condition, he rented it out for a dollar. And everything else had been free. Everything? He called it Community Radio.

The Liberty Bell Bank loaned him twenty thousand dollars with the transmitter and license as collateral. For the first time, he amounted to something. He amounted to twenty thousand dollars. The certified check burned his inside pocket, blazing with the promise of indisputable value, tugging him up to the heavens of respectability. With the power of that number, he could roll with the train into Champlain Station, stride down the streets he remembered, turn suavely onto Flora Avenue and up to the old door.

The boy who answered his knock gazed up at him with his own eyes. He was wearing navy blue cotton shorts and a coarse shirt of faded white linen. He had Max's shoulders, Max's streaked blond hair, Max's compactness, but Dale's own eyes. A deeper howl than the wolf, the recognition of his own, Dale smothered by lifting the frightened, resisting boy into his arm. A letter from Marie had told him the boy's name was George.

George Wylie's first memory was his father's rough hands, unfamiliar, leading him by his fingertips away from dark succulent 17 Flora Avenue through the crisp, burnt-pumpkin, scarlet-leaved air. They walked away from the bustle of the east-side streets, across the Monongahela River, to the curvy big houses that danced around one another as dauntingly as grand ladies. They were so rich, so gingerbread, so haunted.

The boy lived in a house of women, much the way his father had. The whirl of household machinery ignored him, the steamy yard of laundry, the gagging slops hauled out to the gravelly alley, the beef of requirement chewed at the dinner table, the treasury of the berry jam in the risky larder. Passing between the laughing skirts of the boarder women, avoiding the somnolent, shadowy propriety of parlors, George ran toward sweet and away from slap, praying to the expected god in the quiet before bed. His mother loved him with her tender gazes. His grandmother loved him with her guiding hands. Despite all the busyness, despite the full dinner tables and the crammed halls, he was alone in a house of women. His father was a whispering among the boarders. George Wylie, though he didn't know it, was born lonely.

As they crossed the river, mother sulked with grandmother behind them. Father stopped the family outside the biggest and curviest of all the houses, a mansion on Larchmount Crescent, the fanciest street in town. "Well, boy, what do you think?"

"Fine," little George croaked.

"Which room do you think you'll want for your bedroom?"

"Dale Wylie," interrupted grandmother. "Don't give that boy ideas of what he can and can't have. You'll fill up his heart with envy."

"All right, what do you think, Mother?" The adults seemed to be talking about things they weren't talking about.

"None of my business."

"Tell me, though, what do you think, Kitty?"

Mother said nothing. The Larchmount Crescent house was three or four times the size of the house on Flora with lawns on either side and tall hedges screening the view in a ring. "A good, solid house," grandmother said.

"It's ours. I bought it yesterday."

George could hear the women saying nothing behind him. Father drank in their shock like Ovaltine steam. George had only one question for his dad: "Will the boarders like it?" But there would be no more boarders. They didn't need the boarders' money anymore. George just wanted his father to stay. But he curled his hand into the roughness of his father's because he knew that he would go. The house at least was grand. Here was an early lesson for George Wylie: The grander the house, the lonelier it is.

The house on Larchmount Crescent was collateral for seven separate mortgages, which Dale used to raise capital for a binge of spending.

He bought Atkinson's town paper, *The Atkinson Register*, for ten thousand cash, with an agreement in monthly promissory notes for fifteen thousand over the course of ten years. That price included the oldest building in town, on the highest hill—he moved the radio station in and forced the six reporters that came with the building to move their desks into the hall. The employees already worked for minuscule salaries and he slashed them further. In the early thirties the possession of a job rated about the same as possession of a soul. At the same time, he raised his rates. With the newspaper and the radio station, he held a town monopoly on advertising.

As the profit margins crept up, he could leverage higher sums against the properties, with which he could buy more papers, more radio stations. In 1935, he took over *The Rainsview Sentinel* and KMPS in Bracebridge. In 1936, *The Fargo Herald* and *The Callister Standard*. At that time, the purchase value of a newspaper was calculated by taking the annual profit and multiplying it by ten. Working out the annual profits, especially during the years of turbulence, was a problem. The owner always wanted to pick 1927 as the year to establish the business's profitability because that year combined high commodity prices with a fast-growing global economy. Dale accepted that assumption, which made his opponents believe they'd pulled one over on him, then he would apply the incurred debt obligations of that year over ten years, too. The sellers always believed they were realizing a huge bargain—the 1927 price for a paper in the middle of the thirties—but Dale knew that the optimism of 1927 had incurred its own costs.

Once he owned a newspaper, Dale cut costs in half. Cut everything. In half. Since the purchase price had been based on ten times the profit margin of a single year, the key was to double that profit margin immediately. "A penny saved is a penny earned" is a mistaken aphorism. A penny saved exponentially improves the ratio of profit to investment. Among his junior executives, Carnegie was famous for never asking the profit, only the cost of things. The work of the owner is not to create or to add value but to make desirable things cheaper. That's it. That's the entire trick. Everything else is an accident or a by-product. Dale understood.

His ideal newsroom, he claimed in a later interview, consisted of three people: One to write the articles, one to sell the ads, and one to make sure the writer and the salesman were spending the least possible amount of money. Dale Wylie converted his cheapness into a spectacle, an object lesson for the employees. It is true—and not merely legend— that at *The Atkinson Register* every reporter had to hand in a pencil stub before receiving a new pencil. Dale banned notebooks. Reporters used scrap paper for their interviews. At *The Fargo Herald*, Dale discovered the model that he would apply later to his newspapers across the world: the 20/2 system. He demanded a twenty-percent profit margin and expenses worked out to both decimal points.

Even at this early stage, Dale didn't bother his editors about anything other than money. The political positions of his papers were irrelevant. If he bought a paper with a strong left-wing sensibility, it kept that sensibility. He never bothered his editors with calls to support one or another of his friends in a local political battle; he had no political friends. Even later, when he controlled some of the most influential press outlets in the world, he never imposed his own view. Other proprietors used newspapers as playthings of their opinions. Dale used them to make money.

Dale's acquisitiveness quickly transcended the obviousness of cash. Money was just a means to borrow more money. The Liberty Bell Bank lent him so much that they couldn't stop themselves from lending him more. Each business plan promised to fulfill the debt he already owed them, and so they ran deeper and deeper into funding his business. Those bets, in the end, turned out to be among the most profitable the Liberty Bell Bank ever made.

Larchmount Crescent was the distant, shadowy home he returned to if he ever needed to reassure himself that there was a purpose to the leap of number into number. The upgazing boy. The unhappy women who had nothing to complain about. The house admired from the street. The car admired on the street. Respectability.

Wading through the thick grasses of the backyard that ran longer and wilder toward the ravine, George heard his father's voice calling him. His father was the world. What did the world want with him? At the milkman's door, a smiling gray-flannel colossus, all glasses, waving a heavy arm.

"Come inside, Georgie, let's get you dressed."

"I am dressed," George answered.

"You are dressed but you're not properly dressed. Now come on in."

Dad smelled of cigarettes and gasoline and alcohol, talk and money. He brought talk and money into the silent, drab house.

A whole suit of strange clothes had been arranged on George's bed, a burgundy blazer, gray flannel trousers, a starched white shirt, a burgundy-and-gray striped tie. They were a strange dress-up. His father helped gently, clumsily, tucking him into the uniform, smoothing the creases with a butcher's palm, each article of clothing more uncomfortable than the last.

"Are we going to church?" George asked.

"Even better. We're going to Hamilton College," his father answered.

"Dad?"

"Yes, son."

"Why can't I go to school at home?"

His father's pause, perhaps to concentrate on the ribbon architecture of the tie, perhaps to contemplate thoughts deeper than ties, bloomed into petals of nothing. "Georgie, you are the first in the family to go to Hamilton College. It's one of the most expensive schools in the country. You should be proud."

"Dad?"

"Yes, son."

"Why do I have to wear these clothes?"

"Because they're respectable."

George thought while his father lassoed the tie over his neck. "Dad?"

"Yes."

"Is respectable the same as uncomfortable?"

Dale's laughter, somewhere in between a peal and a cackle, had the caramel warmth of a man who smokes and drinks with all walks and all stations in life, and the creamy ease of the father's happiness spread deliciously under George's skin, though he didn't get the joke.

They rode the black car to the school. Outside the pressed iron gates of Hamilton College, where the wealthiest coal and steel families from Pittsburgh bought their children's placement at Harvard and Yale,

Dale and George scrutinized the other boys, all in the school burgundy and gray, bright, clean-cropped, shouting and larking as the jaws of the school swallowed them, a portal to a grand digesting future.

"They seem friendly," Dale said.

"They're friendly with each other because they're friends," George said.

"Go make them your friends."

George pecked his father's sandpapery cheek. The distant and unpredictable gods are the ones we must obey without fail. In the photographs of his childhood, George Wylie always wears the same dumb smile on his half-pleased face. This smile he placed on his face for his father.

Dale watched his son dissolve into the crowd of the uniformed elite, drifting into the school's gates before driving away. He had won. He had a son in Hamilton. No one would be able to say he wasn't respectable again.

In November 1937 a stranger arrived at the office in the belly of the *Atkinson Register* building on Mott Street without an appointment.

The stranger, dapper in double-breasted Harris tweed, assiduously brushing snowflakes from his shoulder and stomping fine brown leather shoes on the mat, entered smiling like a high school football star sharing the credit for a winning touchdown. Ms. Ricci, Dale's secretary, who was later to marry into the Stanfield family and become, for 1958, the best-dressed woman in Cleveland, Ohio, noticed that he wasn't wearing boots or a jacket. He wouldn't give a name either. He wouldn't listen when she told him that Mr. Wylie was very busy and had no time for peddlers. He said he would stay in the waiting room until Mr. Wylie was ready. They had business to discuss. No, he wouldn't say what kind of business.

A few minutes later, Ms. Ricci, hearing the sound of soft scuffling and scraping, peeked into the waiting room where the stranger was hefting the chestnut leather sofa to an angle more available to the door.

"What do you think you're doing?" Ms. Ricci asked.

"See, with the chairs like this, when the occupant of the office comes out, he can see who's waiting for him right away."

"I think Mr. Wylie knows how he likes his chairs."

"I'm sure that's true, Ms. Ricci," said the stranger, "but, you see, soon his office will be mine and the waiting room can't look so shabby when people are here to see me."

When Dale finally allowed the stranger into his office, the man who stood before him was in many ways his opposite. Having lived on the road, separated from his family, Dale had grown rotund and sloppy, waddling around in his cheap suits. The stranger strode into every room with the glamour of predation. He had his shoes shipped in from New York, his suits from London; he arrived everywhere freshly barbered and manicured with his smooth charm that mimicked a small town's idea of a movie star.

"What's your business?" Dale asked, affectedly uninterested.

The stranger placed a book of signed contracts on the desk. Straight from the train station, the man had marched down Robinson Street and sold half the stores sectional ads for the newspaper and the other half-minute spots for the radio station. In 1937, to wrest a book of advertising contracts from small-town businesses was as miraculous as slapping down a grasped ray of sunshine, and Dale's initial disbelief lessened only when he saw the signature of Saul Levman, the owner of the Second Moon, the movie house, on one of the tickets. That could not be a fraud.

Saul never screwed up. Dale's skepticism faded to a dull, inexplicable dread. Who was this guy?

"That's an impressive piece of salesmanship," he said.

"I'm an impressive guy."

"I guess I ought to thank you for the business. Thank you."

"Oh, I wouldn't thank me yet. I haven't given you those contracts. I'm trading them."

Dale leaned back, tucking the stage pen into the properties closet of his suit jacket. "What's your price?"

"I want the job of head of sales, either for *The Atkinson Register* or KCUV, I don't care which."

"Take both," Dale said instantly. "But you'll have to fire the other guys."

Firing people was never a problem for Dale's new lieutenant, whose handshake was a silken garrote and whose name, Dale learned only after he'd hired the man, was Jack Taggart.

Dale had little time or inclination to investigate Jack's abilities or origins. The sales grew. Growth was enough. With Jack managing Atkinson, Dale returned to the trains, sieving the prairie for any glints of despair he could buy up. There were plenty of papers for sale in the Depression, plenty of once-big men willing to cash out for a survivable sum. Dale ran his luck through a surging mass of hopelessness, men who couldn't find work or who had given up hoping for work, men who absented themselves from the quest for material advantage as surely as any monk out of legend, drifting into steamy camps with nothing but their bellies and a general fear, a fear of themselves and other men, of their memory and of the changing of the seasons. Among all those sunken faces, in all those irrelevant towns, smelling of stale sweat and unswept horse stalls, Dale couldn't tell whether he was disappointed or relieved never to catch Max's face staring back.

Dale quickly realized that he could save the expense of telegrams to Atkinson while he was on the hustle—any ideas he had for the business, any opportunities he could imagine or any savings he could reckon to squeeze from the already reamed business had already been reckoned up by the time he returned. "Jack, come in here," he would say.

"It's done," Jack would holler, from the back office.

"What do you mean, it's done? I haven't even told you what to do."

"Dale, there's two things you can ask me. One is an idea that's good, that I've already thought of. The other is an idea that's no good, that I'll talk you out of. So either way it's done."

More than once, Jack's mannerisms, the unconsidered turning of his cheek to greet a stranger at the door, the thrust of his eyes through the window down to some disturbance on the street, or the cup of his hand to hold a lit match against the wind, filled Dale with old memories of Max. The warmth. The trickiness. The confidence that comes from being knocked down and standing up again and again. The gamble in both men. You could say that Jack was Max with polish. The irresistible aroma of worldliness swept over their bodies, and gathered love wherever they passed. How long would Dale be able to keep him? How long until the man's talent carried him away from small-time Atkinson?

They took to the road together: the charmer and the cheapskate, twin pistons firing, tight finance and loose credit, investment and salesmanship, determination and *sprezzatura* buying up every newspaper and station they could with other people's money. They never spoke, or rather they spoke about baseball, or the business, or the bright future of media and where they should position themselves to catch the fullest light of its glittering treasure dawn, or they performed racist imperson- ations of the indistinguishable proprietors of the indistinguishable Chi- nese restaurants in the indistinguishable prairie towns, or they talked about when the Depression would end and how the poor really had only themselves to blame, and they traded rumors and gossip, but they never spoke. After working, they would drink together in the cigarette fog of a random tavern, stumbling out into the snow with new women and old songs, on their way to a track or the movies or a traveling bur- lesque show—whirling sequined pasties over shelf hips and the indif- ferent eyes of the women who floated superciliously over their bodily commodification. At the end of the evening, their paths would diverge. Dale would head to a detective novel in the bath at the hotel, and Jack out for more. And Dale never asked what more or how much more or what kind of more Jack preferred.

The war was a big score for the business. Americans devoured news of parliamentary debates in languages they did not speak and the har- vests of farmers halfway across the surface of the earth and battles on faraway oceans as if the information were as succulent as local gossip.

In Pekora, South Dakota, in the spring of 1939, in the middle of negotiations with the stoic owner of *The Agricultural Fair Dealer*, Dale and Jack were dining on wonton soup and fried rice, past midnight, in the Garden of Earthly Delights, when Jack, not looking up from his bowl to take a hefty gulp of rye, said, "I guess I'll take over the negotia- tion tomorrow, boss."

The full moon rose that night. Dale searched Jack's face, but his eyes stayed at the bottom of his bowl. They had shared the road for months and Dale had assumed, like he had to, that his explanations—bad flus, family visits—had been accepted.

"Unless you plan to come in," Jack added.

"No, you take it, Jack."

"The thing about me, boss," Jack said, tongueing a clot of oily rice out of his undergums. "I'm smart enough to know what I don't want to know."

The dread blushed over Dale again. And what was Jack's secret? That's what Dale, shifting in the booth, wanted to know. What moonlit howl was Jack keeping to himself that he understood so casually how to treat a secret life?

The gambling sure wasn't his secret. Not a small town in the whole Midwest that didn't have a back alley door willing to welcome Jack Taggart down a flight of low steps into a gathering of the dentist, the doctor, the lawyer, and the main street storeowners. They loved Jack. At any game they cared to play, he was the best player in the room. His problem was that he would deliberately take odds that he knew were poor, just for the sake of the gamble. When he won, he was vicious. Catching an ace in the hick seed lot back room, he screamed, "Go pick pennies out of the urinal." When he lost, clutching his hair, he stumbled out over the smashed glass of broken bottles, the tossed butts of all those townie sons of bitches laughing, displaying the trophy of the necktie he had wagered on a thin draw.

Dale preferred Jack losing. To cure himself of the sting of losing, Jack could sell dog meat to a Brahmin. He was the ideal hustler: a gifted salesman whose biggest scores lasted mere days, who lived in the begging rumblings of a permanent need for high-profit wins. Jack cut angles for others even when he couldn't himself. He put Dale on to Utah bonds when they were selling at pennies on the dollar; a Western government, he figured, could never stomach the humiliation of a default. When the bonds were later realized at par, the windfall provided a rare cash infusion into the Wylie properties. Later, in the 1950s, Taggart picked the sites of the Texas oil drills. Jack Taggart was always lucky for the Wylies, even if he was a curse on himself, and the curse spilled over his life in periodic, mesmerizing waves of degradation.

While Dale checked figures, Jack sat across the train table in a pool of self-disgust, rumpled, gambled-away, and Dale never spoke; he usually waited until the mud puddle of Taggart's mood, which sunk into clotted self-pity, inevitably evaporated as they pulled into the next town, where he could earn it all back in commission, which he almost always managed to lose again at dice or cards or in the darkly magical whisking of stones into cardinal corners that the degenerates called fan-tan.

Dale was surprised when Jack, flummoxed in his usual way, broke the silence. They were pulling out of a dense, flat, brambly odor of cattle in the dark of the train station in Sioux Falls into the clear disconcerting light of the foothills on their way to Oregon, to investigate a few papers that might be up for grabs.

"How long we been doing this, Dale?" Jack asked.

Dale looked up from the latest batch of telegrams. "You've been with me almost two years now."

"How long we going to keep doing this?"

"Until I'm sitting on a throne of diamonds on a pile of money that reaches to the moon."

"That's what you need?"

Need? How could he talk like there was an end to need? A boy in Hamilton College who would sometimes be a wolf, who would someday share in the beastliness, someday need to hide. That would do for a lifetime's neediness. Self-pity makes men stupid.

"You'll do it forever," Dale tried. "You can't not do it. You are a force of nature."

"I'm broke, Dale."

"So what? You'll earn it all back in Portland or wherever we're going now. Where are we going?"

"And then lose it again?"

"And then win it again, like you always do. I'm not your mother but you could stand to stop the gamble when you're up for once."

Jack shot his cuffs, badgered his nose. "I'm broke in a deeper way."

"Don't kid a kidder," Dale said.

Jack rubbed a hand over his stubble. "I've got to tell you something that I don't want to tell you."

Again Jack filled Dale with dread, an after-lemony drying in his mouth, like his chest was a squeezed sponge. "Are you sure you want to tell me then?"

"I don't know who else I'm going to tell. That's about the size of it. That's about where I'm sitting right now."

Jack Taggart's secret was a family in Florida, a wife named Scarlet and a son named Lee, starving in Sarasota. The cash Jack was gambling away wasn't entirely his to chuck in fistfuls on the bonfire.

He was begging Dale for a loan. Dale never gave him a loan. On the train in the foothills, Dale instead made the shrewdest deal of his life. He agreed to take care of Jack's wife and son, so long as Jack worked for him. He would set them up in the coach house behind Larchmount Crescent—which meant, incidentally, that he could write off all repairs on the property as business expenses. And he would send Lee to Hamilton College with his own son—also writing off the expenses as a part of Lee's salary. In total, Dale Wylie bought a family, forever, for a few thousand dollars a year. Jack Taggart was unable to stop himself from falling into Dale's arms, shuddering with happy sobs of gratitude, in public, on a moving train headed to the next newspaper or radio station or whatever else was there for the buying.

When Jack's wife and son arrived in Champlain, George watched the boy and his mother arrive from the backyard second-floor window. Their cheap summeriness stood out against the angular skeletons of the October trees, the rusty pillows of dank piled leaves. They were wearing the same outfit: matching cream shorts and orange juice shirts. The mother was a pinup drawing magically sprung to life, a Southern belle Floridified, a pink stick of chewing gum that walked around. The boy squirmed like a drooping humiliated flower. Marie Wylie answered the door.

"Hi. Are y'all the Wylies?"

"I'm Marie Wylie." She offered her hand but Scarlet threw herself into her fellow woman's arms, reeking of rum like an Easter candy.

"I am just so pleased to meet you. Jack has told us all about you, and how wonderful this country is up here. It's a bit cold, though, isn't it? A bit too little of the sun. Look at me, all bubbling over when I've got unpacking to do. This is my boy, Lee."

She reached over to the shoulders of the boy, whose sullenness looked starved, so hungry he'd forgotten hunger.

"Pleased to meet you, Lee."

"Pleased to meet you."

"Ma'am," Scarlet corrected.

"Ma'am," Lee added.

"All of it."

"Pleased to meet you, ma'am," Lee recited.

George could see the ambivalence of his grandmother. Marie disapproved of the woman's liveliness, sympathized with her effort to present herself, hated her colors, liked her manners. "I hope you find the coach house to your liking," she said.

"I'm sure we will. I know we will. Now, I'd better skedaddle and help the movers organize our things. You know how that can be."

Marie restrained herself from offering any help. You never know with Southerners. She might be taken seriously. "Good luck with that. See you later."

Scarlet bumbled over to the coach house, passing a flirtatious remark to the most heavyset lifter, a mass of mover, who lowered a credenza to leer at her curves as she sashayed into the house. Lee was left in the wake of the moving men and furniture, an afterthought lounging on the grass, studying a local civilization of ants. He had a sunburned face, eyes like spilled ink. George drifted downstairs; his father would want him to.

"You must be Lee," George said.

"You're George, right?" The bright boy lifted x-ray eyes.

"That's right." George curled on the other side of the thickening ants in the grass, great adventurers in a hidden world.

"They told me we were supposed to be friends." Lee held out an arm crawling with half a dozen bits of black.

George nodded with automatic admiration. "That's what they told me, too."

They talked about ants. Ants never needed to know if they were important or not—every one irrelevant as the next. Already they had recognized that neither of them was used to talking, not to other boys or to themselves, and that they both were living in dark silent houses, and neither of them saw his father much. George and Lee shared their loneliness, which is a stronger bond than mere companionship. They were imitating their fathers. Who isn't?

As he grew older and richer, Dale preferred the movies to people. It was at the Paradise Theater, in Champlain, that he saw *The Wolfman*—all right and all wrong—and after the show, he wandered through the old neighborhood in a daze of half recognition, until he found himself standing outside the nearly derelict storefront of MacCormack and Sons.

Dale stooped to enter. The offices were the same, exactly the same, but lower, grimmer. The dusty corners, the windowless rooms with the same sturdy stools he had polished, the same anxiety-riddled clerks, and MacCormack himself, turning to fix his gaze on the interloper.

"Look upon him," he declared to his clerks. "Look upon that man."

Dale knew MacCormack could smell the death on his own business. The big hardware stores with their immaculate supply lines and their hammered-out logistical systems would finish off small outfits like MacCormack's. The old man had gone ragged in his desperation. He kept going, no matter what. If everyone who knew he had no chance collapsed, capitalism would dissolve in its own acidic mist. Every business is a tragedy, every last one. It either eventually dies or becomes so big that it belongs, truly, to nobody. Business maintains its furious optimism to mask this terminal condition.

"Look on that man," he shouted to his clerks. "Look upon the man who has come out of the wilderness. He has come out of the wilderness and the question always with such men: Is it a prize or a loss? Beggars and lords are all the same."

"Hello, Mr. MacCormack."

"They always want something more, men like this man. Their appetites are of such a kind that they can never be satisfied. Tell me, have you come here for a job or to walk over me? I can't tell which, Dalie, though I always knew you'd come back for one or the other."

Dale throbbed with pity for the wobbly old trader, a cunning man crazed by his own wiles. It was MacCormack and Sons but MacCormack had no son. Business is a way for men to give themselves fathers and sons, fathers who grow cold and die, sons who run away, and money to bind them together, money to tear them apart. The room stank of sentiment.

"Thank you," Dale said.

"Is that what you came here to say? Right. You've had your say. Now go."

Dale rose out of MacCormack and Sons as if out of the tomb. He didn't need any more fathers. And his son was going to Hamilton.

"I didn't go to school in Florida," Lee Taggart admitted to George in the car on the way to their first day of third grade.

"Just watch me. I'll show you. The big boys tell you what to do and you have to do it. And then when you're a big boy, the little boys have to do what you say. It's fair in the long run," George said, trying out a phrase he had heard his father using.

"What are the big boys like?" Lee asked.

George stared like a philosopher-king out the window at the piles of gravel and ashes that would cram every corner of Pennsylvania if the men of that state had any say in the matter. "They're big," he declared.

The first week at school, George became the proof of his own lesson. George's housemaster, the redheaded lesser son of the attorney general of Connecticut, tipsy on smuggled cider and the arrogance of sixteen years, decided to ratify his first day's control over the under-lings through a demand for toast. George brought toast to his chambers, where his housemaster was hosting. The toast had blackened edges. The housemaster smashed the plate out of George's hand and declared that George was to strip down to his underwear and stand out in the rain. The other upperclassmen mumbled approvingly. What's the point of cruelty if you never display it?

The rain was near freezing, a thick, sleety wall. George had been told to stand outside in his underwear in the rain. Therefore he stood outside in his underwear in the rain. Lee found him before the curfew bell, by which time George had been enduring the cold for nearly six hours.

"They're asleep now, George," Lee whispered. "They're all asleep. I think you can come back now."

George straightened. "They haven't let me go yet."

"I don't think anybody wanted you to stay out all night."

"No. Maybe not."

"So why don't you come in?"

A thick smile, a mild smile, cracked open.

The next morning, the Hamilton masters on their way to classes discovered George standing outside in his underwear in the rain, in a state well beyond the point of embarrassment to the school and en-croaching on territory dangerous to their individual careers. Inquiries were made. Discussions were held. Letters were written. Suspension? Required. Even if his father was the attorney general of Connecticut.

After the fever, a long dream of ice in his blood, George woke up to find Lee waiting, legs crossed and reading *White Fang* in the steam-pressed, light-soaked infirmary.

"They've suspended the housemaster and you've been transferred to Warwick House," Lee said.

"And no fagging duties," George added.

"No more fagging duties."

George smiled mildly. "I told you. Do what the big boys say and everything will work out."

After his stand in the cold, the other boys at Hamilton College imbued him with a kind of fearful exceptionalism. He had no friends other than Lee but the rest of school reserved for him a separate place. He was so obviously capable of things they were not. His will must have come from a place of either total wildness or total control. They acknowledged his extremeness with cautious respect, and so his only real intimacy in childhood was with Lee.

The boys returned to the house on Larchmount Crescent for weekends of hockey. The Wylie chauffeur, who laid the backyard rink, was a Boston ex-pro who made ice with a sense of cosmic responsibility. When ice is made carefully, with instinct for the point of freezing, the calm certainty of the layering amounts to an artistry of the transient. They played one-on-one without goalies, with lumps of coal for posts, replaying Stanley Cup goals from descriptions on the radio, debating the merits of the curvature of their Micmac sticks, until the neighborhood boys began arriving and the game started widening. The only rule was no cherry-picking, which gave them a chance to argue, following the hurly-burly of sticks and skates with the hurly-burly of justification. Every game ended with both sides winners in their own judgments.

The friendship between George and Lee had a dark margin, and they could tease out their joy only so far. When night fell, Lee would have to slip across the ice to the coach house, where no one ever saw his mother, where even the milkmen and the bread men and the men from the general store learned not to knock but to leave their offerings on the stoop like devotees to a silent idol. Lee entered the coach house each night and escaped each morning like a continuous sacrifice continuously reborn.

George wondered if he should tell his father about Lee's invisible mother. Then again: Tell him what?

On George's thirteenth birthday, he learned that he was not an ordinary rich kid with a distant father but a monster out of legend.

"I got something to show you tonight," Dale whispered, leaning in with his smell of railways and leather and Brylcreem as the black forest birthday cake was cleared away. The whole family encircling the massive dining room table seemed to look away at once.

His father led him outside, to the edge of the rink where the evening was setting in scratched and shaved purple reflection. His father's arm was on his shoulder, a rare experience, and the frozen air shivered with vague significance. Dale pointed up to the moon rising over the world for the three billionth time or so. "Better hurry," he said.

He led the boy to the door into the basement, a door George had never seen opened, and then down closed concrete stairs. There were three large connected cages with a large door. George had not known that he had been living in a house of cages. To cage what? Father and son walked without comment into the largest, whose door clanged shut. Dale started shouldering off his suit, then unbuckling his pants. "You better get naked, son. You may as well see."

Dale gestured to a hanger on the back of the cage and George began timidly to unbutton his shirt. They were really going to get naked? The dose of fear was mixed with absurdity.

"I don't know if it'll be tonight, my boy." Dale hung his trousers over a wooden press fold in the corner. Why was he being so meticulous in his gestures? Why wasn't he explaining?

"If what will be tonight?" George asked, turning to pull his sweater over his head.

Already in the cage with him, a gray wolf, menacing in its calm, panted with killing in its clear eyes. George called for his mother and tumbled against the bars of the cage, bumped his lip, the taste of blood in his teeth. He looked back. The wolf had cocked his head, curious. The roar of the fear slowly diminished. The wolf was Father. George thought: Of course. George thought: The house of my parents makes sense. George thought: I have always known that my father is a wolf. Only the name of his origin had escaped him. George thought: I too am the wolf.

From that night, George Wylie spent every full moon in the cage. Sometimes his father was with him and sometimes he was away on business. When the transformation came, engulfing George's flesh in agony, shooting the boiling blood into his eyeballs, furring his skin, razoring his teeth and claws, Dale happened to be home, and they woke up in a naked heap together. Dale said, "Now you know."

George knew but at school he found questions intruding: What did he know? He knew the wolf was another nature. He knew the wolf was a secret. His mother never mentioned the monthly trips to the basement. No one ever offered any explanation, any possibility of meaning.

Were they alone in a private mystery? Or did every family in the world huddle underground three days a month?

Perhaps he could tell Lee. But Lee was sprouting in his own furies. It began when Lee made the Hamilton College hockey team and George didn't, which made no sense. George was an excellent defender. He could scallop-skate backward, and Lee couldn't. Lee was only good at the long pass, and two-line passes were illegal in the interschool league anyway. But Coach Tomson was always respected for the unusual selections he made. He never played favorites: He frequently picked the least likely, the least popular kids. The Hamilton Hellcats always made the league finals anyway, didn't they? Even the weak players, the slow-footed forward, the dekeable defensemen, were tokens of Coach's transcendent comprehension of hockey talent, his deep insight into the game.

It was as random as the wolf. Coach Tomson had stared into their hearts and uncovered the mysterious reality only he could see. Lee could play. George could not.

WylieCorp became an empire in 1947. The empire had an elaborate, unique constitution: Dale's will, a contract of succession which he constructed so that none of the firstborn male children could abdicate, nor could the company be sold out from under them. If the company collapsed, the family collapsed, and vice versa. He wrote it to be unbreakable. He had been scared by the collapse of the Soltanto chain of grocery stores. Old Enzo Soltanto had built a single store in Seattle into nearly a billion dollars' worth of fronts before he died in a brothel in 1936. In some of Dale's districts, ads from Soltanto's amounted to twenty percent of all buys. The two Soltanto sons, one a moron, the other a gambler, drowned the property like a puppy. The business could have survived one or the other but together their squabbling had ruined all hope. That wouldn't happen to WylieCorp. Dale would leave behind clarity, above all.

Dale Wylie's life passed by windows looking out onto fleeting landscapes. A man who sits by the window of a train owns an ersatz wisdom. He knows that everything passes. A clump of evergreen, a clump of deciduous in yellow, then red, a farm that needs paint, a shiny metallic silo, a Presbyterian church, a boy standing in a slough staring up resentfully as the engine of the world chuffs past, two girls in red hats, a clump of evergreen, a rusty abandoned truck, a rusty abandoned forklift, a rusty abandoned bulldozer, a sign that claims JESUS SAVES. One thing after another. Never his brother. One thing after another after another. The slow shudder into the station brought stuttering confusion. How are we supposed to live in the here and now after an endless mocking stream of theres and thens and thens and theres? His will was an answer of a kind: the business would not die.

Dale stopped for an occasional three days at the cottage in North Lake with George. For them, that scarred country was a rich void. They could run as wolves for days through the clear-cut wasteland, lapping waters from the translucent creeks and chasing down the fawns, shredding the throats of pawed hares, digging up squirrels, sleeping piled together in cougar-dug holes at night, then chasing through the morning in the camouflage of high grasses, the useless forests remaindered by the mills and the new forests springing up in sapling and brush. Their severed lives in school and on the road healed without scar, and they were simply father and son. Terror washed away from their skin in bliss. There is no luxury more intense than running through the country of yourself.

One morning, crumpled and aching on the cold hearthstones of the North Lake cottage, Dale returned to his humanity and George was not beside him. Dale found his shirt and slacks where they always were, behind his bedroom door, and, tossing them on, stumbled out and down to the lakeshore, to alleviate the quiet sadness that always followed the beastliness in Alberta.

George was already up, hugging his knees, looking over the lake at the sun infiltrating through the screen of pines. They sat in a failing silence.

"Dad? Are there any others like us?"

Dale breathed and pretended to consider. "I told you about your uncle Max."

"Yeah, you told me about Uncle Max. Nobody knows about Uncle Max, right? Maybe there are others that nobody knows about."

The crisscross yellow of daybreak was looming on the water. Dale breathed in the air of the past, cleansing and ugly. "I'll tell you the truth, son. Max is probably dead, or he's straight wolf."

"But he could be alive. He could come back. What if there are others out there like us? What if the world is full of us and everybody knows? What if we keep it a secret for no reason?" George looked at his father, slightly embarrassed by himself.

"Uncle Max isn't coming back," Dale said. "And he's the only one I know. And my father. Nobody else. We left nobody in Abermarley."

"What about the Taggarts?" George asked.

"You've seen something with Lee?" Dale was curious.

"No, but he hasn't seen anything of me."

Dale yawned. "I think that might be your answer."

George flopped back in the grass, ruminating, and Dale left the boy to his thoughts. The idle thoughts of youth are the subterranean pipelines of our lives. A moment of startled languor can twist a fate, through underground angles, underworld passageways flowing with nameless spirits. Fathers can only ever half understand anyway. George wanted there to be other wolves, with all the chambers of his heart. If there were other wolves, his secret life would not be the same as his family life, and the curse would not be the inescapable rage in his blood.

There are many aristocracies in the world, aristocracies of title and of money and of talent. But no aristocracy rules as thoroughly as the aristocracy of boy athletes.

That winter the ice on the rink between the houses on Larchmount Crescent was either empty or crowded; they played with the lads or not at all. Lee was permitted on the overnight trips to the academy farm, where the celebrated hockey players, the chosen ones, missed an entire week of school. Booze and dirty magazines, too, the envious school whispered, to the hardest-working boys.

Everybody played, the sons of steel mill owners and the sons of unemployed steelworkers, all the young men eager to forget for a couple of hours the desperate vanity of their fathers. Everybody played until the early darkness began to settle, and one by one they slunk away, with final insults and promises of minor revenges until only George and Lee sat on a snow mound untying their skates.

"I'm glad you're still willing to play with a crabby failure like me," George said. He was thinking about Christmas, and about Lee's Christmas in the coach house, whose curtains never even ruffled.

"I'm quitting the team after Christmas," Lee said.

"What?"

"I'm not going to play for Coach Tomson anymore."

Lee was unlacing his skates with mechanistic ferocity. The last of the light was collapsing and soon mothers and aunts would be hollering, but not for Lee. Never for Lee. His house was silence. The rumors George had heard about the coach "in the corners" must be true. The boys found enough courage for a single look and glutted on horror and compassion. Then the stars began to rise up, and the moon.

Dale lived for Alberta, but even that cherished respite soon vanished. The boys were soon to go. George would be off to Harvard in the fall. Lee was going to Blind River, Minnesota, as a sales assistant for the Wylie radio station WKPG, his first step in joining the company.

The compensation was a number. Dale was shaving in the train, the hot foam slicked on his cheek, the blade lifted a fraction below his left ear, when the tumult of calculation from fifty different companies, debts and revenue projections and realized profits and implied obligations, reconfigured and then resolved themselves into a single figure. Twenty million. He was worth twenty million dollars. Two with seven zeroes. Catching his own eye in the mirror, Dale began to bark with laughter, his jaw clenched, unable to stop. Then a howl triumphed up and out of him, ending in anguish. The memory of Max's eyes, flush with dumb-luck money, coming to call him into the night.

There was nobody else to call but Jack. He found his employee in a hotel room in Maine, the silvery laughter of various women pealing in the background. "What do you want, Dale?" Jack asked. "I'm busy. I told you to leave me alone when I'm making deals."

"I just had to tell you. Twenty million. I'm worth twenty million."

"Good for you. Why are you calling me?"

"I thought you might like to know."

The silence crackled with distance and suppressed indifference. A hard woman's laugh rang out like dropped change. "Listen, Dale, you gotta decide right now. Do you want more?"

Dale didn't need to think. "I do."

"Then leave me the hell alone, you dumb rich bastard."

Before George and Lee separated, before the end of what they would have to call their childhoods, there was time for one more revelation. On the night of their graduation ceremony from Hamilton, George took Lee down to the basement of Larchmount Crescent. The leashes, the cages.

For a few moments, they inhaled the smell of animal life, the perfuming rot and consumption and rage.

"Did this come with the property?" Lee asked.

"My father built it. He built all of this."

"For himself?"

"For both of us."

Lee opened the cage, gingerly creaking the joints, surprised at its realism. He stepped inside and closed the door. Lee's blank gaze posed a kind of question on the other side of the bars: Are you going to tell me or aren't you? The secret fell out of George: "Three days out of the month, we are wolves. We chain ourselves down here. I don't know if there are any others like us."

Lee was still. Eventually he moistened his lips with a tongue tip. "I guess we're even," he said.

"I guess."

They were children of the same secrets. Even in the deepest, most unspeakable matters, George was practical. One lesson he had learned from his father without ever having to be told was that no matter what nightmares came roaring out of him the business had to go on. Someday the business would pass to George and he himself was not smart enough to run it; Lee would be. He knew all of this when he was seventeen.

One final mystery remained. When Lee no longer returned to Larchmount Crescent, the coach house was empty. Outside the door, the newspapers stacked up, the milk soured on the stoop. Apparently, the boy, who was no longer a boy, had been living alone. And Scarlet Taggart? No one—certainly none of the Wylie women who had lived beside her for ten years and more—could say whether she had left or when. Once called, the police discovered a neat, well-maintained suite of properly decorated, thoroughly swept rooms. Were they dealing with a murder or a failure to cancel subscriptions? Lee was riding a train to Blind River, unavailable for questioning. Jack Taggart was somewhere in the South swallowing up newspapers and radio stations. Dale was in Atkinson, George at Harvard. What would they know anyway? Ultimately not even a missing person report was filed. There's too much oblivion in the world to keep track of it all.

THREE

S ix weeks after the party, "the personal concierge to Poppy Wylie"—
that was his title, right under his name—answered my seventeenth
or eighteenth request for an interview: "Ms. Wylie will grant you a
media availability," the e-mail read. I called Leo at home to exult but he
was away in Los Angeles for an audience with an idol of his own. Kate
shared in my triumph, though she was more amused by my excitement
than the note itself.

"Now we know what you give the woman who has everything," she said.

"A personal concierge?"

"Fame. The love that moves the sun and the other stars."

Ordinarily with an interview like this, I would have thrown myself
into preparations. The key with celebrities, even pseudo-celebrities, is to
remember details of their lives they themselves have forgotten—movies
straight to video, childhood indiscretions hushed up long ago, friends
abandoned decades previously, any detail that gives the interviewer an
asymmetry of information. But I had been preparing to interview Poppy

since her limousine had curled up outside the house in North Lake. My childhood had been preparation.

Poppy Wylie's personal concierge was a fastidious blond man named Marcus Koenig, a professional of the eccentric protocols and mannerisms of the ultrawealthy. The shade of overcome insecurities haunted his bright confidence. Maybe terrible acne as a kid? Maybe growing up gay in a small Midwestern town? Maybe a drunk mother? Maybe all of the above? Like everyone else on Poppy's staff, and there were at least a half dozen, Marcus wore pressed chinos and a pleated white shirt, the cuffs rolled perplexingly to the midpoint of the forearm. With slightly effeminate sandals, the look bordered on cabana boy even in the marble-paneled octagon foyer of a suite of apartments by Central Park.

Marcus led me to a small side table in the passageway off the kitchen, where a contract the size of a small book waited. I flipped through the pages. A standard attempt at post-interview approval. Marcus frowned judgmentally when I lied, obviously, and told him I'd sign it later. What was he going to do, disappoint his mistress? At first I disliked the man's affectation; he seemed to be imitating a butler he had seen on television. Later I understood how much effort went into maintaining the chaos of Poppy's life. Nothing requires more concentration than the enactment of whims.

I was Poppy's whim that day, so Marcus guided me into a gumwood-paneled library whose view of the park was pure will to power—as if the whole of New York had been built as an immense shrine around the patch of trees right there. Her magazine spreads spilled over the low table, *Vogue* from 1988, *Tattler* from 1991, *Esquire*, all informing me what I already knew: I was meeting one of the most beautiful women who had ever lived.

And yet I almost failed to notice her, still as a fallen leaf on the window ledge, her face darkened by the flood of light behind her.

"You made it," she said, beginning to wring her hands nervously. Her impossibly elegant silken black blouse and pantaloons could have served either as a pajama or a ball gown. She could have taken off her watch to go to bed, or put on diamonds to go to the Oscars. "I hope this is the right thing," she said. "Leo told me you were all right."

She had already spoken with Leo?

"Leo would know," I said.

"He told me you're old friends."

The phrase was quaint, but it would have to do until a more accurate one came along. "I've known Leo forever, or since I moved to the city anyway. I knew him before his accidental marriage."

"He's not married by choice?"

Mort Wilner taught me that you have to give confidences in order to receive them and therefore I dished about the shotgun wedding, the confusion of class, the difficulties of marrying when you're still infatuated. I contributed to the economy of pretended intimacy and she matched my contribution.

"There's no right journey, is there?" She was leaning over her legs, stroking their sheer surfaces, then sat up straight, with her hands on her lap.

"Tell me about your journey," I said. Her hands had stopped wringing. Her shoulders had relaxed. I had her.

I knew I would have to wait for material about Ben. Poppy had fifteen minutes of prepared material, which she repeated on a half-varied loop. It was *HELLO!* magazine stuff mostly, with a whiff of Oprah, about the horror of addiction, about how she had loved modeling but how there was a price to all that superficiality. I shouldn't dismiss her telling completely. She put the old story rather well. When your profession is having your photograph taken, you become a surface, she said. Her journey had been falling through surface after surface. That's how she put it. I let her ramble, nodding and feigning concentration, waiting for her to exhaust the topic. Then I could move in on what I really wanted to know: Why her brother had been lying naked in the Alberta snow. What she had known. The beastliness of her family.

Marcus and a fleet of servants entered and performed various rituals almost as though we weren't there. At promptly 10:30 a.m., a half glass of champagne and a carved half grapefruit sprinkled with brown sugar appeared at Poppy's side. At 10:45, Marcus pulled the blinds down to exactly three-quarters height, and I noticed he had taken off his shoes. All the staff had. The rule for midmorning was everybody barefoot, apparently.

After she had said the line about falling through surfaces for the third or possibly fourth time I began to edge, gingerly, toward the question I cared about. "And your family? How did they deal with your drug use?"

She sniffed and lit a cigarette, an aquamarine Sobranie just to add to the absurdity.

"My family were very loving, but they had no experience with secrets. And I kept everything from them. My family is close but I've always been different."

"You're adopted, aren't you?"

"My adoption doesn't matter as much as it does to some people."

I paused some more and her eyes flickered through the creamy smoke, seeking reprieve from the awkwardness. "I don't want to paint myself as a victim, as a poor little rich girl, but I will say that money creates problems in families and when that money grows to be billions, the problems that follow . . ." She drifted into a glazed reverie. "And it's not as if my parents were the kind of people who went to therapy. When you combine an addiction with unlimited resources . . ." She shrugged.

"It's harder than you think being a billionaire," I declared.

She squirmed. "I am responsible for my journey. I alone am responsible for my journey. It's just that when you belong to a public family, one of the deepest cravings you can have is the craving for privacy. Heroin is the ultimate privacy. You have no name to live up to. You have no name."

"Did your brother find it hard to be so wealthy?"

"Yes, I think he did," she said cautiously, then quietened. She was not so desperate for celebrity that there were not some doors she was willing to slam shut. I kept mum in hope, but then her eyes drifted to a distant horizon and her voice turned tour guide, as it had at the party in the Four Seasons. "I never met my grandmother or my great-grandmother. My own mother never met them either because they died before my parents met. The men were making the fortune and the women waited at home in Champlain."

"The men were in Alberta . . ." I suggested.

"Yes, and the women were in Champlain. I hated Champlain. Too small. They make you work all of that out in rehab. What are you running from? I knew right away when they asked that question. Champlain. My mother always cherished the memory of George's mother and grandmother. Kitty and Marie. They never went anywhere. Not me."

Maybe I should have declared to her openly: Your family are animals. I'm just not that good an interviewer. I'm still a polite boy from Alberta and I have little truck with the impossible. "Do you think that need for privacy is part of why your brother died the way he did?" I asked instead.

The smoke drifted over her like a city.

"I sometimes think that if I understood my brother's death, I could understand the whole history of my family."

I could think of nothing to say.

"If I could understand why he was out there naked in the snow. Do you know why?" she asked.

"I was hoping you could tell me."

She shrugged and smiled softly and I shrugged back. Our one moment of genuine connection was a profound ignorance.

Poppy put out her cigarette abruptly, then distracted me again. "How well do you know Anna Savarin? Do you go to each other's houses?" Poppy asked like we were old friends gossiping.

"I'm sorry. I don't know who that is," I said.

"I thought you knew Ben. You don't know Ben's wife?"

"Oh, Anna. I know Anna as Anna Wylie," I covered. "I did meet Max, the boy. At Sigma's birthday party."

"WylieCorp now technically belongs to Max, and through Max to Anna Savarin. Savvy Anna Savarin."

"I never managed to meet Anna," I said.

"Anna hunted Ben. People believe it was a sweet story, that they met at the Orange Blossom Ball at Hamilton College, and they did. They did. She hunted him there. That was the first place she hunted him." A tangent whisked her elsewhere. "Anyway, I think my journey is about leaving all that behind. And I think that what I have to share with the world is bigger than that. Every family has its secrets, its past."

With that question, our interview turned away from the chance of Ben, and I had no choice but to watch it go, at least for the moment. She had danced me around the edges of the room in which her brother's body lay and out the door again. I would have to think of another way in while she went through Part Two of her prepared material. I knew I was about to hear about The Cause. I had been expecting it. In *Down and Out in Paris and London*, George Orwell said that every waiter in Paris had to dream of opening his own restaurant. Not because the waiters were ever going to open restaurants but because the fantasy of opening a restaurant was necessary to endure the state of being a French waiter. Rich people are the same with their causes. Poppy needed to believe in something larger than herself to survive her narcissism. She lit another Sobranie, while I waited for her to unleash her justification for her own deification, the reason she deserved to be larger than ordinary people, a figure of public consciousness.

Zinc. Zinc was her cause. Zinc would cure everything. She explained: Countries with higher levels of zinc consumption are more peaceful and prosperous than countries with lower levels of zinc. Yeast has zinc. Countries that eat flatbreads are more violent and poorer than countries that eat leavened bread. Children with low levels of zinc perform at lower levels in schools. She supported charities that provided zinc supplements to poor countries. She wanted to raise awareness. She wanted the world to be aware of zinc.

About ten minutes into this simple explanation for all the world's problems—as I searched for ways back to her life, to her family, to the world of subjects people might conceivably care about, to the secrets I cared about—Marcus approached her the way a priest in Babylon must have approached the stone idol in the temple. She excused herself as if she were going to the next room for a pen.

Only Marcus returned. A sudden panic fluttered to my throat: What about all my questions? What about Senna? And Lou Reed? And her brother's body in the snow? Then admiration waked in the surge of regret. These rich people always manage to finagle the best of the situation.

"The media availability is closed," Marcus intoned.

"Just like that," I said.

Marcus returned my devastated smile with what amounted to fellow feeling. We were both creatures of her whim, lifted and dropped. "That's how she works," he whispered. "She goes." He said it with an almost Buddhist compassion, the way another might say "youth goes" or "the world goes."

I wandered into the park. All celebrity interviews end in disappointment, of course. You're supposed to encounter a person; instead you strike a deal, both sides making various arrangements with competing vanities. I had asked her about Ben and she had told me about the women around him. I had asked her about Alberta and she had given me Champlain. In my manifold failure, I sat beside Shakespeare's statue and tried to draw a connection—any connection—between the properties of zinc and a family of wolves.

No connection came. My interview with Poppy, my growing sense of the Wylies as a whole, had been, from the beginning, a movement backward, and not in the revelatory sense of heading upstream toward some mysterious source at whose origin all would be explained. They put me back in my childhood bed and covered me in heavier and thicker and darker blankets. Poppy was the living flesh of the men whose dusty papers I shoveled and sifted, and from her I had learned nothing. But that nothingness, I came to realize as I looked up at Shakespeare's bird-shit-streaked forehead, contained the most vital lesson of all. The Wylies didn't understand themselves. They knew no more about the meaning of their story than I did, probably less. They were not in possession of a secret that I could take from them. We shivered together in the same mystery—the wilderness that extended infinitely within them.

The contours of my obsession changed after the Poppy interview but its force remained. I had rung the tuning fork but couldn't find the spot to hold its meaningful vibration against: To North Lake or Champlain? To Dale or George or Ben or Poppy? To New York or China? To the moon? Anyway, I still had a story to write, and my interview with Poppy would serve that function well enough: I had my two quotes and a description at least. I could say that she had "deflected my questions about her brother's death." I sussed out a few other grains of mild significance as well. I remembered Poppy had said that her parents were not "the kind for therapy." A subsequent afternoon at the library coughed up the Winter 1958 issue of *The Journal of Pastoral Psychology*. George would have been twenty-four in 1955, living in Boston.

A Report of Lycanthropy as a Narcissistic Delusion:
The Case of G
By Roman Blom

Initiation of the Case

In 1955, during the course of ordinary practice, a quiet, respectable young man approached my office without referral. Having no familiarity with the psychoanalytic process, he initially had great difficulty expressing his reasons for seeking treatment. Following standard practice, I refrained from offering G any means of flight through social pleasantries, although his patience was immense, a fact which I interpreted as a sign of the strength and profundity of his psychopathology. Toward the end of our seventh session, he overcame his embarrassment and confessed to me the reason for his visits. He suffered the delusion of lycanthropy. At the time of the full moon, he tied himself in the basement of his house with a stout leash and brayed at the moon. These episodes typically lasted three days and three nights.

The delusion was not limited to himself or his own ego-creation. He believed that his father was a werewolf and his grandfather and his uncle had also been werewolves. His family had controlled their condition, over the course of generations, by means of physical restraints and occasional "holidays" in a family cottage in the woods of Canada, where their lupine nature was permitted wider scope. The reason G had sought treatment was in hope of a cure for his "condition."

The patient proposed a course of hypnotic suggestion. For obvious reasons, I considered the treatment a null option. I mooted behavioral treatment, a common approach for severe psychosis, in which category lycanthropy typically falls. G's lycanthropy was quite circumscribed, however, and the harm therefore more limited, opening more traditional avenues of the "talking cure." The patient complained that his condition required isolation three days a month. He complained also that the transformation into the wolf was painful, often leading to blackouts. His secret wolfishness was the source of a deeper malaise and alienation, too; he worried that he could never be understood because of his condition. Despite the normalcy of lycanthropy in his own house, he was worried about how it might affect his capacity to have a relationship with a woman. He confessed that, at the time of our interview, he remained a virgin, and his primary reason for seeking counsel was that he doubted he could be intimate with a woman, either physically or emotionally, until he understood and conquered his "beast." I suggested to him that maybe he should find a woman who enjoyed his beastliness. He doubted such a woman existed. I assured him they did. He admitted that he probably would not want a woman who wanted him as a wolf.

The Patient's Milieu and Childhood

The patient developed within a mostly normal family environment and had revealed no tendencies toward psychotic manifestations, either in school or at home. He was born in a well-to-do family in the environs of Pittsburgh and had no criminal past. His father traveled on business frequently. The primary family unit included a grandmother and a great-aunt who aided the mother. No servants were ever hired even though the family could easily afford them. His explanation, which he clearly believed, was the need for secrecy about the wolf. The women of the household almost never vacated the family mansion, either, not even for shopping. This self-sequestration sprung from the same source, according to G: the family's lycanthropy. When I asked if they had left their house before his father had made a fortune, he acknowledged that they had. "That's what money is for," he told me. "So you don't have to deal with a lot of people."

As a boy, G was educated at an all-boys' school in the city during the week. He spent the weekend at home. This bifurcated status of home life and school life, in which the former was exclusively feminine while the latter was exclusively masculine, led me to a conjectured diagnosis of lycanthropy as a repressed expression of the fear of castration, as found in Freud's famous Wolf-man case:

> It would seem therefore that he had identified himself with his castrated mother during the dream, and was now fighting against that fact. "If you want to be sexually satisfied by Father," we may perhaps represent him as saying to himself, "you must allow yourself to be castrated like Mother; but I won't have that."

Following this line of inquiry, I concentrated in our biweekly sessions on his relationships with his mother and his grandmother.

They were stern but loving women. G's father was "a visitor in the home," returning to be locked up during the nights of the full moon.

Around this stage of our therapeutic process, the patient described a repetitive dream which became very useful in our analysis. In his dream, which had begun in childhood, he was a wolf, exactly as in his monthly delusion, a red-tinged brown timber wolf. He runs across a field of snow, looking backward and forward, and as he runs he cannot tell whether he is chasing or being chased. When he realizes that he cannot tell whether he is chased or chasing, the patient wakes. This dream was the clearest initial sign that the patient's condition had more than one cause. The dream implies a fear and a wish simultaneously, a wishful fear and a fearful wish, embodied in the doubled desire of the wolf.

I then began to investigate the milieu of the patient's relationship to his father, who was for the most part a ubiquitous absence in G's young life. His father was a successful self-made millionaire who suffered many years of hardship and "life on the road" before his years of triumph. This led me to the diagnosis of lycanthropic expression as a way of reasserting a bond by mechanism of fantasy. I enquired with the patient if his lycanthropic incidents were completely regular, to which he replied that they were, although, on reconsideration, he believed that his uncle and his father had experienced a period of prolonged wolfishness during a stay in the wilds of Canada. This period in family lore was vague, almost never discussed, as it represented a financial and personal failure for the brothers. It was also revealed during our discussions that the brothers, the patient's father and uncle, shared a bed as children. The uncle was also a murderer. He had killed a man in a dispute over a dog.

My suggestion of possible incest and the repression of incest were treated as entirely risible, which I noted as a possible instance of repression. In a different session, the patient's tongue had slipped in the classic sense when he incorrectly called his uncle by a similar-sounding name belonging to a famous homosexual actor. When I noted the parapraxis, the patient merely shrugged, claiming that he had not heard the rumor about that actor, which was nearly impossible as G's business involved a familiarity with current events.

For the father, for his uncle, and for the patient, the onset of lycanthropic incidents occurred simultaneously with the onset of puberty and therefore must be related to the release of sexual life in the genital zone. Other signs pointed to the repression of illicit sexuality as a root case in the cathexis of G's delusional lycanthropy. The patient, on following the practice of dream recovery, noted that his recurring dream of being a wolf had begun at his private school. This school is notorious in the Pittsburgh area for its various pedophilia scandals.

We had made substantial progress, although admittedly without the satisfaction of a complete diagnosis, when I made a significant medical error. I scheduled an appointment during the full moon, at the discovery of which G accused me of not taking his condition seriously. My jarring misstep recalled to him that his purpose in seeking treatment had not been to investigate the causes of a delusion but to cure himself of what, in his mind, constituted a "real," i.e., material, transformation. He accused me of indulging my own curiosity. Following the standard therapeutic model, I assured him that I believed his delusion, but he clearly no longer trusted my good faith. He wanted me to accept the "reality" of his condition. I explained that, due to the method, I could neither accept nor deny the evidence. I explained that, in my psychoanalytic practice, the "real" is merely another therapeutic category. This answer failed to satisfy him.

Attention to the Dreamwork

Following my error, the patient began losing faith in the capacity of the therapy to release him from his "condition." He increasingly desired to escape his recurring dream, which he described in plaintive terms: "I'm stuck. I can't tell whether I am running away from something or running to another thing. Do you see what I mean, Doctor? Am I running into somebody's arms? Am I running to eat? To sleep? It's the confusion that's so unbearable. It's the confusion that wakes me."

We began to place the dream in the context of the fairy tale cognates, given the iconography of the wolf. The vast majority of the fairy tale dreams, as Freud has articulated, are the realization of simple childhood wishes. The nature of the wish kernelled in the patient's dream was confused, however, for the content of the patient's dream was exactly *the suppression of a wish.* In the dream, he was unable to ascertain the nature of his wish. The suppressed desire—in fact, the wish to understand his own wish—was the content of the dream. The desire he was suppressing was suppressed even in a dream. He had managed to remain secret even to his own unconscious. "That sounds like me," he agreed when I suggested this diagnosis to him.

In an insight quite accidental to the dream life enquiries, the patient recalled one pleasure of his lycanthropic delusions: the experience of the women smoothing down his long-haired wolf flanks. He could also recall being fed raw meats of various kinds, both beef and game. These new memories led to a novel conjecture, that the delusion was in fact a narcissistic expression of the genital libido, which caused the neurosis formation. The delusion and the dream were both responsible for deflecting the patient's entry into the world of men out of the world of women. The dream was a perfect encapsulation of the search for sex in a feminized world. The wolf symbolized his penis, the site of the expression of genital libido. He could not be sure whether the women were chasing him or whether he was chasing them. They were the completion of the summation of the patient's spectrum of desire.

From this insight into the nature of the dream, the problem of the root cause of the werewolf delusion was easily unlocked. The patient's lycanthropy manifested itself as compensation for the father's absence in prelibidinal life. Seeking to establish a tight bond with his absent father during the brief times of their togetherness, the patient imagined that he was leashed with his male relatives. This unity provided protection from the *vagina dentata* of an all-female household. The patient feared the absence of his father, and simultaneously feared being swallowed by the women of the household. Therefore he became a beast in the basement. What had been stalling us in our therapy was the simultaneity of the cathexis: the fear of castration and the fear of the absent father.

Conclusion and Supplementary Notes

The patient left analysis shortly after this breakthrough, prematurely in my view, claiming that he had been cured of his delusions and his dreams. He insisted on my assurance that the process of our therapy would be discreet. Profound delusion in a single symptom may be connectable to dual cathexes in other cases. The key to the case was the series of paired oppositions that presented themselves, the father and the uncle, the dream and the delusion. The figure of the wolf, which itself bifurcated into a repetitive dream and a narcissistic delusion, stood as the connecting icon between these various paired opposites. The split of fantasy may itself be one of the figures of the fantasy. The hunger of the wolf feeds him.

The Wylie women died together in the winter of 1960. Danny Swift and Alfio Belpaese, snow removal men working for Champlain Township, noticed a drift curling up and spilling like an obscene white tongue through an open window on the first floor. To Alfio and Danny, trepidatiously investigating the freezing dark halls and then traumatically stumbling on the corpses, the women looked more still than dead—Marie posed palely on her red-satin covers in the bedroom, Kitty on the kitchen floor as if she had sat down one morning and simply forgotten to stand up. The whole town of Champlain whispered about suicide pacts, about murder followed by regret, about simultaneous accidental heart attacks. Champlain's coroner, questioned at the Rotary Club or the hockey rink or the waffle house, would say nothing. He told his wife, who told everybody else, that Kitty had probably collapsed from an aneurysm and Marie, immobile in bed, had starved to death.

One fact was not in dispute. The Wylie men were elsewhere. At the moment the coroner's report was declaring pneumonia the official cause of death, Dale was forking steak into his mouth, mid-negotiation for a television station in the barroom of the Hotel Vancouver in Seattle, George was shading his eyes from the glare of the sliver of Atlantic visible from the Wylie offices on Fifty-second Street in Manhattan, Lee was unsheathing from a manila envelope the production schedule of a paper mill in Butte, Montana, and Jack was tossing down the iced dregs of a Pimm's with gin in a topless bar in New Orleans.

Dale rushed back to what he would have to call home and arrived just in time for the funeral. Graveside, the rest of the mourners were half-remembered boardinghouse women who had traveled from as far away as Texas and Maine and Florida, and who leaned in to articulate, with phrases borrowed from women's magazines, the angelic selflessness, the seasonless generosity, the womanly givingness of Kitty and Marie Wylie. Dale was surprised by the dark. His heart was surprised to find itself drowning on a moon-heavy tide at the fancified gravesite that his wife and mother had orchestrated on the most expensive patch of Tender Hill Cemetery. Their monument was ridiculous. Carved from Carrera marble by a Baltimore sculptor who wore a lace cravat and quoted Walt Whitman at every opportunity, the grave lifted itself in a sickening boney glow. Even in the rain, the other graves seemed rotten by comparison. Kitty and Marie had splurged on immemorial grandeur after a life of scrimping cheapness, of pennies wrung from stained laundry. They had economized on a joint funeral at least. Dale was the only man there other than George: Who were these women who had been his?

The mechanism of WylieCorp had been rolling for thirty years, the whirlwind of credit sweeping all before it as the fifties blossomed into the sixties. Moths had fluttered from the closets. Children skipped down the thoroughfares where the Better Business Councils had paid for the planting of sugarplum pansies and buttery daffodils. The memory of the war was folded up like a wedding dress and tucked, with embarrassment and glee, in the darkest corner of the national basement. Tumescence was general. Women's dresses opened, fluffed, fuchsiaed, shortened, acclimatized to patterns, paisleys, checks, polka dots. The lawns went shaggy. Bellies grew in the widening of the world's prosperity.

Dale had widened, too. He weighed two hundred and forty pounds and was worth a hundred million dollars. He had hustled for forty years. Then the women died and he stopped. He returned to the house on Larchmount Crescent and couldn't figure out the purpose. Why had he run through the country buying up whatever he could on whatever he could borrow? For what? For whom? And why had he written his will so George would have to inherit this miniature empire of zeroes? What did it matter? The questions swarmed over him, like ants over a peony, and like ants over a peony they picked and scraped and chewed the truculent ball until the rest of his life and its vast fortune crashed open in splatters. The simplicity of money had opiated his soul for half a lifetime and now he was living the nightmare at the end of envy: What if money means nothing?

The major transformations within the Wylie business, the decisions that set the company's course for the next three decades and turned them from local American millionaires into global billionaires, emerged as a more or less random response to the aftermath of the women's deaths. Dale's move to England, Lee's rise to COO, George's never-ending tour of the companies—they all came out of grief. Business continues no matter who decides that business doesn't matter. Business is synonymous with change itself.

The transition was brisk. In April of 1961, Dale declared George CEO of North American operations. The executive committee of Wylie-Corp swirled into a suite in the Algonquin Hotel in New York for an emergency meeting. They found George chatting cheerfully with Lee Taggart about Gordie Howe. The Wylie kid, seemingly unfazed by the death of his mother and grandmother, smiled at each member of this ingathering tribe, inquiring about various scrupulously recalled wives and children, commenting on the prospects of the Yankees, noting the loveliness of the early spring in Central Park, patting backs, shaking hands. Once everyone had settled around the boardroom table, George excused himself as if he had forgotten his briefcase in the hallway. Lee Taggart remained. The next-youngest man in the room was twenty-two years older.

"The news is this," Lee said. "I'm COO. I'm the power."

Jeff Turgeson, V.P. of ad sales development, northwest division, couldn't swallow a laugh completely enough.

"You're fired," Lee said.

With the brevity and brutality that would become his trademark, Lee Taggart's era at WylieCorp had begun. In the decades that followed, his efforts would convert the Wylie business from an aggregation of American companies into a transnational corporate empire. Oil money flowing in from the Texas investments poured into the purchase of legal publications and pharmaceutical journals. He began to sell off some of the less profitable newspapers as well. Lee Taggart foresaw the death of print in 1960. He worried about the possibility that a device would be created which would permit the broadcast of a newspaper into the home by means of radio. This single insight, murky and imprecise as it was, served as the intellectual basis of the Wylies' later fortune.

*   *   *

With the spring, a torrent of hunger and disgust began to flow through Dale Wylie again. He couldn't just sit around waiting to die. He despised the stuff of Larchmount Crescent, the doilies spread over the armrests like the untearable webs of very proper spiders, the useless piano nobody ever played, and the vulgar just-wrongness of everything that takes its smack of despair from women straining to be the same as all other women. Dale longed for the self-reliant huff of his powerful armpit in some anonymous hotel. But he knew that he would never return to the road again. Dealsmanship was his lost religion.

The threat of irrelevance caused a decision as wild as Alberta. Dale decided to move to Abermarley in Scotland.

"Why Abermarley?" George asked when they met to discuss the proposal in the WylieCorp offices. His father pitching him was strange, but the pitch itself was stranger.

"Expansion," Dale answered. "There's a little newspaper there that's up for sale. *The Abermarley Gazette.*"

George failed to understand. "There are newspapers all over."

"Britain is the second-biggest newspaper market in the world, and it would be a toehold."

The idea was so ridiculous that George wondered if it was some kind of test. Would it be proof of his poor judgment if he agreed? Then again, what was he going to do, deny his father his own company's cash reserves? The choice made as little sense to George as Alberta had made to Marie Wylie forty-odd years before, but he agreed.

Dale kept his explanations to himself. Sometimes he believed that the possibility of a home pulled him there, the possibility of a place that might mean more than money. At other times he believed that the memory of his father was carrying him backward, a return to roots, or that he simply wanted not to be bored in his old age. The truth was that Dale had no idea why he moved to Scotland. Nobody can give a name to instinct; we can only pretend that we know why we do what we do after we've done it.

Abermarley itself was old-world, a Scottish coal mining town of ten thousand, black men against green hills. It was a mining town but not like American mining towns. The men of Abermarley were not men who believed they could get lucky. They trudged from the mine to the pub to their wives to the Abermarley football club and then back to the mine. They bought what they were expected to buy. They enjoyed what they were expected to enjoy. They discussed the weather or philosophy. The local points of pride included a thirteenth-century church of cut stone, a cast bronze statue of the unknown soldier raising his innocent eyes in the middle of the roundabout, and the first rural post office in Scotland, a single room of redbrick, duly commemorated with a grungy plaque.

The business of the *Gazette* was simple enough. Dale moved in and cut everything in half.

For Dale, there was another point of interest, a small low house on the outskirts of town. An ancient knobby walking stick of a man he met in the Five Bells pub, whose trade was knowing all local affairs of no particular interest, informed him that Dale's father had been born there. The same figure of limping wisdom, in an accent as thick as sea foam, noted that the Wylies had been gamekeepers for the ruling family for hundreds of years. The low stones of a handmade wall squatted next to the private forests of the local manor.

The neighboring property, tucked behind the welcoming green

hills, was the county seat of Lord Fallis. Formerly secretary of information during the Second World War, owner of *The Record of London* and a string of nearly two dozen small newspapers in Scotland and the northeast of England, along with the mine in Abermarley and interests in Sumatran rubber, Lord Fallis was a Great Man who needed to ensure the G and the M stayed capitalized. He had Great Problems: *The Record of London*, through which he waged a one-man war on the ninety-five-percent tax rates for high-income earners; the Conservative Party; his four idiot sons by his first wife (who had committed suicide in the proper English fashion by opening her bluehearted blood to the gilded porcelain of a Parisian hotel *salle de bain*); his new wife; his new mistress; and the family estate, which consumed vast sums on upkeep. He would not, of course, have wasted the time it took to micturate on a nobody like Dale Wylie.

One morning in November, among the detritus and the ashen odor of the morning after Guy Fawkes Day, Dale was waiting for the bus outside the offices of the *Gazette* when Lady Fallis, née Marguerite La Montée, emerged in the lovely gray air of the main street. Loveliness was her profession. Her gray tweed suit, her gray eyes, tender in an unspoken but evident distress, bloomed with luxurious melancholy and warm restraint. Every person on the Abermarley street, her subjects, acknowledged her by not looking; she passed through the crowd on the high street with a berth of honor. So when Dale introduced himself and inquired if she might need assistance, to the townsfolk he may as well have walked into a painting of fairies and spoken to the diaphanous changeling queen.

Lady Fallis, as it turned out, had left her money at home and could not send a parcel on account. Dale lent her five pounds, which was paid back the next day via a greasy messenger boy from the estate's stables, who approached Dale's suburban cottage with the greatest suspicion.

The loan to Lady Fallis, however, had paid interest, even in twenty-four hours. Along with a note of thanks, she invited "her generous savior" to a shooting party the Saturday following, called at seven for eight.

Dale walked up to save the expense of a hired car. The driveway looped through the shutter of birdsonged English forest. Arriving a little before seven, in his walking clothes, carrying a bottle of Krug as a hostess present, he found the front door closed and presented himself at the servants' entrance—he managed thereby to commit four social faux pas before opening his mouth. The servants had no idea what to do with him. The butler stewarded the strange American to the library, leaving a footman until he could assure himself by speaking to Lady Fallis that the man was not an impostor.

Dale had not realized that a shooting party called at seven for eight meant that one was expected to arrive not slightly before seven, but well after seven, expecting to shoot well after eight. One was expected to bring one's own riding reds. And if one did not ride, one might as well choose to wait until before noon, to coincide with the midday meal. He was alone in the library for a good hour as the hunting party, consisting of Lord Fallis's sons and their various society friends from London, descended. The local gentry arrived in their Rolls-Royces or rode over from the neighboring estates, and the servants roiled in hubbubs of liquor and boots and chaotically curious leashes of slobbering hounds. Dale introduced himself to people who could not have cared less about his existence and who lowered their voices, once he had moved on, to ask who had invited the clerk. At eight-thirty, Lady Fallis appeared like the long-suffering wife of the spendthrift drunk in a two-act melodrama to apologize for Lord Fallis's absence. He was in his study on matters of urgent business; he would join them for lunch. Lord Fallis's eldest son, Roger, led the party in his father's place. They walked out in a daze of clomping and barking and yipping, while the servants scuttled back to prepare the luncheon. Dale, a merciful servant suggested, might care to look over the grounds.

They were fine grounds. The Fallis estate offered among the finest examples of French gardens in the whole of England. Elaborate geometries of boxwood spiraled with the effortless declension of a shell down a low hill, on the far side of which sat an infamously dangerous coal mine, and the town's oldest graveyard, old bones and old stones that sat stacked over each other like rotting books. The near side presented itself in perfected quartered gardens that opened onto a series of fountained terraces and spread down to a small lake beside the woods, where anxious families of deer drifted and scarpered. Dale, flummoxed by ignorance and contempt, wandered up to a fake ruined abbey which one of Lord Fallis's Romantic ancestors had conjured onto the crest of a hill, just visible from the pleasance on the west side of the castle. There, among stones deliberately constructed to imitate decayed civilization, Dale Wylie leaned his head back and howled at his own stupidity. What the hell was he doing there? Why on earth had he left America? Why would anyone abandon the community of free men?

By the time he walked down from the abbey, to the ivy-trellised garden table at the center of the grounds, the calm pools of cucumber soup had nearly evaporated into the chatter of the party. Dale bowed to apologize and Lord Fallis, at the head of the table, may or may not have acknowledged the gesture with a ruffle of eyebrow. Lady Fallis sat Dale beside the count and countess of Strathmore, graciously half covering her evident unhappiness at having invited an outsider into the house.

In person, Lord Fallis was the very figure of the post-imperial Englishman, maintaining exactly the right level of delusion—a fine balance between enough savvy to keep what belonged to him and enough blindness not to recognize the parasitism of himself and everybody he knew. He lorded over the lunch in a mustachioed silence, nodding or frowning at the dishes and the conversation, complete in his complacent self-regard. For most Englishmen, the niggers begin at Calais; but Lord Fallis was an English gentleman; the niggers began at his bedroom door, and he slept alone.

"And where are you from, Mr. Wylie?" the countess of Strathmore asked, after their introduction.

"I'm from Pennsylvania—an American, I'm afraid."

"How interesting. And what brings you here?"

"I recently purchased the local paper."

"Ah," said the count, who was at that moment desperate for money. "One of the lads from the village."

Lady Fallis explained how Dale had rescued her from embarrassment at the post office, and the countess said that it was nice to see that chivalry still lived in these uncertain days, and the count said indeed, and asked Dale what he thought of the smoked salmon they were being served, and Dale said that narrow Scottish rivers often produced better fish than their wider American cousins, and the crisis was averted.

In hindsight, it was a very interesting party. If only they had known how everybody was going to die, the company might have enjoyed one another. Monty Wychwood, a somewhat notorious rapist in society circles, choked on his own vomit while partying with the Rolling Stones in France in the mid-seventies. Lord Fallis's youngest son, Richard, crashed his car into the American embassy in Morocco and was shot by sentries who were spooked by the recent bombing in Lebanon. The count of Strathmore, on an ecovacation to see the gorillas in the eastern Congo, was hacked apart by rebels and his body parts strewn along the hiking trail. The countess died in 2006 by the side of the woman with whom she had been living for twenty years, Lady Fallis, who had returned to her maiden name, Marguerite La Montée. The hunters were not boring people. Yet they insisted on boring each other.

Dale was seated as far from Lord Fallis as possible, on Lady Fallis's left side. Conversation had turned to his son Roger's hair, which he had grown long; he could be confused with a "rock'n'roller," somebody's aunt declared, with crafty suggestion. Lord Fallis, scrupulously intent on his shoulder of lamb until that point, made his only pronouncement of the luncheon: "Perhaps Mr. Wylie can help you with that, boy."

The table failed to understand.

"Why would Mr. Wylie know what to do, darling?" Lady Fallis asked.

Dale answered. "I believe that Lord Fallis is referring to the fact that I am the son of a barber. But I assure you that we only ever did three basic cuts, and I doubt your son would want any of them."

Awkwardness lingered until it dissolved in its own propriety. Lord Fallis, helpless in the welter of centuries of breeding, could not stop himself from offering tobacco to his guests, and then immediately began to leave for his postprandial solitude. Dale strolled after his host into the rose pleasance; everyone else assumed the old man reckoned his duties discharged.

"Lord Fallis, excuse me, I may never have another chance."

"What's it?"

"I'll be brief. I want you to sell me the rural papers."

"I'm sorry?"

"I turn around papers. That's my living. And they're sapping you, I know. Sell me *The Aberdeen Globe* anyway. You don't care."

Lord Fallis's eyebrows rustled again.

"I'm afraid I never discuss matters of business at personal functions."

"I understand. Send me a number."

"Number?"

"A number. A price."

Lord Fallis blinked. "I've heard that in America everything has its price," he murmured.

Two days later, the boy who cleaned the knives and boots brought over the offer. Even Lord Fallis's stationery was godlike, yellow with age, the ink soaked into its weight, the number written in a broad, circuitous hand: two and a half million pounds. This for a paper with revenues of a hundred thousand a year. Two and a half million pounds was exactly the amount of seed money Dale had arranged on sufferance from the North American operations.

A rough roaring laughter swelled from Dale's gut, suffusing him with angry joy. He was glad of the insult. It had taught him why he had left America. He realized at last, through the dim lightening of envy, the motivations of his incomprehensible instinct: to conquer the old world. He relished the hunger. He basked in the envy. He was home again, at last.

In 1963, George began his tour of the family's North American properties, while Lee Taggart managed the business from the offices in Manhattan. The tour had been Lee's idea—George would gather the information only an owner could gather from the companies scattered over America and Lee would be left alone to run things in New York. George could also pick up what Lee had learned in the field as a kid, how the individual mechanisms of the businesses worked. But WylieCorp had changed from when Lee had started out in Blind River. Sometimes

WylieCorp acquired two or three properties in a week, and all over the world. George's tour became less a chance to gather information—the only information that really mattered to Lee and George was the size of the quarterly profit margin anyway—and more a chance to impose the Wylie spirit on the widening empire.

The visits were always the same, coming without warning; the chief executive of the factory or newspaper received a call at 4:58 p.m. that Mister Wylie would arrive the next morning at eight-thirty. At eight-thirty, the executive team arrayed themselves in the lobby, waiting for the owner's limousine and entourage. In their anxiety, they barely noticed a young man in a cheap suit pull a Dodge Dart into a far corner of the parking lot. Often George had to introduce himself. His years at Harvard had served him well and he knew how an aristocrat should behave. He never offered advice on the running of the company but he always brought a bag lunch of a peanut butter and grape jelly sandwich, an apple, and a Coke, and insisted on eating in the cafeteria. Kings displayed their power with splendor. The Wylies, growing richer than kings, regaled the world with their stinginess.

George was smart enough to understand his function, as an icon of property. He recognized that he filled a need in the heart of managers and workers. Somebody had to own things. His work was being there, existing. He watched in silence so the people who worked for him knew they were being watched. Every company was the same no matter what it made. He didn't care what they made. He cared that they saved as much money as possible. Soon he didn't bother going to New York. He made his arrangements out of Champlain and kept moving, company to company, town to town.

Into even the most quotidian dream a blue tiger may stride, and into the life of a George Wylie, a Lavinia Thibodeau.

Lavinia Thibodeau was famous by 1963, midway through her seventh world tour. At the age of twelve, in 1952, she had been described as "the prettiest performer in the Province of Quebec" by *The Montreal Gazette*, worshipped as much for her devout Catholicism as for her meticulous performances. Her precocious, traditional playing, at a time when every middle-class girl in Quebec was chained to the parlor piano, thrust her into the provincial iconocracy. Her father, an archconservative supporter of Quebec's corrupt, nationalistic Duplessis regime, dressed her in the party's blue for every concert. During election seasons, she even wore shoes with red soles, which she flashed to the chuckles of her knowing audiences, matching Duplessis's slogan *Le ciel est bleu, l'enfer est rouge.* (Heaven is blue. Hell is red. Blue was the color of the Unione Nationale, red of the Quebec Liberal Party.) She stuck mostly with Mozart and church recital music and won the Rubinstein Prize and the International Mozart Prize by the time she was fourteen.

At seventeen, she discovered the modernist compositions of Alban Berg. Even the possession of such music amounted to sin in her house, and she stashed the leaves under her mattress like pornography. She learned the music without playing, simply by studying. At a concert three days after Duplessis's death, she blazed onto the stage in a scarlet ball gown, an absurd luxury fringed with her grandmother's handmade lace. Instead of the Mozart piano sonatas Nos. 18 and 23, she sat down at the piano, lifting her legs to reveal light blue stockings, and strayed out into the great mathematical wilderness of Berg's sonata No. 1. She was booed offstage. Her father never spoke to her again. She had rejected the order of things.

In the shipwreck aftermath of that concert, she drifted, in her scarlet dress, to the Montreal home of a libertine aunt, whose house on the Plateau was a refuge for experimental artists and proto-Separatists. They called themselves the neantists—the name they gave to their rejection of tradition and religion and politics. Instead of the cruel certainties of Quebec under *la grande noirceur,* everything was to be light. Painting was an experiment. Sex was an experiment, and money and underwear and music. The bedraggled, filthy guru of the neantist group was the composer Lefevre (better known as T.T.). Arrested seven times for homosexuality, and later beaten to death during the 1971 riots in Kingston Penitentiary in Ontario, he wrote the music of dumb luck. In his early "Goldfish Symphonies" three aquariums lined with musical staffs divided the stage, one each for the woodwinds, brass, and strings. Wherever the goldfish swam, the orchestra played. He also composed a violin octet, "Musical Chairs," which worked exactly like the children's game except that the children playing were the performers of the music. For Lavinia, T.T. composed his most famous and disturbing piece, the "Duet for Piano and Lovebirds." On the 1963 tour, the tour that was to swallow George Wylie's life, Lavinia performed Mozart's sonatas Nos. 18 and 23 before the intermission, with T.T.'s duet following.

George often went to hear classical music. On his endless tour of every town in America where WylieCorp owned a company, the ritual of the concert hall was appealing. He didn't know who was playing when he went to see Lavinia. He was in New York, staying close to Carnegie Hall. That's all he knew.

At the appointed hour, the polite conversation dutifully lowered and the overheads dimmed. To dutiful applause, a French-Canadian woman in an overdramatic scarlet dress and with a classical name walked onstage. She smiled and bowed and sat down at the piano. As the young woman plunked out some rather cheerful Mozart, George considered his plans. He was supposed to head to New Orleans the next day, to visit *The Louisiana Sentinel.* The concert was good for planning things. The woman onstage was lovely but not lovely enough to disturb his composure, and the music lifted and dropped itself like a languorous youth on a willowed bankside. The melodies passed like well-mannered paintings. Everything was charming, easy, and the conclusion was obvious. The crowd was pleased that it knew exactly when to applaud.

George stayed in his seat during the intermission while the stagehands raised nets and dropped hoops from the ceiling. The net was enormous and very fine, like a malaria net, and the men raising it all wore black suits with white collars, like the surplices of priests, hollering to each other in pea-soup-thick patois, veiling the stage in a translucent scrim, a thin cloud.

After twenty minutes, the crowd filed back in. The overheads again dimmed. To dutiful applause and polite laughter, the woman entered carrying a cage of lovebirds. She released them into a chirruping—a gasp at the irresponsibility. The lorikeets fluttered into the net and back to the hanging hoops and she sat to play.

This music was not pretty. This music was not polite. This music shivered. The crowd who listened vanished into irrelevance. George was alone with the woman, gorgeous in her transport, caught behind a vague net there for the breaking. You could say that George Wylie fell in love, but *absolute recognition* would be more a precise phrase, abyss calling to abyss. The birds flew and cooed, paused on the hoops, and whenever they landed on the piano itself, Lavinia stopped playing until they fluttered off, which once took seven awkward minutes. Lavinia's concentration remained pure: At the still center of the swooping vibrancy and delirious chaos, she seemed to dance around the music and the birds rather than conjure them up. Her own beauty resonated from the stage, too, a delicacy that was not fragile, a tender mastery over the sense and nonsense the music wrought.

The music ended only because all music ends.

From that moment George followed Lavinia Thibodeau. From Pittsburgh to Philadelphia, from Philadelphia to New York, from New York to London, from London to Paris, and from Paris to sixty-two other cities. At each show, he bought the front-row seat on the left aisle. He sat at the front, on the left, mildly smiling, always. He sat until the show ended, and the custodians had swept up the lorikeet droppings and the musicians had drifted away to whatever comforts they could cadge from foreign bars and alien churches. George stayed until they asked him to leave.

One of Lavinia's entourage first noticed the strange, dumbly smiling American in Leningrad. He had been in the same spot in Helsinki three nights earlier. How had he managed to fly to Leningrad? How had he managed a ticket to the show? A week later, in Moscow, Lavinia peeked from behind the curtain to glimpse her complacent admirer, who sat smiling in the front row, on the left. Who was he? Why was he there? His relentlessness began to unnerve her: He kept coming and coming with his mild smile, his silence. And he always stayed until the end.

In Rome she sent an usher to ask him to leave. She could not play with him in the theater. He was happy to leave, he said. He would never want to upset Miss Thibodeau. But he was there at the next concert in Berlin, and at the next in Stuttgart, where, after the performance, a few of the stagehands, drunk, emerged to tease him as he sat in the front row, mildly smiling. Lavinia watched as her coterie swirled about him, this strange man who just kept showing up. Her friend Rosette, who maintained the lorikeets, stripteased drunkenly in front of him but again there was no reaction. They spoke to him in French and he didn't answer. He couldn't answer. He smiled mildly.

The tension resolved itself in China, half accidentally. George stepped off the plane in Peking to a greeting committee of a single Chinese official, a man no taller than five feet, radiating concentration and poise. "You are Mr. Wylie, are you not? The American businessman?" he asked from the tarmac at the foot of the plane. The little man's English was fluid, inflected with Oxford.

"I'm George."

"My name is Pi-Lin."

A proffered handshake awkwardly met a bow. George returned the bow as Pi-Lin extended a hand.

"The people of China would like to demonstrate to you the wonders of the worker's paradise."

George mentioned that he had a concert to attend.

"I will personally escort you to the concert of Madamemoiselle Thibodeau after the tour. Your bags have been quite taken care of." They strolled through customs. The guards, catching the faintest glimpse of George's guide, deferred instantly, although the man wore the same gray-green Mao costume with cap that everyone else was wearing and was physically distinct only insofar as he was shorter than the others. "As the chairman says, our bureaucracy is our great strength," Pi-Lin said as they passed the final gate into a Jeep driven by a flinty-faced military officer. How had they even known he was coming? And what was he doing? The little Chinese man startled George out of the reverie he had fallen into at Carnegie Hall. It was as if his father had picked him up at the airport. What does it all mean, son?

They first visited a pharmaceutical factory that smelled of candy and ammonia, where George was lectured for half an hour in Chinese about the virtues of socialism while six hundred workers, wearing face masks the entire time, listened in rapt tranquility. They visited a school, where George was honored by an assembly of a thousand children singing what Pi-Lin explained was a poem written by Chairman Mao about dawn rising red in the East. They visited a construction site, little more than a patch of bald ground, where three men in hard hats pointed at the dirt and Pi-Lin described the immense tracts of convenient modern housing that would rise from it. George smiled mildly wherever they went. He was good at visiting grim institutions he didn't understand. It was his regular job, after all.

The tour concluded with a banquet. More than a hundred men and women sat around an ovoid table smoking perpetual cigarettes and slurping vodka from teacups.

"And where are we now, Pi-Lin? Who are all of these people?" George asked. They had grown familiar over the course of the day.

"These are your people, Mr. Wylie. These are the editors and publishers of all the newspapers."

"They drink and smoke like editors and publishers, I'll give you that."

Among the chattering Communists, as unexpected as a baseball through a skyscraper window, Lavinia Thibodeau in her hallucinatory scarlet dress arrived like luxury itself, like the refutation of utilitarianism personified, like elegance refined into a goddess. George's throat went dry in gratitude and anxiety. He had no idea what to say. If only he could play music to her instead.

Pi-Lin, scrupulously suppressing his obvious pleasure at having orchestrated the awkwardness, offered introductions.

"Miss Thibodeau, welcome. This gentleman has traveled a great distance to see you perform. We are truly honored to be able to have two such luminaries from the West together with us."

"The honor is ours," Lavinia said.

"A pleasure," George said, stupidly, to Lavinia.

"I'm sure it is."

He leaned in, his words flustering around her almost tangible odor of lavender. "I want you to know that I had no part in organizing this. It's as much a surprise to me that you're here as it is to me."

"It's no surprise to me," she said. "You seem to show up wherever I go."

That was all the conversation they were allowed, being displayed like fragile white trophies at opposite ends of the banquet table. The distance between them, George thought, was roughly the same as the distance between his seat in the front row and Lavinia onstage, a narrow abyss. The journalists swooped up dozens and dozens of delicacies, then a Communist Party delegate gave a thirty-minute speech about how the printing press had been invented in China. Before they left, Pi-Lin presented the guests with fountain pens decorated with Chairman Mao's face set against a rising sun. Then they rose, and Lavinia left, turning to the back of the room without even a gesture his way. He had missed some kind of chance. The last rustle of her red dress out the doorway was like watching a species go extinct.

George and Pi-Lin drove back through the dimly lit streets crowded with evening loungers squatting against the walls or around lamplit mahjong conversations.

"How powerful are you?" George asked his quiet host.

Pi-Lin pondered the question like a fable. "It is impossible for any-one in China to answer that question precisely."

"I want to know who I owe. Was meeting Miss Thibodeau your idea or the party's?"

Pi-Lin nodded, paused before he spoke. "There are certain elements within China, even within the party, that imagine that someday there will be a connection."

"A connection between what?"

"That is exactly the question. Between systems? Between continents?"

Out the window, a seven-year-old girl was selling red peonies from a steel bucket. "Stop the car," George ordered. Pi-Lin barked at the driver, and before he could be stopped, George leaped out, bought the whole bucket with a roll of bills, and brought them back to the car. "I must support any capitalist in China on principle," George explained.

At the hotel, George handed Pi-Lin a business card. A name on a piece of luxury paper. A vaguely defeated smile passed over Pi-Lin's gaze as he held the card, then a restored determination visibly thickened in him. "If there's anything I can do for you," George said. His host bowed.

After Peking, the Thibodeau entourage never looked George's way again, not in Singapore, not in Honolulu, not in Sydney. He followed the music all the way to Quebec City, the final stop on the world tour. Lavinia played the "Duet for Piano and Lovebirds" for the last time, and all the old fans, who remembered her as a young girl wrapped in the azurine blue of her father's politics and the farmers' sky and the Church's heaven, booed her as she began to play. They had come for order. She gave them the beginning of their revolution. They spat, stomped out the door hurling insults and their Playbills, hurling seat cushions, ripping the fine netting, spuming rampant sugar water and bird shit. The tune of accidental beauty dissolved into riot. The birds flew away, perching in the rafters and then escaping through the high windows into the winter air, into the freedom that would surely kill them.

George sat in the wreckage, smiling mildly. There was nobody else but him. After the sixty-three epiphanies, after so many concert halls in their antique frosty glamour, the shuddering taxicabs, George's mission had its satisfaction. Through the torn netting, her eyes mascara-soaked, Lavinia Thibodeau floated to the seat beside him, and into his ear whispered the words: "I suppose we should eat something."

WylieCorp had barely noticed the absence of George. Lee was running North America just fine and Dale was in the middle of buying the two largest media companies in England, becoming, in the process, one of the most powerful men in the country almost accidentally.

His first big purchase was NWM. North West Media was a bankrupt mess. The conglomerate of international investors that controlled the license for television in England's northwest, particularly for Manchester, were willing to sell NWM for the price of its debt, 3.56 million pounds. Dale Wylie sent letters personally to all the executives of WylieCorp, which included the editors of the newspapers, offering to let them in on the stock he was raising for the purchase. Nobody could understand what Dale understood: NWM couldn't win at virtue. They had been trying to compete with the BBC, producing worthy news programming along with expensive dramas. They were fighting for the wrong territory. While the company drifted in the limbo between fire sale and bankruptcy, Dale cannily rounded up the syndication rights to dozens of American shows. The costs for these shows—shows like *Gunsmoke, McHale's Navy, Combat!, The Jetsons, The Lucy Show, The Beverly Hillbillies,* and *The Virginian*—were almost nothing. NWM held the only license for the region. Dale paid a few hundred thousand pounds, on extended contracts, for the lot. Local shows, required for a broadcast license, were produced on the cheap—documentary programs that spun single news stories into hour-long discussion panels and rock-and-roll variety acts. Essentially for no outlay in risk, Dale Wylie controlled a fifth of English television.

On the day of purchase, Dale imported a cost-cutting army from the American branch of the company. He himself immediately fired one-third of the staff. Within three months, the profits had already paid off the syndication rights, and Dale announced himself by purchasing a house in Kensington Palace Gardens. The rising property values meant that he could mortgage the property immediately after the purchase, several times, for a much higher price than he paid for it. The NWM deal made him an unignorable sum of money, and so easily that not even Lord Fallis's influence could exclude him any longer.

A letter from this period of conquest survived at North Lake:

13 November 1963

The Countess of Strathmore

Haverford House

Dear Mr. Wylie,

As you may well guess, the purchase in Kensington Palace Gardens, much more even than the annual report on North West Media, for which success let me congratulate you, has provoked an intense groundswell of gossip. I'm afraid that it will not all be to your liking. However, since you've requested all pertinent information, I will record it here.

I received a letter from my cousin, Georgette de Villiers, in which she guardedly enquired as to your situation, both financial and matrimonial. I responded with caution. To be specific, she asked about "the recent American émigré, who is I believe some kind of an oil baron." She attached a well-circulated letter from Baron Whitefield, which contains a description, which he claims he received from the Waburtons of Pennsylvania: "He is, whatever he may claim about Scottish origins, a filthy Jew and everybody knows it." Baron Whitefield goes on to describe, in his inimitably crass style, that "all the bitches are in heat for his money." I feel confident in assuming, from this comments, that the prospects of your marrying are much discussed in London society.

The purchase of such a magnificent domicile is deeply resented. The previous owner is claiming openly that the price was too high not to sell, but that he regrets the sale already. He reportedly told Lady Asquith who told Mr. Fey that "he pities the old place," presumably for whatever improvements you are planning to make.

So these two subjects are the dominant motifs, your plans to marry and your plans to renovate. You may, of course, provide me with any information about your intentions which you wish me to disseminate. If I might add my own gloss of the above remarks, they are nothing to trouble you, Mr. Wylie. They are the typical assessments that any new entrant into society must face.

I will send you any new information as it arrives.

Yours truly,

C. S.

The house in Kensington Palace Gardens was chaperoned by embassies, a squat and unloved princess of property maintained by a caretaker as lonely and devoted as a lighthouse keeper. Dale was never there. He was never in Abermarley either. He lived with the money as the money rolled drunkenly into the offices of NWM, which were grubby even by the standards of Wylie buildings, scratched out of repurposed factories on the outskirts of Manchester. There, in the pulsing twilight of that harbinger city, Dale made the deal that established him as one of the most powerful men in the world.

Lord Fallis sold him *The Record of London*. Dale had never fantasized such a possibility. He had hoped to buy the string of rural papers and possibly the handful of radio stations that the Fallis holdings controlled in the southeastern counties. But never the *Record*. Lord Fallis was a friend of Prince Philip, and he ran the *Record* much the way the British aristocratic families had been running their declining estates. Every morning, at around ten, a chauffeur brought him to the Fleet Street offices, where the elevator was held (while his employees took the stairs) so he could whisk himself directly to the top floor. He kept his four moronic sons on the board. They all arrived by chauffeur, too. Lord Fallis's workday consisted of reading the other newspapers, lickspittle conversations with the sitting prime minister, and the occasional disemboweling of an editor. Long lunches, good sherry, and a hearty measure of influence—why would anyone cede such a life to another? In an interview a decade earlier, Lord Fallis himself had bristled at the notion of abandoning his duties: "Offering to sell *The Record of London* would be like offering one's wife to a houseguest," he had said.

The influence of the paper made such minor considerations as its profitability seem ludicrous. The *Record* selected who was going to be the leader of the Conservative Party in England. *The Record on Sunday*, its sister publication, doled out definitive theater and restaurant reviews— the terror of the city. What was the profitability of the Church of England? Or of the royal family? Or of the cliffs of Dover? The paper had been losing money steadily for decades, but it was impossible to change its financial structure, given its social position and the strong union that controlled every aspect of the printing shop and the newsroom. Dale speculated that Lord Fallis was just tired of losing money. His friends thought that money was not so much the problem as his waning interest in the cause of Conservative politics and his waxing interest in a twenty-four-year-old Argentine masseuse. Editors at the *Record* believed a distaste for his sons was the secret motive. He knew his four boys were all disasters-in-waiting, this line of argument went, so he ensured that they would destroy only the family fortune and not his beloved *Record*—a flattering attribution of motive. Whatever Lord Fallis's reasons for selling, Dale was the only obvious buyer. With the NWM profits cresting over several hundred thousand pounds a week, and looking to rise, he was the only man with the resources to broker a deal.

Pausing in Monaco just long enough to lose his life's savings at baccarat, Jack Taggart proceeded, as ordered, to London. Dale showed him the books: The money flowing in from NWM serviced debt on an undeferrable schedule. The North American property had soaked up the oil funds. Lee had imposed strict internal controls to prevent leveraging the information management divisions. They had bought too much too recently and had no obvious institution from whom to borrow.

"Fallis doesn't know we're gambled out," Jack said.

"He thinks we're buying things with our own money. That's my guess."

Jack snorted. "Couldn't get laid in a bucket of dicks," he said, a nostalgic turn of rudeness. "How much do we need?"

"Eighteen million pounds and change."

For a week, Jack and Dale retreated to Abermarley, to the old stone cottage on the edge of town, where they stalked the antique forests of Lord Fallis's grounds and concocted what would turn out to be their contribution to the history of money: the interior bid. The idea was to combine stock with debt obligations. Instead of cash, the parties would be sold second-class nonvoting stock that could be purchased back by the first-class stockholder if the terms of debt repayment were completed. The sale of dreams: Jack and Dale found a way to buy a company with the idea of its own future profits.

The rest was patience and secrecy. Any hint of the coming bid, any suspicion of its mechanism, and stock market speculators would instantly rip the throat out of the deal, feast on the exposed entrails. The bid had to be negotiated with the *Record*'s board of directors, and their offices were all on Fleet Street. Fortunately, nobody knew Jack Taggart, the emissary. Dale, like an Egyptian deity embraced by the impenetrable darkness of a granite naos, waited in his Abermarley cottage. Six weeks he waited, drugged by television, waiting for day. Then the light broke. Jack called. The Wylies owned *The Record of London*.

London took a sudden and appalled intake of breath. Instantly, Dale Wylie was the foremost newspaper proprietor in the country. A cheapskate American upstart had bought off Lord Fallis himself. The British press understood Dale Wylie so little that on the day of the transfer of ownership photographers bunched at the front doors expecting a triumphal procession. The day before, Lord Fallis hadn't shirked providing the tabloids with a bit of drama when he had personally supervised the removal of his desk, a nineteenth-century oak battleship of furniture. As he was overseeing the grand decline into a moving van, he declared: "The oak heart has been in my family for two hundred years. No one will ever convince me that I've sold it." The reporters didn't notice Dale arriving because the bus stop outside the offices of the *Record* dispensed passengers on the other side of Fleet Street. Only one photographer, a refugee from the first round of firing at *The Abermarley Gazette*, recognized the man stooping to pick up a happy jagged silver moon in the street, a crooked sixpence—the image that defined the Wylies ever after.

Through the back door, held open for him, into the private elevator, held open for him, into his office doors, held open for him, Dale found Jack Taggart sitting on the floor, because there was no desk, examining the books.

"You're not going to believe this," Jack said as Dale entered. "All four kids have cars and drivers."

"I believe it." He turned to his secretary. "Fire all the drivers on staff. Fire everyone who held a door open for me. Fire the other secretary."

Dale and Jack had passed so much time guessing at the rot in the *Record*'s systems, but they had guessed wrong. "Look at this. They have a bureau in the Ukraine. Can you imagine? You have three reporters living off your fat in Kiev. It's a hell of a world. You have work to do here, buddy," Jack said.

"I think you mean that *you* have work to do."

"I don't think so, Dale. It's going to be tricky. You won't be able to run it like *The Atkinson Register*."

"Nonsense. Everything I've ever bought runs like the *Register*."

"Not by me, sunshine."

"When will I see you again?"

"I'll catch you at your funeral," Jack said quickly.

Dale called back his secretary. "Bring me a desk the newsroom has thrown out."

In New York, George showed Lavinia his true nature in a cage in the Presidential Suite of the Plaza. Three days later, he woke up in Lavinia's arms. She had crawled into the cage with him, and he could half remember, in potent unconsciousness, a woman smoothing his flanks.

"Are you all right?" he asked.

She eventually answered, "It's like a fairy tale." The smooth post-bestial satisfaction, aglow with its new relaxation and the city light and a woman he loved who knew his nature, may have been the happiest morning of George's life.

New York in 1964 was the city at the end of metaphysics. Nobody questioned the eccentric beautiful foreign woman who led a quite wolf-like dog on a stout chain out of the hotel into the park in the evenings. She took him into the bank when she needed money, and into Macy's when she needed shoes, and into a chophouse, where the animal gnawed rare steak and bloody bones at her feet. For the rest of the time, George and Lavinia walked together as people, as lovers, drifting and roaming, allowing surprises to surprise them, boredoms to bore them, fears to frighten them. "I can't tell," she said one morning, when they were snaking through Sheep Meadow, among the lounging picnickers in the bright day of all possibility.

"What can't you tell?"

"I can't tell whether I prefer to walk with you as a man or a wolf. Right now, I think I'd rather you were a wolf. I could let you off the leash to run through all these picnickers."

"Don't ever let me off the leash."

Love turned the beast into a game. They could pretend, for a while, that even monsters are put on this earth to be happy.

George and Lavinia stayed in New York until Lavinia became pregnant, then moved to Pennsylvania. Lavinia adored the house in Champlain even though the roof was dripping and the rooms were barren and dust-clotted and the wallpaper had begun to peel from the corners.

George resumed his tour of the family companies that fall. The executives found his blandness terrifying, provoking furies of cost-cutting. Once he accidentally showed up to tour a cardboard box plant he no longer owned. Lee had sold it and George hadn't noticed. The mistake added to his legend. The Wylies owned more than they themselves could remember.

And every month the wolf brought George home. The rise of the beast was almost a pleasure. Lavinia would bring down flesh and water. She would wait until he turned, and three days later he would wake up naked in her arms. Six months after they moved back to Champlain, however, George woke up alone. The house was silent and a terror flushed over his cold flesh. He pulled on clothes and stumbled up the stairs to find her waiting on their bed, holding an infant. "He came early," she said. She was apologetic even though he was the one who couldn't be there for the birth.

Tenderly confounded, he picked the boy from her arms. To hold a son, to have another of your name, is to know how many fates worse than death there are, how many numbers less than zero. How are you supposed to live, to breathe air and eat food and drink water, with your heart wandering out there in the wild world?

Dale Wylie
Kensington Palace Gardens
May 4, 1965

Dear George,

A boy. Terrific. But you know what a boy means. We must prepare for what he has in him.

Some notes on inheritance. Now that we have the *Record* the English will love us. I assume they'll give me a title, and it will be hereditary, and the nature of the agreement means that you will take over the company and the lordship and all the rest of it. That's the will I made. I could tell you that it was for death duties or I could say it was to avoid taxes or I could say that I bound your future and Ben's future and Ben's grandson's future to my own little moment in time in some purely financial logic, but we both know it would be a lie. I made the contract because of the wolf. I have gambled with all of us, I recognize that.

Where you live is up to you, but I advise you to stay in America. I can't tell if it's the war that has made the English so contemptible but I've met the queen now and I've been to Buckingham Palace, and the palace is a prison and the queen has the sadness of the prisoner-in-chief. I've met whores in Atkinson who are more fully human than her. I miss lumberjacks. The last lumberjack I met must have been a decade ago. That was a man. He asked for nothing and he gave nothing.

The British are waiting here to be bought and sold. No wonder the colonies are shrugging them off.

I admire so much your ability to listen to people who know. So few rich kids can.

Love,

Dale

In May of 1968, Dale abandoned his American citizenship in order to be knighted the First Lord Wylie of Abermarley.

The celebration that followed the ceremony was at the Dorchester hotel, which then possessed the largest ballroom of any luxury hotel in London. Seven hundred and twenty-three guests passed an honor guard of Beefeaters. On the Park Lane side of the hotel, a wall-sized photograph of 17 Flora Avenue filled forty-five feet by nine and a half feet. On the other side, a similarly sized photograph of the house in Kensington Palace Gardens. And in between, the room had been filled with spruces, the trees from which newsprint is made, imported from the American West. The opulence was literally wild.

Prime Minister Harold Wilson arrived early, pausing to discuss the unrest in France, youth in London, the history of revolution and its causes, the possibility of having to foot De Gaulle's bills again. Jack Taggart showed up. His tuxedo looked rented, cheap, borrowed off a prom kid. Bedraggled in his age by never-slowing fits of lust and losses, he must have been out of money again.

"How much is all this costing us?" Jack asked, looking around, shaking Dale's hand.

"Business expense," Dale offered.

"Champagne and claret are business expenses in England? How many waiters did you hire for this affair? These look like professionals, too. We should have brought in the reporters from the *Record*, had them scrounge around. Make 'em work for their checks."

"The day I take advice on expenditures from Jack Taggart is the day they come to take me away."

"I don't know," Jack said, inspecting the rafts of canapés circulating among the spruces, and the ruffled, gilded tables, each a travesty of lavishness. "I'm starting to worry. This looks like exactly the sort of thing I'd do."

"The bar's free," Dale added, gladhanding his old buddy forward. Rita Hayworth was next in line, and after her the shadow minister of defense, and after the shadow minister of defense, the Earl of Duquesne. Far down the long line of beauties and powers, terrestrial deities of celebrity and the marketplace, he noticed a couple waiting their turn, the man smiling mildly, the woman draped in an extravagant scarlet dress that, even within the glittering of London society, rose like lipsticked lips pressed against train station glass. Between them stood a small, confused boy in a gray flannel suit, a lost pup among the knees of the grand old world. Dale recognized his own in the boy: his first glimpse of Ben Wylie.

"Dad, I have some introductions. My wife and son."

The woman was beautiful, eager to meet him but slightly afraid, too. Ben looked so much like Max, Dale tried to pick him up. The boy struggled in the stranger's arms, moaning and howling, and Dale quickly returned him to the earth. "Poor kid, I'm sorry he had to meet me among all these people."

"We thought we'd bring him to see you in all your glory," George said.

"At least there are trees," Dale said.

Lavinia smiled. "We'll all feel right at home."

Then Prince Charles, at the time a young, awkward guardsman, strolled up and Dale automatically extended a hand. "Hello, Charles. I'm Dale." By the time he turned back, his son and grandson had slipped away into the crowd.

After the meal—maple-glazed duck with orange rice and Christmas salad—Dale gave himself a brief toast, from under an arbor of expensively imported evergreen:

Ladies and gentlemen,

If I may speak a few brief words.

I came to England after my sixty-fifth birthday, because I didn't want to be bored in my old age. I have lived among you for only a brief time, though I hope indeed that the master of ceremonies allows me a little longer. I can say, in all honesty, that you have never bored me.

My first newspaper I bought in Atkinson, on the border between Minnesota and North Dakota. I am still, I fear, an Atkinson man. But I hope that I have managed at least to coat
myself with a good London veneer. The lessons from those early
days remain. I remember once, in the province of Alberta, I was
caught in a hailstorm. Hailstorms in Alberta can be a serious
business and a neighboring field of dairy cattle were murdered
where they stood. I survived with my brother by hiding under
thick newspapers. Then after the storm, we went through the
field gathering the stones into our rolled-up newspapers. I can
still recall the taste of those hailstones. Life has no more sa-
vory delicacy. If only I could order for all of you here a rolled-up
newspaper full of hailstones from Alberta. But I'm afraid even
the Dorchester lacks that chain of supply.

I tell this story because it encapsulates what I believe about
newspapers. Many of you have asked me why I don't use the
paper or NWM to espouse the perspective on affairs that I share
with many of you, although I'm afraid not you, Prime Minister.
I have lost friendships because of my refusal but I keep my nose
out of my editors' business because I believe that newspapers are
not for politics even though they must be political. Newspapers
are to keep the hail off your head and to gather up the hail once
it's fallen.

I think, if I do say so myself, that my papers make good hats
and good cones.

It's funny, the older I become, the more I think about the future. The less future you have, the more you cherish it, I suppose.
I won't trouble you with my plans for the Wylie Corporation,
which are mostly my son's plans anyway, but I will tell you a little

story, which I heard about Lord Fallis, if he'll pardon the mention of his name. When I was very new to town and making impertinent inquiries even then, he asked one of his subordinates, "Who is this Wylie? Where is he from?" And the subordinate answered, "Well, he began in a town called Atkinson, which was too small for him so he moved to Pittsburgh. It was too small as well so he moved to New York. New York was too small so he moved to London, which looks like it will be too small for him as well." "Where will he move next then?" Lord Fallis asked. The subordinate considered. "I suppose, sir, to hell."

Friends, I am not ready yet to make that move.

George sent Lavinia home with the boy after the speech. No point forcing them to endure the infinite vanity of old men. The frail bodies of the London elite lounged in glitter. All the hectic business of the flesh had ached away from the river of the old people's souls, exposing the grime-soaked shipwrecks of their fundamental desires: for more money, for more power. A stray policeman, needling a way through the whirling gears of the silvery tables, appeared at George's side. George was needed, the bobby whispered, about a matter pertaining to his father.

In the Presidential Suite, the most sumptuous room in the world at that time, on the edge of the unmade bed, sat a woman who, despite her state of shock, wore the most perfect mist-gray silk ball gown, matching the ephemeral pearls of her eyes. She was Lady Fallis, née Marguerite La Montée. On the bed, Dale Wylie's naked corpse sprawled. The first Lord Wylie of Abermarley, worth nine hundred million dollars, had lived less than twenty-four hours with his title.

*   *   *

Dale's death would be Ben's first memory. Little Ben worried that his eyes had killed his grandfather, which made sense: He had seen him and then he had died. The rest of the business of death was a spontaneous grand adventure. In London, the disappointment of the hotel room with its weird dream of a mustard paisley-patterned carpet, mother distraught and annoyed and worried about father, who was missing. After the dreary roar between airports, the regular house filled with kind, distracted women dressed like crows and the sadness that weighed down the house like perfume-soggy drapes was the opposite of the hotel: He could run out on the new-minted spring lawns. Out to the abandoned house with its jangled locks, to the fringe of the trees. He could run wherever he liked except on the stairs. The house was so playful with shadows that the knock of a ghost on the door hardly surprised the boy.

This ghost had matted and grizzled gray hair and his raggedy clothes were worse than the men who helped the gardeners, a yellow belt pulled crossways across his narrow waist, and a stuffed blanket under his arm. The ghost hugged Ben's father. Nobody ever hugged Father.

"You look just like Dale," he said.

"Uncle Max," George said.

George and Max flew Dale's body to Alberta, then drove him together to North Lake, so he could be buried, as he requested, "somewhere in the middle of nowhere." Ben and Lavinia were following in a town car. George drove. The man beside him was all stooped, gray rags of beard and open-air eyes and hands curled on his lap like claws. Max was unused to sitting still, his eyes wary, almost tauntingly alive. They had nothing in common except their natures.

"Do you have any children?" George asked, for something to ask.

"None ever seemed to come along," Max answered. "Not for lack of trying."

George began again. "So where have you been all this time?" He knew it was the question he wanted to ask his dead father.

"I've been in paradise," the gnarled man said with a smile.

"Alberta?" George guessed.

"You've only ever been a wolf in a cage, haven't you? I can see that. Dale was that way, too. I've nearly starved, I'm not saying I haven't. You haven't had anything to eat, the cold, the death. But then that ripped-up field mouse, his little guts that didn't want to die. Jesus himself never had a greater feast in heaven. That's the paradise I've been in."

A little while later, after he had tried to understand and failed, George asked, "Isn't that hell?"

"After I killed that wop, I was out west, you know? I went to work in this valley, Turner Valley, where they had discovered gas, and they weren't very good at it. They flared off about thirty percent. Just burned it up. The whole place smelled like rotten eggs, and not a little, I'm saying, not a nosebleed Sunday whiff, but the real stench of the stuff. And let me tell you, among the men there I wasn't the roughest. I wasn't near the worst guy. And I was a murderer. And why I'm telling you is that the place was heaven."

"Alberta in winter was heaven?"

"The gas kept the valley warm all winter and the deer and the antelope would come to graze off the wildflowers. A cougar came down from the mountains. Work for the asking. Hunting wherever you looked. Perpetual summer in the heat of flared-off stink. And no questions. That's heaven."

They drove in silence for a while, leaving behind the cottage country, where people play at the wilderness, for the starker country. "I need to know one more thing," George said. "Have you ever met anyone like us?"

"I'd leave that." George waited for another bleary rant, another smoky-voiced gush from the rusty pump.

"I've always wanted to meet another wolf," George continued.

"You're meeting one now."

"But there were rumors of others, wherever you've been?"

"There are werewolf stories all over. Because there are men and there are wolves, that's why. And dogs, and dogs who are like men, and men who are like dogs. Men who are men and wolves who are wolves."

George turned his face away. "I have this sensation sometimes that I'm already dead, that I'm seeing the world frozen, or that I've just died, and everything flashing up is the past, the dead past."

Max laughed. "You need one of those headshrinkers."

"Already tried."

A guffaw scraped its way out of Max's inhuman throat. "Then maybe a good run in the woods. Although, in a way, I know what you're talking about. In a way. After Turner Valley, I stole a truck and ran to the bush after trading in Edmonton for three ponies and a kit. I launched out. And about two days later, I bought Mags. My wife. Fourteen-year-old Indian girl and I bought her for one of my ponies, a Winchester rifle, and a box of cartridges. I'll tell you something else. That's the best bargain any of us will ever make, even Dale. She sure was ready to leave her old man, too, so I'm pretty sure it was a good deal for her. Anyway, we lit out and she'd been learning to read from this old English Bible that the missionaries were handing out, and the first thing I did was rip out all the pages and tie them up for kindling. How she roared. Laughed her ass silly."

Something moving beyond the window startled him. He was not used to cars, maybe not used to windows either.

"So we went into ranching country and built a little cabin and a day's ride away was a ranch and another day's ride the other way was a hotel for rich American sportsmen, and I would go to work for the ranchers and steal 'em blind and Mags would go down to the hotel and guide 'em and rob 'em blind, and pretty soon we had a pretty good thing going. She set up our little cabin in the bush. We had geraniums all year round and good beef too, 'cause I would tail a few away at the end of the year, you see, and she would kill them. The way she slid a knife into a bullcalf heart, swift, painless, on the down breath, so it never even knew it was dead. That's a woman. And I remember she took the pictures of the dresses out of the magazines and put 'em all over our walls and it looked good, like a real home. And I lay with her, man and wolf."

He closed his eyes, squeezed them shut, as if he were trying to relive the scenes of his memories. They opened full of naked tears.

"Why did you come back, Max?" George asked.

"I want to know how my brother died."

"There's good news there," George said. "He died fucking a British lady in the most expensive hotel room in the greatest city in the world the day he was knighted by the queen."

Max shuffled the tears off as laughter. "That wouldn't have upset him too much, I think."

"A proper British lady, too. The wife of an eighth earl of somewhere."

"Good for Dalie boy."

They drove into increasing wilderness.

"So why did you come back now, Max? Why not sooner?"

Max mused for a while, coughing, as they cut through a valley of pointless barren stone. "I suppose I couldn't ask him for money anymore."

In a town car with his mother, after driving to the end of an infinity of snow and boredom, as they pulled into the driveway of a stone cottage on the edge of a frozen lake, Ben saw his father with the grizzled man, the ghost from the doorway. They were shaking hands. They seemed happy and sad at the same time. Then the man began to run. Though he was a very old man, he ran fast across the snow toward the forest, and passed into the snowy trees leaping, and as he leaped he turned, midair, into a wolf. A black wolf. Ben's father kept waving as the wolf vanished into a cover of aspens. Ben looked back to his mother, whose smile was calm and understanding, the magical transformation a matter of every-day unconcern to her. She had seen the miracle but said nothing.

FOUR

The cab throbbed on the curb outside Kate and Leo's as I waited for them to finish screwing. The driver wasn't bothered by the wait. He could see the meter ticking over fatalistically, the *New York Post* related the city's various degradations to him in four-hundred-word nuggets, and a Starbucks venti pumpkin spice latte brightened his intermittent banter in Ibo over the Bluetooth. His life was rich with things. I had only my thoughts. My thoughts were still commercially viable then. Eight thousand words on the Wylies—enough to be cut down to four thousand—waited on my MacBook in the apartment, begging to have fresh detail, to be scoured by my anxieties and then, most gloriously of all, to be sold.

Fifteen dollars and forty-five cents later, the Stathapolouses sauntered out, Kate in postcoital lululemon, with her hair satisfyingly moist, Leo in aviator sunglasses and a padded green vest under a heavy brown wool suit jacket, like an English count strolling to shoot pheasants in a soggy Norfolk field or, rather, like some Guy Ritchie purchaseable version of same. He might have looked all right, too, if not for the deer-stalker cap with the flaps buttoned up.

"I'm not letting you in the car with that hat on," I said. Kate and I shared guffaws, hers as light and truculent as marshmallow foam.

Leo popped the trunk and put his suitcase inside. Kate swiped the hat from his head. Leo frowned poutingly. How much of his attention must be invested in navigating the shipping lanes and coastal shoals of these class oceans. "I guess I should have worn my Beaver Patrol trucker hat instead," he said.

"You don't have to impress the fish," Kate said, kissing him on the earlobe and tumbling into his thick Greco-Roman shoulders. Their glow in this moment was succulent: Marriage is the blackest of black boxes but I could never have imagined that a marriage with shower-sex could be so near to collapse. Kate waved us away, brimming with the morning light, leaving the waning glow of her cupidity in the rearview mirror.

"Sorry we kept you waiting," Leo mumbled.

"As long as you pay the fare."

With that arrangement, we set out for La Guardia on the twelve-hour journey from the world's center to the ends of the earth, from New York to North Lake.

Leo had claimed he wanted to fish Alberta. He provided an excuse I could give my mother: I was coming up to show one of my city friends the great outdoors, and I hinted at vague professional benefits. The truth was that I needed to suck more information out of the Wylie cottage. I had only gone over the place once and if I was sure of anything, I was sure the Wylies had more secrets. Leo heard about the trip and asked to join me. For the fishing, he said.

My mother never would have believed me if I had said I was just coming to see her. If I had said that I was just coming to see her, she would have assumed I had cancer. If I had told her that I was coming to ask her about the Wylies, she would have said that I shouldn't bother, she knew nothing. But for a city friend, a possible professional ally, she would buy steaks from the Mennonite butcher in Mint Lake two towns over.

The drive from the airport in Edmonton to North Lake takes five hours, a full tank of gas, and the complete resources of my spirit. The moment I sit down in the car, I always remember when I came back from university for the summer, working at the ice-cream parlor in town that served maybe a couple hundred customers during the season. I had mentioned to my mother one night after work that Ian Reed, the town lawyer, had come in for a cone of maple walnut. "Now, doesn't Mr. Reed have it made," my mother said to me. "I hear he naps every single afternoon." To my mother, the definition of success is an afternoon nap every day. I'm not even sure she's wrong.

In the smaller towns outside Edmonton, the land is all stands of scant trees and stones and stones and a few more trees and a little lakeside water and stones. Whenever I travel south, I have contempt for the fecundity, the resplendence, the welcoming embrace of nature. Who can respect the whorish givingness of the tropics? The vastness of the north, what my ex-wife used to call "the boreality," is unfathomably proud. Rock juts up from the roadside like endless mangled fangs. The atavism of the forest rises in the throat like relief. New York and London and all of Europe and the United States, you think as you drive, have built themselves an imposing ruse of self-importance, shunting away and forgetting that one way or another the wild will swallow them up. But here we know. We are swallowed. We know that we don't matter any more than a tree or a stone. The darkness in the woods makes everybody a child, every story a fairy tale.

Past Niggonipa, Leo roused himself from his twisted car-nap for a Double-Double at Tim Hortons, which he sipped the way a tourist to Iran might sip sekanjabin, sampling local color.

"The Wylies drove up here every month?" he asked when we sat down in the car.

"They flew. And not every month."

"There's an airport in North Lake?" He was just beginning to recognize the foreignness of his situation. Border control in Calgary had seemed to him like an amusing Old World ritual. Soon I would tell him that the print edition of *The New York Times* wasn't available here, and he wouldn't believe me.

"I remember their floatplane when I was a kid," I answered.

"Your little town must mean a lot to them. It must have cost a fortune to get here. And those people are cheap."

At that irrelevant moment, I remembered Leo's engagement party, half of our youth ago. At least I think it was his engagement party; there couldn't have been that many parties between the time he met Kate and the birth of Sigma. Leo had not yet acclimatized to the rarified air of big money then and, as soon as I arrived at the mansion in Connecticut that Kate's cousin had volunteered for the occasion, he steered me down to the cellar. The musty cavern was full of French *premier crus* from the sixties and seventies. Thousands of bottles, and many thousands of dollars a bottle, and all of it, every last dusty bottle, spoiled. The ignorant sons had forgotten about their father's burgundies and Bordeaux, hadn't regulated the temperature, so the wine had dissolved into itself. We picked out random bottles—a 1968 Margaux comes to mind—and the liquid only rolled to the three-quarter measure.

Leo and I must have stood in that amazing underworld of gorgeous detritus for fifteen minutes while the party above us fizzed.

North Lake will always be haunted to me, and not just by my father, who stares up from the skeletal October aspens, and not just by the Wylies either. North Lake is haunted by the former me, hick me. Leo could see as well as I could the cheap prettiness of the houses, the abandoned lumberyard with its dinosaur rust, the big lawns, scrupulously raked and edged, the swings in the antiquated schoolyard making forlorn perpetual pendulums. I remember, when I briefly studied aesthetic philosophy in school, wondering why the professors cared about the beautiful and the sublime. I grew up among the pretty and the cute. Porcelain angels behind parlor cabinet glass. Gilt chickadees suctioned to kitchen windows. Barbie dolls with knitted pink ball gowns to cover the spare toilet roll. For Leo, all this business was the surface of Mars.

My mother was standing at the door as we arrived. She suits the wilderness on the edge of town. With my father's pension and the few scraps of savings, she lives on next to nothing. She shovels her own roof. She makes stock from the saved bones of her dinners. She is a real person. I don't know if I've met another. She kissed Leo on both cheeks; she must have heard that they do it that way in New York.

"Dinner's ready," she said as I lifted the bags out of the trunk. "And I've given your big-city friend the guest room."

"It's beautiful here," Leo said, ignoring the offhand remark about his urbanity.

My mother peered apologetically at the landscape, the sparse aspens in the far and lonely fields darkening. "It's beautiful in the mornings in June," she said.

In the kitchen of my claustrophobic youth, with its wildwood flower wallpaper and its photographs of a dozen ancestors I couldn't name standing stock upright in their oblivion, at the wooden table on which my father relished his final meals, we ate steak and potatoes the way I like them, with canned peas. The canned peas made Leo a true anthropologist. Greeks cannot eat tinned food. They can force it down their throats but they can't eat it. We talked about the drive up, and about Leo's job, and about the fishing around North Lake, and about Leo's family, and about Sigma, and about how profoundly men had changed in the arena of child-rearing over the past twenty years, and we didn't talk about my divorce or the absence of offspring. Leo and my mother together: It oddly worked, like a pale blue suit with an orange shirt. I interrupted their conversation about what constitutes a really good butcher. "Leo here knows the Wylies," I said.

"A bit," Leo demurred.

My mother smiled. The local connection. "They used to live over a little ways."

"Did Poppy ever live there?" I asked. "She's the daughter."

"The Oriental one," my mother said. The word stung my twenty-first-century propriety like a hornet. "Never. I've never seen her. The ladies only stayed up here a few times. It was mostly the men."

"How long ago?" I asked.

"Before you were born."

"Mom," I said. "We're gossiping here. We want to know the details."

"I know, dear. That's why I'm holding back. Isn't that the secret of storytelling?"

My clever mother coaxed a tinfoil laugh out of Leo. Shared mockery was a bond he comprehended. "Let your mom tell the story in her own way." At that moment, I realized Leo had also come to Alberta for the Wylies, not the fish, not for me. Why?

"It's not too much of a story," said my mom. "It's more of a scenario. It was always the plane landing. Do you remember that, son?"

"I do. Circling down." Like a maple seed, a half helix. I am from irrelevance.

"Nobody knew the Wylies," she said. "They never brought friends with them. We could catch little hints, bits and pieces."

"What did you see, Mom?"

"Me specifically? I went over one afternoon with your dad. He wanted to know if they still needed yard work. The men. It was Dale and George. They were half naked. Scared, too. Though how anyone could be scared of your father . . ."

"I guess they came here for the privacy," Leo said. I noted that he had finished his canned peas, a gesture of true friendship.

"It must be more, I think. They're all buried here. All the men anyway. Always a hearse from Edmonton. All three of them. And Americans, too."

"How odd," Leo said. He was speaking differently around my mom, having already, in the course of an hour, adapted to a new social reality.

"We all thought so."

Leo placed his knife and fork accurately on the plate. "I've been to the family tomb in Champlain. Looks like an oversized birthday cake. That's where all the women are buried."

Why would he have ever visited Champlain? Why would anyone visit Champlain?

"And the men are all buried out back in the dirt without so much as a marker," my mother added, shoveling a mouthful of potatoes into her pursed mouth like the delicate peasant she is. Like I am.

For dessert, Saskatoon berry pie—a true prairie delicacy.

The next morning Leo and I fished one of the lakes of the Wylie property, right next to their cottage. The lake is small but livid with trout, currents of snapping flesh coursing and charging within the clarity of the water and the labyrinths of the low, mossy stones. Simple trout, to me, is the most delicious fish in the world—a flavor without ostentation or resistance.

Leo asked, "Are you taking me to where they found him?"

"That's about two hours north," I said.

"You mean there's north of here?"

Leo did not know how to cast a line, so I had to teach him the rollicking roll, the release and fade, a gesture with its own countrified pimpish swagger. The half hour of fishing was ribald, ridiculous. We caught seven two-footers as easily as casting. Leo was cheerfully amazed by the sportingness but he left the scaling and gutting to me. Leo has not traveled among the wealthy long enough to realize that true aristocrats relish menial tasks so long as they're completed in the wild. Prince Harry scales and guts the trout he catches.

Even though the land is all regrowth, replanted from clear-cut, the Wylie territory is the only place in the world where I sense the original meaning of wilderness. The place is an affront to human dignity. The longer I spend away from Alberta, the more Albertan I feel myself becoming. It's as if I gather all the terrors and incomprehensions I can muster in the larger world, in the quiet unspoken corners of other people's observed lives, private and public, and carry them, in the buckets of my eyes, to the terrors and incomprehensions of the trees and the rocks and the wolves and the eternal cold. I bring my own wilderness with me wherever I go. Like the Wylies.

While I was threading the fish by their gills through a branch I looked up and Leo was gone. Through the passage in the trees, I could see him sneaking into the Wylies' cottage. I found out later from my mother that they were no longer paying for its upkeep. I had broken in many times myself. Still, I raced to their door with outrage scouring my throat. By the time I arrived, panting, I could tell he had taken something. Later, I discovered it was a bird book from which I had already removed the important document. There is always the chance he filched something else, I suppose. Later, when I scoured the place myself, I found a trove of letters from the London years and Ben's diary from Hamilton College in a cardboard box under scattered tennis rackets.

"Why?" I asked him.

He smiled an art dealer smile. "Just wanted to see how the other half lives," he said.

"You are the other half."

He shrugged like a teenager caught smoking. "You're just as curious," he said. "You've been asking about Poppy and Ben all weekend. You've been asking your mom for gossip."

"There's a difference between gossip and breaking and entering," I said.

"These are the Wylies," he said. "What can you possibly take from them that would matter?"

He breezed past me. With a quick turn of my eyes, I checked. In the corner by the window, the Paul Klee received the declining light with grace. My heart full of blood cooled at its crimson squares, its blazing civilization. At least *The Wolf* was safe.

*   *   *

I was in bed with my ex-wife several weeks later when I learned that Leo had fled the groomed lawns and shoveled walks of provincial morality for the wide, empty beaches of limitless globalized cash. He had run off with Poppy.

My ex-wife and I often slept together after the catch-up lunches we insisted on putting ourselves through whenever she came to New York on business. I would order a salad to show I was taking care of myself. She would order chocolate mousse to demonstrate the daring will-to-pleasure in her new life, knowing that I knew that a woman in her late thirties who eats chocolate mousse in public at lunch is not lacking for the various intrusions of men. The loves and despairs and appeals and abjections in our conversations were a gooey palimpsest of crisscrossing questions: How did we ever get married? How did we ever separate? But we always followed the grotesque hour of mangled, throat-constricting chatter with a splurged hour of illicit and informed sex.

It was November. I remember the rotten cardboard gray of the city skies and the bare branches of the pear tree that girded the view from the hotel bed. The slope of her nudity brushed along me—the beauty of naked women after the business of copulation is lovely, like the smell of old paper, a loveliness to be inhaled, held in the lungs. She adjusted her duchess neck onto my shoulder.

"I'm only seeing guys in their fifties from here on," she said blithely.

"Less demanding?" I guessed.

"They've given up. If you have an ass, and they can touch it, that's all they ask. Plus he's made partner. He just travels, collects art. African art, but still."

My wife was cheating with me. Brilliant. The hard bridge of the back of her head readjusted against my shoulder, and I knew she was comparing its comfort with the comfort of the partner's. By the weather passing across her face, lips curling, the moist front massing behind her eyes, I followed the pattern of her thought down to its source, the primordial sadness in her cosmopolitan eyes: poor young men or rich old men. She could have one or the other. Cake or its eating. Then her eyes bristled with a wave of cruelty and I no longer knew what she was thinking.

"You're lucky," she said finally. "Being a single man in your late thirties is like being a woman in her early twenties. Everything's in your favor. For once, you're attractive because of your age."

"Who wants to be attractive because of a number?" I asked.

"Who wants anything they have?"

She had always complained that I could never enjoy what I had, that once I possessed anything, the possession lost all value in my eyes, and the familiarity of the criticism diminished the ache in my heart.

Then she shattered the familiar with a dropped elbow.

"Your pal Leo didn't want what he had either," she said. "He's following my general plan. You should join us. We'll all screw people twenty years older than us for the money, and then when we have the money we'll all screw people twenty years younger than us."

"What do you mean about Leo?"

Then she told me. Her surprise was genuine. Putting the knives back into the drawer she had accidentally stuck a blade into my neck. As she left, her quick and angry kiss, a droplet condensed from the fine mist of our lust and self-loathing, sat on my cheek, an inconsolable tear-pearl. She left me in her hotel room with the flat gray fugitive sky cackling with black lightning branches. I lay there alone with all the times I've been abandoned running through my veins like a seventh whisky, although Leo's departure from his wife, I knew even then, was by no means unfavorable to me.

I couldn't stop myself from imagining where Leo must be standing, in torpid privacy, on some lugubrious sheltered beach, inspecting the unowned stars winking over the fished-out sea, no doubt wondering with his unfathomable ambition where was higher, what was next. He had floated away, from me and from everyone. Leo had floated up among the careless gods.

Nobody knew where, exactly, they had floated to. Nobody could name that inequitable Utopia, the Shangri-la of the oligarchs where all things are possible with money, leaving the rest of us in the quotidian ruins of our squalid little lives to dream inchoately of their beautiful omnipotence. I had no time to gauge how Leo would make his entrance into the story I was writing. The day after my exchange of carnal mementoes with my wife, Mort Wilner called, and I rolled around to the offices of the *Standard*.

"How's the piece going?" he asked.

I had my enthusiastic patter down, vague in outline but spiced with detail about the family, about the times they lived in. The men whom she had dated were, each in their way, representative of their time, which was the outline of my theory of her love life.

"Representative of their time," he mused. "That's not bad."

"And now there's a new guy, and I know him. I've known him for years. My buddy Leo."

"That's perfect," he said, with wildly exaggerated cheeriness. "Except no. No, it isn't." Mort held a letter up across his desk, just as he'd once held up a graph to fire me. "This is a letter from WylieCorp's legal firm. Shall I sum it up?"

I took the letter.

"It says they gave you a contract before the interview."

"I didn't sign it," I said.

"They say you promised to sign it. But it doesn't really matter, you understand? They can sue us until we bleed, for fun."

I made some gesture of outrage, but he stopped me.

"It's irrelevant," he said. He held up the letter. The letter was money. Who is stupid enough to fight with money?

My story was dead. Hope wasn't far behind. What means or reason could I swagger up for staying in New York now? There was enough begging space on my Visa for another two months' rent, maybe. Even worse, a digital advertising firm I had been writing for occasionally had offered me a permanent job—a terrific, well-paying job as a copywriter—in Toronto, and to refuse might be the act of a crazy person rather than somebody charmingly obsessed with New York City. The crisis was coming, one way or another. What was the point of all the Wylie papers, my rented basement archive of a family that craved nothing more than to be forgotten forever? Poppy Wylie was my own private celebrity; the Wylies were a private secret. And what is that worth? Everyone has one of those. A new hunger began to creep into my guts. My wife had been right—no one can earn a place in the money anymore.

By the time I turned up in SoHo, Kate had already redecorated. Interior design was her mode of protest against the injustices of the universe and the inscrutability of fate. The living room had been wallpapered with a sepia-washed scene of Brazilian beach-bathers, the carpet was blue shag foam bearing aloft the elegant, floating furniture. I selected a recliner with lifelike horseheads for armrests, comfortable in a Mongol way.

"Everything in this room used to be local," she said. "Manhattan designers. Locally sourced. Now everything's from as far away as I could manage. Isn't that silly?"

"I love the carpet," I said. Rich women with their fabrics are like bikers with their tattoos—always looking for a chance to discuss the finer details.

"I ordered the blue from Lagos. The wallpaper's from São Paolo. The lamps are from London. All the best lamps come from Northern Europe."

"I like it here," I said. Then added in a splurge of confidence, "*The Standard* gave me the kill fee for my piece on Poppy today."

She thought about it. "I bet Leo taught her how to block it."

"Maybe. Or maybe she knew herself. Anyway, I've been paid for my silence. And I'll never be able to write about it. Not ever."

"Maybe a novel?" she suggested.

I stroked the mane of the armrest horse to calm the beast, steady its youthful wildness. My story was now mere space on my laptop that I wouldn't bother to clear out for its insignificance: one-sixteenth the memory of a song. The chair made me want raw flesh. "I think we should drink brandy," I said.

She rose, walked to the bar, and returned with two vase-sized snifters, alighting near me on the floor, her legs tucked under her knees, a middle-aged siren on invisible rocks about to sing.

"He sent a 'Dear Kate' text," she said. "Divorced by text message. I wonder if that will be something I can tell my grandchildren."

"It probably won't happen to that many people."

Her initial burst of laughter petered out timidly. "He should have at least told Sigma."

"Sigma doesn't know?"

Sarcasm staticked her voice, a ragged leak of maternal anguish. "I can't bear to tell her. The story's too embarrassing. Daddy left Mommy. A kid might understand that. But Sigma can't yet understand a text saying 'You should know, I'm with Poppy.'"

"That was all it said?"

She nodded. "We had an old-fashioned marriage while it lasted. With our own lives. Everybody knew."

I was supposed to say something, anything, a word for our mutual dignity, a glance at a beggar instead of handing over a coin, but I had nothing. I had not even a glance to offer.

"Now we'll have a rather traditional divorce. I suppose I was just a rung on some ladder."

"I don't know," I said.

The brandy stung her nose and she hacked at the alcohol on her throat. "Isn't it supposed to be the villains in melodramas who drink brandy?"

"I mean, how is he going to survive? He barely knows her."

Her smile poured out shadowy elixir. "What, you think he'll miss his friends?" She laced the last word with all the ghosts of friends she couldn't have because of her money and all the friends she had only because of her money. Then she cheered up. "Marrying money is the oldest job in the world. I guess it's good that men are doing it now."

Nothing seems to be able to cure me of the belief that life is happening elsewhere. In Kate's living room, as we spotted the haven of drunkenness, and the winds began to drift in that direction, even then, at that moment, I wanted to talk to Leo. Leo has the gift of making others forget his failings, maybe because he forgets them so easily himself—a prestidigitation of conscience. Kate longed for him, too, I could tell. That night envy bound us more tightly than love ever could. In the luxurious appointments of a grand house in the most prosperous city known to human history, we lounged on the latest furniture with excellent brandy, considering our comparative poverty. Together we stared into the chasm between ourselves and the real money, the money that enables the fulfillment that eludes ordinary life. I left before I tried another sort of fulfillment.

I was glad of the night's emptiness as I stumbled out the door. The twin mysteries were crucifixion then: How do we ever live with people? How do we ever abandon them? I walked home, or rather I walked back to my place between the home I was too good for and the home I had broken and the home I craved. I knew my way and could not be more lost.

The vestibule of the house on Larchmount Crescent had no space for art, not even for a mirror, just a small table for keys and an awkward closet, but the narrow passage was a haven for Ben Wylie. He was a weekender at Hamilton College, which meant that on Monday mornings, the other boys lay in wait at the gates to chuck snowballs at him as the chauffeur opened the limo doors, and on Friday evenings the chauffeur drove him alone through the early winter nights back to shadowy Larchmount Crescent, with its flitting servants and its warmed-up dinners under the half glow of television. In the vestibule, he was not at school, not at home, safe in the refuge of in-between.

On the night of his thirteenth birthday, Ben arrived home to find his mother waiting for him there, curled on the staircase in a scarlet dress. He had hoped his mother would come home for his birthday. She took his coat, teasing the fringe of his shoulder-length hair with a curious, tender judgment, and then amazed him. "Your father wants to speak to you," she said.

What could have brought his father home? Death? Disease? Had someone at the school called to tell his father that he was a mediocre student? That the other boys were rough with him? Had the business collapsed? Were they poor now? His mother piloted him into the dining room, where George sat, hands crossed like an undertaker preparing to discuss the bill, at the wide oak dinner table where they almost never ate dinner together. A brown manila envelope crouched by his elbow.

His parents left him with the envelope and waited in the garden while Ben learned that he was born to a lonelier fate than money.

To my heir, Ben, whom I love,

I may as well say it straight. You and I are wolves. Once a month, during the full moon, I become a gray timber wolf. After three days, I wake up as a man again, with no memory of the experience. I know how strange that must sound. When I was about your age, my father took me down into the basement and showed me. It will be shocking for you when you see the same change in me, I know. My hope is that I can spare you the horror of ignorance at least.

You're awfully young to have to deal with these problems. I don't want this letter to frighten you. There's no reason to be frightened. There is pain in becoming a beast. There is also an ecstasy. To me, the saddest moment is the ache following the retransformation, when I wake up and I'm human again. After the terror and after the violence comes the loneliness. I've spent my life trying to cure that loneliness. Sometimes it goes away of its own accord. Sometimes under the loveliness of your mother's music, it doesn't seem to matter. But it's never away for long.

My cure for loneliness has been the search for others like us. My dad only knew about Uncle Max. You might remember Max because he showed up at your grandfather's funeral. Dad told me that he

never met a werewolf outside of the family, though he'd had his sus-
picions. He believed that Lyndon Johnson was a wolf. He believed
Hermann Goering was. He opened up to me all that he believed, all
that he had sussed out of his little reading because he was not that
big a reader of books though he read every newspaper he could get
his hands on. He believed that Lord Wellesley, the former governor
of India and the Duke of Wellington's brother, was a werewolf, but
he was only guessing that after reading a series of biographies. He
named a bunch of other names, from every walk of life, and I've
run all those guesses down, and there was nothing to any of them.
He may have wanted to please me. Or maybe he dreamed them up
because he was consorting with a lot of lords and so on, who could
trace their families back by millennia, and finding werewolves at key
moments in history made him feel grander. I don't really know.

I have spent my life searching. The business has taken care of
itself. I discovered a simple truth about business, which might serve
you well later: Hire good people and leave them alone. I discovered
it more or less by accident. Lee wouldn't let me turn WylieCorp
into a holding company. The deals he was finding were just too
sweet and, for various reasons, I felt I owed him a chance to see out
his vision. You will have to make your own decisions. Just let me say
that opportunities are not inherited. When Lee goes, you should
probably structure the shares around income-bearing properties.
Just my opinion.

My search has taken me to every corner of the earth. To Peru, to
Catalonia, to the Gobi Desert, to Nigeria, to Oman, to Baffin Island, to Delhi, the Middle East, behind the Iron Curtain. I'm going
to tell you what I know.

There are two references to werewolves in antiquity that matter.

The first comes from the very first work of literature, *The Epic of Gilgamesh*, dated about 1700 BC. In a list of the men that the goddess of love has destroyed, there's this:

> *You loved a shepherd, a herdsman,*
>
> *Who endlessly put up cakes for you,*
>
> *And every day slaughtered kids for you.*
>
> *You struck him, turned him into a wolf.*
>
> *His own boys drove him away,*
>
> *And his dogs tore his hide to bits.*

The other important reference comes from Ovid, a poet who lived around the time of Christ. His poetry collection, *The Metamorphoses*, described King Lycaon of Arcadia, which was an idyllic country in central Turkey. At a banquet in honor of Zeus, King Lycaon butchered his own son and cooked him into a dish for the god to eat. In his rage, Zeus transformed Lycaon into a werewolf:

> *My thunderbolt struck the king's house to ruins,*
>
> *And he, wild master, ran like beast to field*
>
> *Crying his terror which cannot utter words*
>
> *But howls in fear, his foaming lips and jaws,*
>
> *Quick with the thought of blood, harry the sheep.*
>
> *His cloak turned into bristling hair, his arms*
>
> *Were forelegs of a wolf, yet he resembled*
>
> *Himself, what he had been—the violent*
>
> *Gray hair, face, eyes, the ceaseless, restless state*
>
> *Of drunken tyranny and hopeless hate.*

It's hard to tell whether the werewolf is a victim or a monster, isn't it? For many years I had a recurring dream, though it has lessened since I met your mother. In this dream I cannot tell whether I am chasing or being chased, I am just a running wolf. And that seems to be the same as in Gilgamesh and Ovid: Are we outlaws? Or are we poor shepherds?

The earliest records of werewolves were written by a French historian named Giraldus Cambrensis. He never doubted that encounters with werewolves were real.

> Is such an animal to be called a brute or a man? A rational animal appears to be far above the level of a brute; but who will venture to assign a quadruped, which inclines to the earth, and is not a laughing animal, to the species of a man? Again, if anyone should slay this animal, would he be called a homicide?

I have always been surprised by how much compassion the commentators feel for men like us. Nonetheless, our inclusion among the human race has not always been a given. The most famous werewolf in France was a young man named Jean Grenier, who lived in the sixteenth century. He confessed to killing more than fifty children. The president, or judge of the case, refused to believe that Grenier was a lycanthrope: "The president went on to say that lycanthropy and kuanthropy were mere hallucinations, and that the change of shape existed only in the disorganized brain of the insane, consequently it was not a crime that could be punished." The president sentenced the boy to life within the local monastery. He did not enjoy his subsequent life. He began by gorging on a bloody heap of offal and ended without being able to look anyone in the face. He died at twenty years of age.

There are dozens of other legitimate records. I honestly don't know what to make of most of them. They may be something. They may be nothing. I followed every trace, every rumor, into the Amazon, into Haiti, into Malaysia, the Côte d'Ivoire, the Congo, up the Zambezi, and down the Mississippi. The stories would lead me to some place, to the woods where children had seen a werewolf centuries before, to a hill where townsfolk had supposedly hung a wolfman, to a dark prairie where a hunter had been eaten alive by our kind. Always the same question came to me when I got where I was going: What had I been expecting? What had I been looking for? There were just places. Woods, a hill, a prairie. I found no insight, only landscape.

The medical records are even less satisfying, though they're much clearer. The condition of lycanthropy has been well documented. In the second century AD the Greek physician Marcellus of Side saw dozens of lycanthropes. The prescribed treatment was bleeding to the point of fainting. That seemed to be the cure for pretty much everything back then. In modern medical literature, roughly fifty cases have been reported, although this number may be low because patients receive the diagnosis only after having passed through a period where they believe they are wolves, which means that only patients who have a moment of clarity, becoming capable of identifying their symptoms, appear on the record. I think it's safe to say that many more of these poor fellows simply remain in the delusion that they are wolves. Many others cannot remember what they became.

There are variations of lycanthropy, too. An interesting one, recently reported, is the case of the patient who believes he can turn others into wolves. The coexistence of lycanthropy and Cotard's syndrome has also been reported in more than three instances. Cotard's syndrome is a disease in which the patient believes that he is already dead and thus is immortal. It's a nihilistic delusion, and it can even go so far as the delusion that the flesh is rotting off the patient's bones, rendering him invulnerable. In these cases, the lycanthropy comes as a punishment from God, as externalized sexual expression, as inferiority complex, as a form of identification with a despised aggressor, as the expression of primitive id-instincts, as an evasion of feelings of guilt. None of this applies to you or me, of course. They're not wolves, these people. They just think they are. Still, you may find their stories interesting and/or valuable at some time in the future.

I met several wolf-raised children. I thought they might help me understand the fusion of the human and the wild. A girl in Azerbaijan disappeared from her home for twenty-one days when she was four years old. She told her rescuers that she had been cared for by wolves who fed her and kept her warm. Anthropologists have verified her story, but when I spoke with her, she had been telling it for so long, to so many strangers, that the story had spun itself into a myth she told herself, so it was useless.

Shamdeo, the wolfboy of India, was not useless. Mother Teresa was caring for him in Calcutta when I met him, but the poor fellow had been discovered living among wolves outside Sultanpur in the Punjab. I spent an hour with him. He had sharpened his teeth on bones. He lurked in the corners, in the shadows. He was suspicious of everyone but the priest who took care of him. There was something of us in the dark-eyed boy but he would never say what. I realized that, even if he knew, he couldn't tell me whatever it was I wanted to know. I gave up searching after Shamdeo. He was as close as I was ever going to get, and it was nowhere. At least I could set up a small house and an annuity for the poor fellow.

There's one more incident it's my duty to tell you about. I'm not sure what it means but I'm sure it means something, and maybe you'll figure it out someday. Maybe some piece of the puzzle will fall into your hands that never fell into mine. It concerns your sister. You may or may not remember her adoption. Your sister's biological father was a man named Pi-Lin, a Chinese official. Her adoption came shortly after your grandfather died, and before I began my investigations into our condition. We were still in Alberta after your grandfather's funeral. The caretaker came over with the message. It was extraordinary. A man I had met only once before was asking me to bring your mother to Hong Kong immediately. We flew out the next day. A very nervous middleman took us by junk into Victoria Harbor. Pi-Lin met us in the harbor, leaping into our boat. He had a baby in his arms. That was your sister.

Something terrible was about to happen to him, but he wouldn't be more specific. He was to be "reeducated." I asked him whether he would ever come back. He said that it would be sensible to assume that he was already dead. He showed me his delicate short-fingered hands and asked me if I thought they would survive a season making pig iron. I didn't know what to say. He told us your sister's name, which sounded like "Poppy" to us, and Pi-Lin smiled and said Poppy would be a fine name for her. He took one last look at his daughter in your mother's arms, and said, "It's just painted skin." Then he boarded his boat and disappeared into the Cultural Revolution.

The story "Painted Skin" comes from a collection called *Strange Stories from a Chinese Studio*, by Songling Pu. It's a story of secret monsters. In it, a man named Wang meets a beautiful young runaway on the street and brings her home. By accident one evening, he returns home, to his library, and sees a monster spreading out human skin on the bed, painting it. The monster throws on the skin like a cloak and becomes the girl. Shocked, Wang runs to tell his wife and a Taoist priest. The priest tells him to hang a flybrush on the library door so that the monster won't be able to escape. The monster bursts past the door and rips out Wang's heart anyway. The priest pursues and manages to kill the monster with a wooden sword, but he cannot raise the dead man. Only a filthy and destitute maniac raving by the side of the road has that power, the priest says. So Wang's wife begs the madman, who beats and curses her. Finally, when she refuses to leave without the cure for death, he spits and tells her to swallow his spit if she wants her husband back. She finally chokes it down and later that night, as she's preparing her husband's body, a lump rises in her throat. She throws up a heart, which falls into her husband's chest cavity. Her husband revives, with no more harm done to him than a little scar on his chest.

I'm unable to shake the thought that Pi-Lin meant something by quoting this story. Had Pi-Lin seen? Had he somehow known about our monstrosity? If he knew, why didn't he say? Or was it all coincidence, misunderstanding, overthink? This is hard to explain, Ben, but part of having a deep, unbelievable secret is the sense that everybody knows but isn't talking about your deep, unbelievable secret. That's one of the hardest fantasies to lose, the selfish idea that everybody is thinking about you.

I set up a paper mill in Shenzhen, shipping timber from Oregon and British Columbia to be processed into glossy paper and shipped back, and it did turn out to be significantly profitable, I must say, but I was doing it as an excuse to have contact with the Party, and that was a failure. The economic future of China was obvious by then. The port at Shenzhen was like seeing a wonder of the world come into existence, larger than dreams. They won't be giving away their daughters anymore, I thought the first time I saw it. I told the series of apologetic officials that I wanted to deal with Pi-Lin.

They claimed that no one of that name had ever existed. I insisted he did. They blamed the destruction of records during the Cultural Revolution. After much pressing, they admitted that there may have been an official by that name who may have been reeducated. The problem was how thoroughly he had been reeducated. They probably really didn't know. At the end, I again found only a blank.

That's all I have. I've written all my disappointments down in the hopes that you won't have to repeat them. I believe that every person is a creature of inheritance. Life happens between what we've been given and what we leave behind. It's true for everybody but it's doubly true for us. I think I've done my duty. I think my old dad would think I've carried the bucket without spilling too much. But I hoped that I could give you an answer about who you are, who we are, and maybe even why we are. I can't.

At least I can offer you this. Don't fear our nature. That's what it's so necessary for you to know. What it takes some time to understand is that being a wolf is better than being a man. Wolves don't kill things for no reason. Wolves are loyal or they go alone. Wolves don't hide from themselves. I'm not sure that helps. I'm coming up short on wisdom. Maybe this: When you're a man, be a man. When you're a beast, be a beast. Find a woman who can live with both.

Your loving father

As Ben read, his heart fluttered up to his tonsils. A joke? No, he didn't know his father well enough. And besides, it was too detailed, the weird old poems and the medical records. As he read, Ben found himself remembering the time his sister had run away. Before they had sent her to boarding school in Switzerland. The servants had been zigzagging like pinballs through the house, weeping for their jobs, and for the lost child. The police came to the door, knowing nothing, taking statements, asking questions. Nobody asked Ben, but Ben knew that his sister loved to play along the abandoned train tracks. So that is where he went. The fierce beams of his flashlight had arrowed intermittently through the forest, through the swallowing blackness. Just as he expected, she was sitting under pine branches by the abandoned tracks, and had brought with her a small group of her stuffed animals. She whispered to him when he arrived. She said she wanted to see if the stuffed animals spoke to each other at night. He had lain down beside her. Stuffed tigers and dogs and bears and parrots and wolves. When he had brought his sister back in the morning, the blubbering, grateful servants all looked like they wanted to smack him in the mouth.

The last page fell accidentally from Ben's tingling fingers. The surprise was not nearly so rough as it should have been. He had always suspected. Not a wolf. Not a wolf exactly. But he had always known. There are worse secrets.

His parents were waiting in the garden for his reaction. The bone moon, near-full, a faint watermark in the vast longing it overlooked, posed like a beacon over them.

"Are you done looking?" Ben asked.

"We'll be here, my dear," his mother said.

"We'll have every weekend," George added quickly, quickly understanding.

Ben shrugged. "I've always wanted to know what's in our basement."

Ben's material introduction to lycanthropy followed two nights later. The basement, with its labyrinth of cages and restraint devices, was more horrible than the cartoonish reality of his father's transformation. His mother calmed the beast, the prelude to civilization.

The next month, George and Ben shared the cage. At first, wolf-George was leashed to the wall out of reach of his son, but within a few hours Ben understood that his father knew him for his own even as wolf. They brooded together in the night, the wolf's head on Ben's lap, joint musk and warmth. George's howl reverberated shockingly in the echo chambers of the concrete cellar. Ben came to love the sound.

Month after month, Ben waited in the cage. Each moon began with the exciting possibility—today I may be transformed—then, after his father's appalling agonies, there was only the dreariness, the dirt floor, the leashes, three whole days with nothing to do. Terror and love sloped into boredom. In his disappointment, Ben began sketching in notebooks he carried down to the cage with him. He began sketching the wolf, its suppleness, its power, and its strangeness. He drew the wolf's head on his lap. The bars, the leashes, the restraints. He took to studying the momentary agony of his father's transformation, attempting to put that fury onto paper, to convert the memory of the sudden fluidity into an image. Drawing was a distraction from the question that swelled with each passing month. Why wasn't he turning into a wolf? With the lowering of the moon, his father's eyes would look up from his rehumanized face with a mangled hope: This time? No. Then they would dress and leap up to the kitchen, where Lavinia would soothe their disappointment with bacon and oatmeal.

His mother liberated Ben after two years. In the middle of the full moon, the George-wolf sleeping, she led her confused son out of the basement cage.

"I think we should take this as a blessing," she said, as she held her son in the moonlight, sobbing in his absence of beastliness.

"Is Dad angry about it?" Ben asked.

"He's more confused than upset. He traveled everywhere to learn about a condition he thought you would suffer from, and then you escaped. You cured yourself."

"I didn't do anything."

"Nobody knows what they're doing," she answered softly. His mother guided him inside, around and up the marble staircase, to the parental bedroom, where a large red-and-white abstract painting filled a wall. The canvas was clawed on, scarred with impression. "T.T. painted this for me," she said. "He wrote the duet for lovebirds for me and then he painted this for me. When I left my family to tour the first time, when I left Quebec and never wanted to return but still carried that smell of Quebec in my hair." Her loitering gaze hinted at the mélange of what that fragrance must have been: the smoke from maple fires and whore perfume and the slime of salmon skin and mossy stones and sweaty sheets and old piano music and Cathedral incense . . .

"Was T.T. a wolf?"

"No, but he wanted to be. I realized this much later. He wanted to be what your father was. He wanted to be magic." Her eyes were saucers of black water. "I always wondered if I should have explained to him all that I saw, if I should have said, 'The magic is a curse.' He thought that George was a stupid Anglo businessman. Imagine."

"Why are you telling me this?"

She was now enmeshed in the million dewy spiderwebs of her own memories and looked up with a slow and luscious blink. "I don't think either of them would understand. The magic is the curse and the curse is the magic. Can I make you understand that, Ben? Do you understand?"

Ben failed to understand anything. "Yes, Mother, I understand."

She unlocked a cabinet and handed over a raft of Ben's smeared drawings, ragged from the cage. Between their hands, a mille-feuille of paint and shit instead of the inexpressible, the inconsolable.

"Your father has not seen a full moon since he turned fourteen," she said. "Can you imagine?"

The moon nestled like a stone in the tall grasses by the ravine where Larchmount Crescent sloped down to the wilderness. Ben wandered down, as lonely as any merely human soul, to crouch like a stone, like the moon, in the tall grasses. He began to weep. He wept the way only teenage boys weep, from the floor. Eventually he heard rustling from the house. He sucked himself up, for his mother, for his father? It was only Poppy. His kid sister back from school for Christmas. She said nothing. She stood beside him, a little above him, and then began to comb his hair with her fingers. Into the sudden pause of her tenderness, Ben Wylie unleashed the howl he so wished could be real.

That was the year old Jack Taggart died. The second stroke took him at a dog track in Sarasota, and the tragedy of his final moments was that he never saw Seeya Later romp home, paying handsomely at a hundred to eight.

The whole flight to Sarasota, George and Lee had nothing to say, frozen by the death of a man neither had seen for almost a decade. The funeral had been arranged on the pink and floury sand of the Siesta Key beach, where Jack had lived his later years in a little mango-colored bungalow with a secretary named Tammy. Siesta Key was one of the peculiar paradises America has scattered over itself like glittering ashes. A grotesque highway spewed diesel fumes beside an eternal pillow of beach on which sea turtles dug egg holes by night, surrounded by pirati-cal bars and old folks' homes and crab restaurants and little stores selling garish sunglasses and key chains and local handmade pottery. Jack had died surrounded by life's cheaper pleasures.

"Do we have the wrong place?" George asked as they pulled up to the beach address. A party seemed to be under way. Several hundred men and women—buyers and sellers, lovers and gamblers, friends and enemies from the mad, capable, fanatic, gorgeous, moneyed world— had showed up in Technicolor finery: Hawaiian shirts and knee-length shorts, and fluorescent bikinis, and one man in an unforgettable suit of yellow linen, and another in open-necked teal. Stepping out in black from a blue Cadillac, George and Lee plopped like lumps of coal into fruit salad.

"It looks like Dad's people," Lee said.

George waded through the jocular mourners to the rosewood casket, luscious and antiquated, and there he was: Jack. George's memories of the whole rough world of joking, smoking, farting, flesh-squeezing men with their tumblers of iced whisky and their smokes and their dumb puns and their communities of winks and their pockets jangling with change lay dead in the casket with him.

"It's him," George said.

"And I don't know a man or woman here," Lee said.

Eventually, the crowd, exuding tutti-frutti skin cream and tacky cheerfulness, settled into the sand and a buffoonishly drunk obese man in a purple suit took the microphone beside the casket. He was holding on to a fistful of rum in ice with mint like a speaking stick. "My fa-vorite Jack Taggart story," he announced. When a semblance of silence breached, he ran into it shouting: "My favorite Jack Taggart story hap-pened at the track. If ever the track had a saint, it was Jack Taggart. And every saint has his miracle, right? We were driving, I remember, upstate New York, and he asks, 'Want to go to the track?' and I say, 'Sure,' and we're driving and, bam, a white squirrel runs out onto the road. Albino. Nearly killed us. 'Wasn't that a bit lucky,' said Jack.

"So we're at the track that afternoon, it's the seventh race and wouldn't you know it, there's a horse called Whitetail. And Jack comes to me, he says, 'Look at this, it's a horse called Whitetail, just like we saw on the road.' Sure enough and I know what's coming next. Horse is running at a hundred to three.

"So Jack figures this out, and he figures that out, he borrows from this guy, he scrapes from that guy, stuff he shouldn't, rent, kids' money, wives' money, money he has that belongs to other people. Everything and more. On a hunch. You understand? Just on some stirring in that gut of his.

"And sure enough, Whitetail wins and he had to carry the money out in a bag. He had to buy a bag from the gift shop to carry it out. We had to go somewhere, too. Business deal. Now, I know that he lost it all, and I know he made a lot of dumb bets that didn't pay off, but that's how I'll always remember him. Laughing his ass off, rich with the track's money, on the road to a deal."

The next woman in line took the mic. She looked like Teri Garr. She spoke like Teri Garr. She may well have been Teri Garr. "I just want to say that I was with him when he went broke after two days in an underground Chinese casino in New York and I saw him give the last five dollars he had in the world to a rummy off the street and he laughed about it. He laughed just as much as he must have laughed in that car."

A whole line of men and women told their favorite Jack Taggart stories, grasping at his amusing and infuriating brilliance, his unique capacity for incomplete collapse and partial recovery, his fleshy hope.

Some laughed. Some wept. Some railed. Some boasted. Some worked themselves into rages and had to be shushed to mollifying grumbles. Like water running through the earth, money had coursed through Jack Taggart in rivulets and mighty floods, in underground rivers and vast sucking tides, and pillars of clouds that drenched down, and mile-thick glaciers. Like water leaves stories on the earth, money left stories on Jack Taggart. The man that money poured through.

Until the light began to fall, Lee and George listened to the stories money had wrought. Then they drove in silence to the jet. They didn't speak till they were at twenty thousand feet.

"Maybe I should have told a story," Lee said.

"What story would you have told?" George asked.

Lee ran the talons of his hands over his skull, and then folded them virtuously on his lap. "I suppose I have no story."

George understood, as he always seemed to understand with Lee. Their lives ran parallel through a diabolical, inevitable magnetism that imitated friendship at least.

"He was a true American," George said.

"That's fair."

"I wish my father had a funeral like that."

"I wish my mother had."

Ben sucked the thumb of his own contempt, peered down the row of girls leaning against the wall of the gym, and thought: You could never be with me. I'm so much richer than you. I'm just so much richer than you. So so much richer than you.

The annual Orange Blossom Ball between the Amherst School for Girls and Hamilton College was held at the beginning of spring. Ben stood apart. Ben was happiest standing apart, least vulnerable. Over twelve years of coexistence, the boys of Hamilton College had learned to hate Ben Wylie, and he had learned to hate them back. Class warfare is more acute between the rich and the megarich than between the rich and the poor. Moneyed people cannot stand the eccentricities of those with more than them and the richer find the slightly less rich intolerably money-grubbing. There is a world of difference between being born on third, thinking you've hit a stand-up triple, and being born on home plate.

Ben insisted on knotting his school tie as he entered the school and unknotting his school tie when he left, as if the uniform was a tangled net he was caught in every morning and struggled to escape every afternoon. He scowled. He carried a heavy book of Caravaggio reproductions in his satchel. He hated the thumping stadium rock that everybody else liked. He knew he was easy to despise.

So he was standing apart when Anna Savarin came for him. Through the darkened gym, clanging with a brittle "She Loves You (Yeah, Yeah, Yeah)," across the space whose edges were arranged with clusters of boys ignoring girls and girls fascinated with the clusters of boys ignoring them, her eyes came first. Green auras with gray centers. Then her breasts. Anna Savarin cut like cruel fate wearing a delicately patterned pink floral dress. Ben watched the distances between them narrowing helplessly.

"I believe we're supposed to dance," she said on arrival.

"I'm sorry?" muttered Ben.

"It's tradition for the head girl at Amherst and the prefect of Hamilton College to dance at the Orange Blossom ball."

She pulled him out onto the floor. "The Lady in Red" drifted overhead, while Ben's hand on her waist waited, the faint moisture of his palm softening the starch of her dress. Aware of his own smell, the odor of fumbling and indelicacy, aware that he was supposed to say something, aware that he should say only the perfect thing, he shifted his weight left to right, right to left, left to right. "Ever feel like you're being watched?" he asked, nodding his head to the suppressed gazes on the edge of the dance floor.

"They should watch us," Anna replied. "We're role models."

"Not me."

"You're prefect of Hamilton College," she asserted, as if he were questioning her status by doubting his own.

"Headmaster Reynolds made me prefect because the prefect automatically becomes head of alumni fund-raising after graduation. All the other boys resent me. At least thirty of them deserve it more than me."

"Hatred is a sign of jealousy." The maxim instant on her lips.

He was already appalled by her. "I bet all the girls at Amherst love you."

Anna laughed, a bright and silvery sound like the tumbling of knives through the air. "They resent me, too. They resent me as much as the etiquette teacher."

"Because you're cruel or because you're polite?"

"Ask me a less rude question."

"All right." He straightened. "Where are you going next year? That's what I'm supposed to ask, right?"

"I'm going to travel," she said. "Then, I don't know where. Probably Princeton. Like my dad."

"I'm going to Harvard," Ben said.

"Harvard? How very interesting." She was obviously wondering what donation his father was making and he nearly told her about the shrubberies.

"Not really," he said instead.

"No, not really. But you know what is interesting?"

"What's interesting?"

"If you can find us a private place, I'll teach you how to fuck me." Her eyes fixed his with expansive phoniness.

They sneaked through the halls, away from the music and light. Headmaster Reynolds, a defeated man terminally spooked by his wealthy charges, poked his head around the corner at the sound of their rustling and instantly ducked away. Ben froze, hissed, "He's seen us."

"You want him to see," Anna whispered. "That way he won't interrupt."

In the locker room of the hockey rink, among bags stuffed with fish-scented gloves and the splintery planks of the sweaty shin guards, she spread her floral skirt and tucked out her limpid bee-sting breasts.

She showed him what it was. She showed him how it worked.

Afterward, she straightened herself out, sheathed the blade of her smile, and stole away without a word, and he remembered, for some unknown reason, Mrs. Lansing, the mother of one of the boys, from earlier in the week, by the school gate. Wreathed in a fox stole, with its sad glass eyes questioning the whole of the human race, she had sized him up properly, head to heel, the petrified stink of her foundation mixed with rouge. At the mention of his name, Mrs. Lansing's eyes had opened like the delayed headlamps of a Porsche with faulty electrics. "You'll be quite the catch, won't you?" she had cooed.

Alone in the locker room, Ben would have cried if he hadn't just come.

The last time Ben and George shared a cage was the night before Ben left for Harvard. The Wylie men rarely shared each other's company by then. What do mere men have to say to one another? Better to sit in the cage, waiting. After the ancient beastliness flowered up in George's veins, Ben would silently stroke his father's fur in the darkness. The wash of the wolf's lick on his cheek was a rugged bath, lovely and cleansing. One last time, they leaned their heads back together, man and wolf, and howled into the emptiness.

Like many self-deprecating men, George had discovered that the humility he had been feigning all his life turned out to be justified in the end. He had nothing he wanted and nothing to complain about. Hadn't he lived up to his responsibilities? Even if Lee had run the whole business, even if Lee had made all the money, hadn't George found Lee? Hadn't he done exactly what was expected of him?

George sat in his cage, waiting for the beast, worrying about his children. Poppy had finally returned from Switzerland only to flee for New York, buying a pricey white cube of a Manhattan penthouse that was, at least, a decent appreciating asset. George had wanted Poppy to stay in Pennsylvania. She'd been expelled from her school in Saint Moritz—a complete shock to him. Lavinia had shown him the girl's high marks, the class photos with the daughters of the global elite, girls of every creed and color whose fathers owned the world, either through capitalism or dictatorship. In twelfth grade, she had developed a patent with her class for a kind of cheap solar-powered water pump usable in Third World irrigation systems. The news that she had run away was nonsensical. She ran away with a Cherokee boy, too—a boy who was somehow Cherokee in Switzerland. And they'd stolen a car and crashed it, and when she broke it off with him, the poor kid stabbed himself three times in the heart. George couldn't understand how that was even possible. Lavinia had shown him the letter of expulsion from the headmistress and the phrase had been written there: "stabbed himself three times in the heart." Very quickly, he guessed.

So Poppy returned home, spent a tumultuous week at Larchmount Crescent, and moved to the penthouse on Park Avenue. "She will have to find her own home," was all the clarification Lavinia would offer.

His children were gone. His search for meaning had failed. He had been left alone to live out his irrelevant magic.

Ben arrived in Champlain Station after his freshman year, relishing a summer away from Harvard, away from being a "legacy," a "valuable connection," "a good contact." He could do what he wanted. He could hole up in the basement, in the cages, and make things. He could draw and paint for a season. But as he strolled out into that delicious promise, a Porsche 911—silver, spangled—waited in his father's parking spot where he had expected a town car. Anna Savarin's smile lurked in the cool, smooth black interior.

They went slower this time, drove out beyond the cut-down steel mill to a ruined drive-in foaming with yellow reeds, the big screen peeling away.

"The beautiful thing is that you can't talk about this to anyone," she said afterward.

"Why's that?"

"Because you're at Harvard and I'm going to Princeton. You won't be able to ruin my so-called reputation." She was connecting her bra around her back. Her porcelain stilt fingers, elegant as Scheherazade stories, sloped up her back, the hint of her breasts like a delicious rumor in the court chambers of some oriental potentate.

"The reputation of the girls at Amherst Prep is that they take it in the ass," Ben said.

"Is that what they taught you?" She smiled, so far beyond cynicism that she had arrived again at innocence. "That's the Catholic girls at Saint Agnes's. We're WASPs. We screw regular."

Now he laughed. In the field outside the steamed window, a flock of several hundred returning sparrows scoured and hallelujahed the air. She curled up into her knees, pouted airily.

"It's going to be good to hear you laugh when you're an old man," she said.

"What's that mean?" He wanted to sleep but Porsches are not built for sleeping. Screwing, yes, but not sleeping.

"We're going to get married someday," she said. The air wilted, the birds in the sky dropped dead in his panic.

"Anna . . ." he began.

"Oh no, I understand. You don't know. I've talked it over with your mother. We're going to leave each other now. We're going to screw around, live in foreign cities, the rest of it. Then we're going to come back here." She pointed to the kingdom of rusted car stalls, curlicued wires vining over their gratings. "We're going to live together here. This is our fate."

"I don't believe in fate," he said, gulping up a spirit of hope.

"You're one of the only men in the world who has a fate. You're like a prince."

He found himself thinking about his painting. He couldn't tell her. He couldn't tell anybody. "Maybe I won't be a prince. I want to do something else maybe."

"You may want to, but you won't."

The pity in her eyes seemed genuine. The perfection of her manners made Anna's mind mythically unfathomable: Behind those porcelain eyes lurked a goddess or a stooge. Wolves running through the abandoned drive-in brushed against Ben's imagination. He remembered the envelope crouching at his father's elbow.

"What are you doing?" Anna asked.

Automatically, by instinct, he had begun to draw, tracing figures with his finger on her back.

In May of 1987, a photographer from *Spy* magazine—to whom small-town Pennsylvania was as exotic as the veldt—drove his powder blue Volkswagen Beetle to the front of Larchmount Crescent, unfolded a Hasselblad 500 EL/M, and took unremarkable photographs of an unremarkable house. Later Graydon Carter stood over the big table in the Puck Building offices, looking over the prints, exuding quiet fury. He had paid for glamorous photographs of a rich man's house, not this impossible banality, unbelievably middle-American. Kurt Andersen saw the potential, however. Money rendered the banality lunatic. The photograph ran in the "Weirdest Rich People in America" series. *Spy* had ranked the Wylies third.

By 1987, the spirit of the eighties had truly arrived, fashionably late to its own decade. Any residual hopes or values remembered from the sixties had been digested by the Quaalude loucheness of the seventies and then efficiently excreted in the first seven years. The only thing people believed in anymore was home espresso makers and *The Price Is Right*. Everybody agreed. The goal of humanity was to have stuff.

During this time, the Wylies became more than wealthy. The ice spiders of Lee Taggart's mind strung unlikely bonds across the globe—a data entry facility in Manila with a cruise line in Trinidad, a shortbread factory in Colchester with a recycling plant in Seattle, a forty-story tower in midtown Manhattan with a rare-earths mine in the Congo. To WylieCorp, the world was not people or places or substances. The world was numbers. The self-connected threads of the information business, on which Lee had imposed, for tax purposes, a twenty-year period of dividend reinvestment, resolved themselves into an unbreakable knot. The North American profits had bought up the European companies, and the European profits had bought up the Asian companies, and the Asian profits had bought up the South American companies, and the South American profits had bought up the African companies, until the roundelay coughed up a number: 12.35 billion.

The Wylie fortune had emerged organically, like a seed tucked under the soil straining to light. If business models can have beauty, the simplicity and elegance of Lee Taggart's model was beautiful. The information business grew with the growth of the professions, swelling with prosperity yet completely recession-proof; no matter what happened in the economy, pharmacists needed to know what the latest drugs were. The costs of producing and transmitting information halved every two years. As the world prepared to digitize itself the Wylies could let others build the subcutaneous rivers of light; they would paddle along them with their bounties of necessary data. A used-car salesman requires much more cunning and daring to run a car dealership than the Wylies needed to run these transglobal information businesses. Such was the genius—there can be no other word—of Lee Taggart. And the genius of George Wylie was to step out of his way.

The money brought unavoidable prominence. Lee had come to the office one morning with an envelope sent to him by Otto Cameron, an Anglophile bully who was threatening to start a newspaper war in the northeast. Newspaper wars are won by whoever has deeper pockets and George liked his chances. In the envelope were photographs of Lee at gay clubs and bathhouses, with street hustlers in various poses that would once have been called compromising. Both men laughed. "This guy thinks that's the darkest secret we share," George said, and called

the editors of several papers to say it would be a shame if anyone reported anything inappropriate about Lee Taggart.

In 1989, the family's net worth surpassed 16 billion and they entered
the list of the world's ten richest families, which at that time included
the Waltons, the Wylies, and a bunch of Japanese. Despite that wealth
or because of it, George Wylie lived a life indistinguishable from the
everyday existence of middle management. When he appeared at the
Wylie offices on Fifty-second Street, he brought his own cup of soup
down to the basement cafeteria for lunch, scrupulously purchasing a
99-cent coffee so he would have the right to use the microwave. If his
wife was visiting, they might splurge on a bowl of minestrone. He was
unfailingly polite to everyone, offering business tips to the shoeshine
man, whom he never tipped in any other way.

He wasn't a nobody, but he wasn't a somebody either. His reality
constituted the end point of all the struggles of the rich and would-be
rich—a life of fluid, effortless expansion—and yet he never attained
real respect on Wall Street. The traders considered George a cipher, a
conductor between the hardscrabble gamble of his father and the puri-
fied business mind of Lee Taggart, a figurehead, a legal fiction. George
never hustled. He never scammed or bullied or deceived. He never de-
vised strategies or thought outside the box. He never seemed to think
at all. In 1960, he had decided that the free flow of information would
eventually constitute a massive and easy source of profit. By the time the
idea bore fruit, in the mid-eighties, the few who could understand the
significance of his insight regarded the decision mostly as luck.

There was luck, certainly. WylieCorp diversified into every aspect of
the news business—softwood lumber, the chemical plants that produced
ink, the manufacturers of television camera parts—and there were occasional windfalls. One of the camera parts manufacturers developed the

patent for nontoxic inflammable plastics, and burgeoned into a company that now generates a dividend of 50 million dollars a month. In order to mine a rare earth necessary for the manufacture of a television component they were developing, which never turned into a product, WylieCorp purchased concessions throughout central Africa. Twenty-four years later, portable music players all needed these rare earths. The company made 4 billion dollars in straight profit. The windfalls were beside the steady, enormous returns of the professional information division, and the twenty-three percent profit margins of the newspapers whose cyclical nature had been balanced by the purchase of a fleet of cruise ships that ran through the summer season as a counter to the September-to-April run of ad sales.

What Wall Street could never fathom, or perhaps could never allow itself to fathom, was that George Wylie triumphed by doing nothing, by removing himself, by stepping aside. He was absent in charity as well. In other cities, particularly in London and Boston, certain society families dominate by nonparticipation, attending only the biggest parties, donating sparely, intervening in business maybe once a decade. Their power, they intuit, dwells in an aura of exclusivity. Thus the wide culverts and open sloughs between suburban mansions, the gilded epaulets and terse smiles of the Manhattan doormen. More civilization is more opportunity to say "I am not you." The whole world shakes with men and women sieving themselves out. But the Wylies were never strategic in their separation from the world. They simply never showed up.

The *Spy* magazine photograph appalled George. Why would anyone care about them? They were just insignificant businessmen. Then Poppy appeared, to George's horror, in a spread in *Tattler*, dressed in Chinese Communist suit with a little Mao cap, under the title "China Girl." At least she had chosen to be photographed there. The predatory snapshots on yachts and in nightclubs—he tried to pretend they had never happened.

George could have been a new Medici but the idea would have been monstrous to him. He did not consider himself better than a gas station owner who makes sure his station is clean and profitable so that his sons and daughters can go to college. The difference between himself and the next man was nine zeroes. George's contribution to the eternal debate about whether the rich are different from you and me is this: The rich should be different from you and me but they're not.

Ben never showed anybody his paintings at Harvard, not the secret society boys who cultivated his membership, nor the art history girls with their pearl necklaces and nascent sexual dysfunction who would run all the museums and galleries soon. He never took an art class, never showed up at the office hours of the professors. He could never show anybody his paintings for the same reason he could never tell who was a real friend or a real lover. The money sucked all possibility of genuine recognition into its void.

He sometimes hid in North Lake, where winter covered him comfortably. He took long walks over the property, a prairie scattered with lakes, rampaged by herds of elk and their inevitable followers, the wolves. He could return to the cages in the basement to stash his nature onto canvas. His paintings grew claw and tooth, red and black. He destroyed them all, usually after waiting a week to see if he could like them.

The solitude suited him except that he couldn't lock the cage in the basement. With his knees curled up under his chin, he sat naked on the dirt floor and knew that his imprisonment was ersatz. The problem was the same as being rich: He could do what he liked. Anytime he liked he could run out into the snow over the fields into the trees. All he could do was exactly what he wanted.

I am an experiment, Ben thought. Every billionaire is a distinct experiment in what happens when everything is permitted.

At his father's prompting, Ben moved to New York, and to the family holdings at Morgan Stanley. It was 1990, the year the world decided it wanted to be money and nothing else. The Berlin Wall had fallen like a curtain—on tragedy or farce? Capitalism was like the last standing contestant at the ideological beauty pageant and broke down gushing at her own triumph. Cocaine was the confetti at the parade.

The year 1990 brought this item from the *New York Post*:

A FIVE-GRAND DISAPPOINTMENT

A Manhattan waitress was disappointed by a $5,000 tip. Howzat, you're asking yourself now. "I'm pretty happy, but it's less than a measly ten percent," said Sandy Bellman, server at swank TriBeCa eatery Bouley. She was the lucky girl who served a meal valued at over $52,310.59 to a quartet of Morgan Stanley traders. The really pricey part was the fancy French wine that accompanied the ten-course meal. Two bottles of Château d'Yquem, 1885 and 1900, at ten grand a pop, and the Petrus 1945 at $18,000. Ben Wylie, son of the one of the richest men in the world, picked up the tab. "He just handed over a black card," according to sort-of-stiffed Sandy. Don't feel too bad for her. She already has plans for her windfall. "I'm going to take the kids to Disneyland!"

That night began with a Keith Haring yo-yo. Ben had brought colleagues from Morgan Stanley Sovereign Wealth—Fred Corbach, Marty

Shragge, and Eduardo Albano—to watch him make the purchase. They disapproved. That's why he brought them.

If you worked in banking, you were supposed to buy Picassos and Cézannes. For the rich, the art market was merely another market in which to prove themselves, a purer one insofar as it was as unregulated as drugs. Ben's taste was idiosyncratic and superb. Ben's first purchase when he arrived at Morgan Stanley had been a Francis Bacon triptych called *Rage*, a series of human figures scarred and scraped by the paintbrush. He bought Basquiats and Chuck Closes. The Basquiats that he preferred were painted on objects found on the street: pens, Coke cans, the bottoms of shattered vases. The Keith Haring yo-yo would find a place among them. Haring had painted the yo-yo black, with cartoon figures crawling out of yellow labyrinths.

At the Fundamentum Gallery, narcissism was leaking into the street in small puddles of flauntery. Corbach and Shragge wore navy and burgundy Gucci, respectively. Albano had changed, after work, into white linen, tieless. He never could remember that he wasn't in Buenos Aires anymore. Corbach was recommending a prostitute to Shragge—the ownership of people was the foremost imitation of joy they could manage. It is a truth universally acknowledged that a single man in possession of a great fortune is in want of a prostitute.

"You'll come on her neck, of course."

"What do you mean?" Shragge asked.

"Buddy, that's common courtesy. I don't know if you've slept with this level of ass before. This is not one of the heifers you're used to, straight out of Juarez."

"She's a hooker, right? You pay her to have sex."

Corbach sneered. "You've understood that much, yes."

"I though the whole point of a hooker was that you could do what you want."

"You don't understand, do you? When you're paying three hundred dollars an hour, you're in the territory of a sexual actress."

"An aristocrat." Shragge sneered, schmeering the words like a Jew in a German Christmas play. So much realer was he than all these goyim.

"Fucking right. And when I go to the ballet, I wouldn't crack peanuts or shit in the corner. This is a sexual performer, I'm sending you. You come on her neck. Not on her face or on her tits or in her mouth. And if you come on her hair, I personally will beat the living shit out of you. On her neck."

"Is that a pearl necklace?" Albano asked. Albano was attached to a brick-sized cell phone, on hold. Before his companions could answer, a voice on the other end picked up and he turned, receiving a proposition. "What if I were to promise a G on the wine," Albano whispered into the machine. "A G, a thousand," he whispered lower. He looked up, all eyes, asking for approval.

The others colluded with nods.

Albano perked up, hung up, rejoined his party. "Dinner for four at Bouley. No reservation. Ten o'clock Saturday night. I want the love."

Everybody but Albano knew that it's not a get if you have to pay for it. Ben dug in his pocket for the latest treasure, the Keith Haring yo-yo. Spun, the thing was whirling circles within circles.

"This guy owns the most expensive yo-yo in the world," Corbach said.

Shragge was moderately interested. "How much did you pay for it in the end?"

"Thirteen thousand," Ben said.

"You're buying dinner," Albano said, meekly joking but not. Shragge and Corbach laughed at the transparence of the remark, and of everyone, including themselves. Why am I with these people if I have all the money? Ben asked himself. I am with these people because I have all the money, he answered himself.

Trader aggression was roidishly oozing out of Shragge. "I just bought a fucking Warhol of Elizabeth Taylor as Cleopatra."

Ben's turn to sneer. "Of course you did."

"I hang it beside my fucking rose-period Picasso. Wylie, can I ask you something?"

"Shraggie, don't," Corbach warned.

"Why are you so bloody weird and cheap?"

"Shraggie . . ."

"No, it's just a question. He can answer. He's a big boy. What's the point? That's what I have to ask. I mean, don't get me wrong. You're good at your job. Not that you have to be. But what the fuck, man. Why do you wear such shitty clothes?"

The question turned the night into a tournament. For Shragge, every night was a tournament. But the coked-up bluster was contorted by genuine curiosity, Ben could see. He was a mystery to his colleagues. There were things that were supposed to be done. The Connecticut Yankees exchanged high-performance Eastern European women. Old Jews bought boats or farms to show how not Jewish they were. Albano, like the other Argentine traders, played polo in Jersey. Everybody bought Gucci loafers. But Ben was so rich he wore hundred-dollar suits. Ben wore canvas sneakers. He cut his own hair. He owned no business cards. If you didn't know him, he didn't want you to know him. His money was a cloak of invisibility cast over everybody else.

"The reason I don't spend money is because I could buy you all fifty times over," he answered.

The meal Ben proceeded to order was another kind of answer. The

Château d'Yquem was an amber abyss of sweetness with hints of the tsar spreading marmalade on buttered toast. Bouley was at its early peak—famous but not yet profitably famous. Teams of serious servers carried out perfect plates: creamy raw salmon rolled around seagod pops of briny roe, almond-smooth yellowfin tuna brightened with rough-cut chives, then sea scallops blessed with slivers of white truffle. After those dillydallying dishes came an earthen striped bass bolstered by a hearty tomato water, skate homaged with humble artichoke and capers, an extravagance of lobster tail simmered in paprika and port, foie gras befuddled on a bed of pureed quince. Then a shoulder of lamb with parsnips served the way a shepherd in Vivaldi's *Four Seasons* might eat it. Petrus was ordered, thick as blood, with tinges of mulberry, pipe smoke. A bowl of melon soup the color of a ski jacket, to be finished by the tender something-nothing of a verbena soufflé.

After the feast of conspicuous distinctions, Ben excused himself without excuse and took the town car. He prowled bank to bank, emptying every ATM on the Upper East Side until a nice neat brick worth fifteen thousand dollars crouched in his hand. Up to the West Bronx, a neighborhood where you could open up a Kalishnakov and nobody would notice, and where, under the D-train rumble, the hookers paraded, a preview of tortured ghosts. He sought out the youngest. Butt cheeks like ham hocks under silver sequins. Thirteen? Fourteen? Her eyes reflected the neon. He held the money out the window. The girl looked disbelieving at the hallucinatory pile. How much fucking is that? What weird shit is that shit? He threw the cash and she caught it, nestled in her elbow crook like a wide receiver. A brother or a father or a molesting uncle must have played football.

"Change your life," Ben said.

She slunk away, first at a stumbling perplexed walk, then a heel-brokered trot, then a terrified outright run on her tippy-toes. Ben Wylie, weeping with impotence, remembered his great-uncle Max running into the deep forest.

As the driver turned the town car back downtown, the windows rolled by, liquid with the city. One final prophecy from the poor whom you will always have with you—a woman hollering at a bank of busted pay phones, cracked and frazzled and addled and sorrowing and murderous. Her eyes rolling at the spectral town car, she ran up, panting, pounding the bullet-resistant glass, screaming either a plea or a curse. The driver smoothly accelerated away into interstitial New York, the valleys between the mountains.

The thrill of the gift and the panic of the chase ebbed, and then the inertia resumed. He was once again the eighth-richest man in the world being driven home in a town car after some typical rich-guy eccentricity.

How far would he have to drive to hear the howl of a wolf?

George watched the numbers roll in: 16.68 billion, 17.83 billion, 19.64 billion, 22.31 billion. Numbers grew into other numbers, their meanings compounding into incomprehensibility. What can you buy with 22 billion dollars? What do you own?

As his wealth launched beyond the meaning of wealth, cheapness gripped the heart of George Wylie as never before. In 1994 he owned two suits, one a slate gray and the other navy blue. He saw no reason for new clothes when his billions blossomed; rather the opposite. Who did he need to impress? When his briefcase, which he had carried with him to Hamilton College eons before, disintegrated in his hands, he started taking his papers around in the thick plastic bags given for free from the local grocery store in Champlain. Polish luggage, he called it.

To the wider world, the Wylie men were as mysterious as ever, impervious to the scrutiny of even their employees. Their highest-level managers saw Ben and George only once a year. They arrived by subway, wandered in like citizens, George in his slate gray and Ben in ragged khakis. They rode to the top floor. They entered Lee Taggart's office. They spoke for about an hour. They left. Rumors about the content of these meetings ran the gutters of WylieCorp and splashed onto Wall Street. Some said they were little more than presentations of numbers, a personal investment statement. Others believed that George arrived every year with a single guiding business idea. "Information cannot be taxed" or "Improbability is the river in which we fish" or some other gnomic pronouncement. One year, the rumors ran, George uttered a single word: "China."

Their absence made the Wylies into Wall Street myth, icons of the cold indifference of the marketplace, the irrelevance of wealth's trappings to the mechanics of capital, the unfathomability of money. They were as plainly mysterious as how the world works.

Ben agreed to meet Anna Saravin in a diner on Eighth Avenue, a place with a grill and a stream of lottery numbers flowing in from a screen in the corner. This wasn't one of the clean fancified retro weren't-things-easier-when-there-weren't-any-restaurants-except-diners diners. This was one of the grimy run-down I-buy-eggs-for-five-cents-and-I-fry-them-and-I-sell-them-for-ten-cents-so-don't-ask-me-to-pretend-to-be-happy-about-it diners, risen from the ground like a primordial link between mud and the future, embossing a gray-green film over the eyes of the customers.

Anna arrived with a six-foot-seven black man who bristled with glossy bubblegum-colored shopping bags outside the window. She kissed his leaned-down cheek, explained something indisputable, and then dipped inside the diner, gingerly, careful not to dirty herself by brushing against the zinc counter or the coiled mushroom-colored vinyl stools. Her presence dragged Ben down by his lapels into a mortal exhaustion.

"I can only stay for five minutes," she said after ordering a coffee.

"Who's your friend?" Ben nodded to the man on the other side of the window.

"He plays for the Knicks." He was watching. She waved three fingers of her hand as she held the spoon. "You're not doing a very good job," she added.

"Of what?"

"Of living up to your potential. You're going to have to run the business when we're married. You're going to have to understand how WylieCorp works eventually." She sipped her coffee. "You think I don't understand what's going on here? With your poor-person clothes? With your cheapness? Insulting all the other Morgan Stanleys." She was gorgeous with her cruel raw-meat mouth. "Pathetic bluff. Eventually someone is going to call you on it."

Ben shrugged. "I do what I like now."

She looked at him with pity. "You know, I believe that you believe that. Inviting me here to this dive. Let me evaluate your choices. You could have rented a room at the Plaza and fucked me. You could have flown me to Paris. You could have not met me at all. Instead you brought me here." She smiled. "I've met guys like you. You are the crime and you are the punishment. You don't know what money's for."

The basketball player knocked on the window. "Your dog is barking," Ben said.

"Your wolf is howling," she answered, leaning in to kiss his cheek, leaving the soft ephemeral dollop of her ownership. Marked territory.

Ben lowered his gaze while she stalked back into the city. The coffee was chalky, the cream had congealed like wrung linen in a polluted river. The liquid was cold on his lips. Sure she must have gone, he looked up. The Eighth Avenue crowd, the flowing hustle of grit and determination, flustered past the window. A city of soma. A city of addiction and starvation. And there, in the middle of the tumble and roll, Ben saw his mother, wandering among them like an exiled prophetess. Ben believed that he was seeing a ghost. Only supernatural explanations would suffice. To Ben, his mother was a creature of Larchmount Crescent, a goddess who belongs in a temple in a grotto, the grotto of a small Pennsylvania town.

She proceeded into the diner, somehow knowing his precise location. Mother's instinct? Anna Savarin?

"My son," she announced, sitting.

"What are you doing here, Mom?"

"My daughter," she answered. Her distress reared up in her inflection. What had Poppy done? "She won't speak to me." Lavinia looked at her son, with the calm of true need. "How I wish I was embarrassing you with a wedding."

Poppy needed, at last, to be taken away. The experiments in rock and powder, with smoke and needle, had concluded with the expected results; Poppy had worked out their various refinements with extraordinary thoroughness. The typical addict is limited by cash flow. Poppy received two hundred thousand dollars a day from her portion of the trust. She tried to huff every penny.

She had reached bottom near the top of the world on Central Park West. Ben opened the elevator into her private suite, into a mess. Paintings in crates. Clothes in silver and gold torn and strewn on the living room floor and over a zebra-skin sectional and Lucite coffee table. Books of photography, ripped. An avant-garde menorah. A rust-needled pine tree from Christmas past, nearly bare. The main window was smashed, cracked as if someone had thrown furniture from the forty-first floor. The apartment was naked to the sky. A pair of pigeons cooed and strutted over a row of three television sets. The window must have been broken for a while because pigeon shit was spackled over the crack pipes and the gear and a bowl of rot-excruciated tangerines and little green apples and a limp leek, and the stacked catalogues from Christie's and Sotheby's. A Penguin edition of *Strange Tales from a Chinese Studio* lay on top. Poppy was splayed out in new gym wear on the sofa in front of the smashed window, her eyes bruised, her skin flaky.

"Honey, you're home," she said, looking up lizardly.

"It doesn't much look like anybody's home."

"Why is it, you think," Poppy wondered, "that Mother thinks I'll go with you?"

Ben sat beside her. If she decided to jump through the window he could grab her. "I think she thinks we're the only people on earth we can trust."

Poppy fingered a small gold and ruby device hanging from a chain around her neck—it looked like a cigarette lighter—and took two automatic sniffs.

"We've let everything fall apart, haven't we," he said.

She was high but spoke correctly. "It's amazing how it doesn't fall apart no matter what we do." Then she stood up, tottering. "It's all just painted skin, whatever that means."

*   *   *

After dropping his sister at the self-esteem factory in Connecticut—it was called Beginnings, an all-purpose rehab clinic that offered equine therapy and Japanese massage within the secure confines of a barbed wire fence—Ben left his job and his collection and New York and his family. If I have to be an experiment, he thought, at least I can decide what the experiment is.

So he experimented: He purchased a motorcycle and drove around Normandy, then flew the company Gulfstream to Cairo for kushari, then to Rome, where he bought a bronze Christ that had once hung in Bernini's studio for 30 million dollars and gave it to the University Art Gallery in Harvard for the tax credit. Then to Kiev, where he bought the Ukraine's largest steel factory, to Hong Kong, where he pissed in a glass urinal in a restaurant that served red panda meat, to Bangkok, to Mumbai, to Rome again, to Tokyo. He would buy all the Rothkos at an auction or an entire Chuck Close show, sight unseen, and bury them in the family vault in Kensington Palace Gardens.

To see, through the transcendent window of the Maybach, the scenes of everyday life—the homeless man outside the liquor store in New Orleans glugging electric pink wine, the Queen of England inspecting the horseflesh at the races, the gaggle of laughing girls on their way to a twelve-hour shift in a pharmaceutical factory in Shenzhen, a solitary boy climbing the hills of Kenya with fly-fishing equipment, the Saudis in their tasteless stupidity buying platinum toilets. Always the background rumble: Am I living now? Is this all there is? The present, to Ben, unrolled like a painting spilling to the floor in a burning museum.

In the Imperial Suite at the Ritz, at the *fons et origo* of luxury, Ben ordered a hot dog and ate it in the bathroom overlooking the Place Vendôme. The room cost $12,389 dollars a night. In Los Angeles, Ben purchased a Lamborghini Countach, purple as grape soda and equally tasteful, crazy as a fatherless teenager. He thrust the mad machine up the Pacific Coast Highway, through green and blue and gold and white to San Francisco, and thought what a good road it would be to die on. The past fumed away like applewood smoke. All that was solid was melting into air, and the air was heating up. The world was beginning to break up, to shift. Mere geography, mere material, mere human beings—properties to be assumed into the one invisible, indivisible city of money, the one true universal brotherhood all men and women were hustling to join. He saw China rising in furious glory, the ancient civilization back for the most curious revenge in history. Ten thousand souls in a single factory made umbrellas and the imperial nations trembled, forecasting rain.

One evening in London, Ben paid what was then the largest sum ever paid for a Rembrandt: £25,897,543 for *Saint Francis and the Wolf.* He laid the painting outside the cage in the house in Kensington Palace Gardens to receive the flat expanse of the moonlight through the window.

The butler had to bring the phone down to the cage. It was his sister. "Come home," she said, and hung up.

It had been seven years since Ben had returned to Champlain. The rot of the house on Larchmount Crescent was evident from the street, the margins frayed, the grass mopey, a house obviously in mourning and disrepair, although all of Champlain seemed to be permanently in mourning and disrepair. No butler to usher him in here. He knocked and entered to the flicker of women in the dark halls above, maybe

Poppy, maybe his mother. He seemed to know where he was supposed to go by instinct.

At the long oak table in the living room, ancient as winter, Lee Taggart waited. He had grayed. Even his graying was precise. The ghostly color of his hair matched the deferential steel of his eyes, the cut of his suit. Six piles of papers waited scrupulously on the table. As Ben entered, Lee moved as if he had been asleep until that moment, a robot switched suddenly on.

"You need to sign all these," he said, handing over a gold fountain pen.

Ben endured the weight of the instrument in his fingers, dutifully leaning over, scrawling his name mechanically, in silence, over the rafts of English, French, Spanish, German, Japanese, and Arabic papers.

"I was called back for some signatures?" Ben asked.

"I'm here for your father."

"As you always have been."

The old man's knobbly finger divinely pointed to the dotted line, life's fundamental truth. "I'm going to say it just like he asked me to, Ben. I owe him."

"What do you owe?"

"Finish the signatures." He waited on the completion of legal formalities. "What he wanted you to know is that his condition was just a lot more painful than it had ever been before."

"His condition?"

"His condition, the spasms, were becoming agonies, real agonies, Ben. Your parents decided to go together. They didn't want to stick around without each other. That's how your dad wanted me to put it. Don't decide to take it too hard. He wanted me to tell you this way. He wanted me to say it just like this."

"What's going on, Lee?"

Lee collected the papers into his briefcase, and then began to guide Ben by the elbow into the living room. "George was an amazing owner," he said. "He knew exactly when to do nothing." A coffin. A large and well-manufactured coffin, obviously from a well-reputed coffin company. From the edges of the universe, at the fastest speed there is, beams of pure darkness began their rush toward Ben. In the coffin lay his mother, and beside her the carcass of a wolf, smiling mildly.

As the sedation ebbed, Ben awoke with the refreshment of a great agony having passed. Slowly, by stages, his vision adjusted to the cage. The comfort of the familiar basement was smooth in the fresh ache. Lost, he forgot, and forgetting, he couldn't say how long he sat in the cage or how long she was there.

In the half dark, on the other side of the bars, utterly poised, Anna Savarin was patiently waiting.

FIVE

T*he Wolf* saved me. I took the Paul Klee from the Wylie cottage nook and drove it from Alberta to New York—across the thousand-cornered room of America, the fields of the megafarms swaying with genetically modified wheat, the small towns abandoned by their ambitious young people, the rusting derelict cities abandoned by themselves. The country was a highway strung with escape hatches. Every crossroads, every side road, was its own temptation. Who would notice my absence or the painting's?

"It's beautiful," Kate said dubiously when I hung it back over the desk in her study.

"I thought it belonged here," I said.

"That's not what I mean," she said in a voice like moss. "It's beautiful because you brought it back."

Then she kissed me. I wish there were some more cynical, more contemporary way for me to describe it, but kisses will always be antiquated. Surprised kisses are practically nineteenth century, like carnations pressed in leather-bound books, or four-poster oaken beds, or carved opaline silhouettes. She kissed me and I was surprised and it was as lovely as a watermark. Still, I had needed the painting. She could never have taken me without a gift and I could never have come without theft.

The following morning, I crept, shoes in hand, down the elegant stairs lined with Robert Frank photographs from his Mexican period and stumbled on Sigma perched at the granite-topped kitchen island, grumpily consuming an Eggo waffle that had been cut into stamp-sized squares by an absent nanny. She looked up with Leo's suspicious Greek eyes through a tumble of gold ringlets.

"I don't want this," she said, pointing to the waffle.

I know nothing about children or their upbringing so I went simple. "What do you want?" I asked her.

"Pizza," she said, grinning.

In the Miele fridge, a few slices of Hawaiian pizza limped forlornly over the edge of a plate. I passed the dish over cold, thereby earning eternal friendship through ham and pineapple. Kate came down a few minutes later to find me reading Garfield to her daughter from the back of a two-day-old *Post*. The easy beauty of her morning doziness was spine-softening. She tousled her hair silently, gorgeous in an entirely novel manner. She smiled the insider smile upon me, and I was redeemed by its ease.

So began my life in the money or beside it, rather. I still worked. I still kept my Portuguese basement. I still ran my freelancing gamble, just with lower stakes. At the dinners and parties and functions to which

Kate brought me over the next months I remained a spectator to the frictionless young men with their puffy-faced arrogance who fawned over anyone with more money than them, then flashed a dead-eyed contempt on anyone with less. Their backstories were all the same. They had graduated with degrees in finance from Ivy League schools and worked in family holding companies, or circled the network collecting investors for one scheme or another, off of which they slivered livable commissions. The whiz kids, the math PhDs, and the rocket scientists were supposed to have ended this clubbiness, or so I'd read. As far as I could tell, the whiz kids were on salary. Money's job was still to maintain the tribe, to give just enough money to other people's idiot sons so that your own idiot sons would have just enough people to ask for money in their turn.

I think that I offered Kate a kind of reprieve from the wealthy friends she neither wanted to know nor could bring herself to ignore. Plus I was helpful with Sigma. When Kate fell into a migraine, Sigma and I would skip her classes—integrated art or Talmudic math or Serbo-Guyanan dance or whatever it was—and drive Mommy's Audi to the Six Flags in Jersey. Sigma was pure Viking at heart. She wanted to go on all the rides, in every sense of the phrase. At the end of our days out, I would carry her sleeping from the Audi up to her delicate pink room like the exhausted animal she was happy to be. Then Kate would make me the exhausted animal I was happy to be.

One evening in late summer, the cool breeze wafting the faint odor of BBQ pork dumplings through the air, maybe six months after we had begun whatever we were beginning, Kate whispered in my ear the sum she had inherited from her grand old American forefathers: 47 million. That talismanic number, spilt like pomegranate seeds from her whispery lips, was more erotic than any other possible gesture of her tongue. I would not at first tell myself what it meant, but my easing spine, my relaxing muscles already knew. I would never have to leave New York.

"Did you tell that number to Leo?" I asked.

She sighed. "You're not jealous of Leo, are you?"

"No, I just want to know if he knew."

"You want to know whether you know what he knows?"

"Maybe that's it." Actually I wanted to know how 47 million could be unsatisfying, how anyone could want more than that. Kate sat up into the cooling darkness, the moon through the window casting a glow like relevant history on her breasts.

"Leo knew. But to him numbers never mattered. More and less mattered, but not numbers."

"Forty-seven million has to be enough," I said, guffawing.

She almost took offense, then registered that I meant it and forgave me for my ignorance. "You know why you still love Leo?" she asked, and didn't wait for an answer. "When Leo was about six his mother went to live on a lesbian commune in Colorado. His dad had no money. Sales assistant for dishwashers in the middle of nowhere. Leo is one those boys you see on the playground, looking out through the fence. 'Do you love me? Do you love me?' There's no *enough* for him."

"You talk like he was born on the streets of Mumbai or something."

"You can be abandoned anywhere," Kate insisted.

Aren't we all, I wanted to say. Aren't we all the orphans at the beginning of a Charles Dickens novel? Aren't we all Hansel and Gretel, lost in the deep dark woods, searching for the traces of the trail of bread crumbs?

"What are you thinking now?" Kate asked, seeing the unasked questions pass over my face.

"I'm wondering what my excuse will be," I said.

* * *

Solzhenitsyn said that a man who is warm cannot understand the point of view of a man who is cold. I was the warm man with the cold man inside. When we snagged a table at Kajitsu, and the check came, Kate's card snapped down neatly at the conclusion. My non-Platinum equivalent would have been embarrassing, I told myself. Her card was like a cleaver to hack through the gristle and bone of life's little embarrassments.

She paid for the trips. To London. To Paris. To Los Angeles and then Hawaii and then Cambodia because why not, we were practically there. I could never have afforded them. Sometimes neither could Kate. Sam and Ricky, a couple who had invested early in PayPal and whose daughter Sexton went to the same ballet class as Sigma, flew us in their private jet down to Saint Barths in May. I liked Sam and Ricky. Sam was a rotund ex-frat boy with a heart of molded plastic who spent his time waiting for what he called the "next perfect pitch," whatever that meant. He was not instantly bored with me when he realized that I had no money. Ricky was a Long Island princess who had made a good match. She was impressed that I knew one of the wedding reporters from the *Times*, so she deigned to audition her version of a winning smile on me.

The stay in Saint Barths was less exciting to me than the private jet, but good value. Uma Thurman was splashing around the beach with her kids, which is something, I guess. Her presence certainly justified any expense as far as Sam and Ricky were concerned. The horror began as we were leaving. Sam was late for takeoff. More than an hour late. Ricky was worried, though not for her husband or for our schedule. On a private jet, the fuel per hour costs about ten thousand dollars, and it was running the whole time we waited for him, to keep our spot on the tarmac. Sam eventually showed up with Chinese food. There was a chow mein place he loved on the island. Ricky was furious. "For Chinese food?" she shouted. "Are those noodles worth ten thousand dollars?" Sam looked surprised, genuinely. She was suddenly appalled at his taste for luxury? "Look where you are," he shouted back, sweeping his arm around the jet cabin. "What more do you want?"

That's really the question, isn't it? What more do you want? Sigma and Sexton wanted *Archie* comics that they consumed in studied silence in a pool of jet-window light after takeoff. I could not quite manage to hide my discomfort so casually. Kate noticed. After we landed, after we were alone in the cab on the way back to SoHo, she leaned over Sigma's sleeping head and whispered, "We don't have to be like that."

"We couldn't possibly be like them," I said.

"I mean, the money doesn't have to come between us. We can work something out. We don't have to end up screaming at each other in a private jet." It took a moment for me to realize what she meant. For Kate, money was a source of difficulty, of anger and loss. It was so ravishingly naïve I almost told her I loved her. But it was not that moment.

"Don't worry," I said instead. "We'll find some other reason to scream at each other."

Then Sigma roused herself. "Who's screaming?" she asked dreamily.

"Nobody's screaming," I said, kissing the top of her head as delicately as my rough lips could manage, which could never possibly be delicate enough. "Nobody will ever be screaming."

After Saint Barths, for a kind of vacation—a desperate pull for an ending perhaps—I visited Champlain. Number 17 Flora Avenue clung to elegance with an almost charming precariousness in a neighborhood that remains what it was in the early days of the Wylies, a repository of the recently arrived, upwardly mobile, lower middle class, though hardscrabble Sikhs had replaced hardscrabble Scots. The thick-matted dandelioned yard in front and the rusted-shut front gate marred an otherwise impeccable street, groomed by fiercely house-proud new owners.

The property on Larchmount Crescent was rotting splendidly— the roof spider-veined with cracks, the windows boarded, the yellowish bricks crumbling in ever larger chunks from the Victorian façade. The inside of the house was a phantasmagoria of distressed gentility, like a melancholy dream of childhood. The old Edwardian carpets stank of their threadbare decline, the voluptuous wallpaper curling in defeated sheets off the rot-poxed walls, the brass lamps squatting forlornly, and the lovely ceiling moldings dripping small black stalactites. No one had touched the place since George and Lavinia's death, obviously. One of the upstairs rooms must have been discovered by teenagers or drug addicts. The cream-colored wallpaper was scrawled with graffiti that had wept itself into indecipherability, cigarette butts and empties were disintegrating and, in the room's center, I don't know how, a maple sapling stirred out of the floor.

I came back from my tour of the collapsing American dream to find that the money had called. "He's coming," Kate said.

"Who?"

"The gigolo."

Leo hadn't seen Sigma for a year. Kate wanted me to be there when he came. I owed her.

The town car curled up to the curb. Leo emerged in a Prada suit, looking like a schoolboy lover. Prada has a gift: They make clothes that appear expensive in a way that implies the wearer never earned the money to buy them. They have mastered the look of otiose finance. Before the door closed, I caught a shard of Poppy Wylie in a black crepe cocktail dress. It was ten in the morning. A funeral or an all-hours party? Time itself seemed to have lost meaning in her impossible elegance.

"She looks bored, Leo."

At the front door, Leo looked tougher than before, more of a hustler, the shiny suit up close like a leather jacket of a 1950s pimp. His smile stole over his face like a childhood memory but he betrayed no surprise at my presence. "You can't still hate me."

"I think you're confusing hate with contempt."

He looked quizzically up at the sky. "Your heart is full of something black, but not contempt. Envy?"

"We all have to make a living," I said.

"I understand," he said in the spirit of sympathetic benevolence that a corporate raider might demonstrate to an employee he's just fired.

"What do you understand?"

"I understand everything. That's why we shouldn't hate each other. We do what we have to. Now let me see my daughter."

My heart was pumping with some thick, hateful sap. It could have been envy but I'm not sure. He was implying that I had brought Poppy to him so I could have Kate for myself, bumping him up so I could bump myself up. Was that what I had been doing? Was I a kept man? Had I done what I had to do?

I was still in New York, after all.

I went into the kitchen and poured myself a scotch—a seventeen-year-old Bowmore—and when I returned Poppy was sitting in the living room, her regal hands on the horseheads of my favorite chair. She was staring into the distance. Hers was a dazed beauty. And then I realized she was staring at *The Wolf*, which hung in the next room, on the wall of the study. With a pang of terror I could see in her gaze that the painting was an answer to many questions she hadn't thought to ask until then. We both knew that I was some kind of thief.

"I remember you now," she finally said. "North Lake. You're from North Lake. You're from Alberta, aren't you?"

I couldn't deny it.

"I can't think of a better place to die," she said.

"I do everything backward," I said. "I was born there."

"I remember you in the fields. You were standing in the weeds beside a rusty swing set. The caretaker's son. You were husk brown. It reminded me, seeing you just there. You were a boy, so free, so wild."

The thought of my father sobbed to my throat. Her eyes had seen me when he was alive. And when had I been free? When?

"My mother said to me when we were in North Lake, 'You must never tell anyone, Poppy. You must never tell a living soul.'" She smiled at me. "But you already know. You probably knew all along. You must have understood that I couldn't let you tell the world this. You must have known."

"Can I ask you something?"

She seemed a little surprised but nodded.

"Why are all the men buried in the north?"

She wreathed herself in the meaning of her secrecy. She could talk as much as she wanted now. "My mother loved the wolves. They would have called her a witch a century ago. She loved her French-Canadian rituals. She loved Father being a wolf and rising up again as a man. Thought she was in some folktale of the *loup-garou*. For me, my papa was dying. For her, the meaning was going out of the world."

She teased out a cigarette from a pack of Sobranies, put it to her lips, then removed it, threaded it back into the pack. "You have no idea how

I wish I'd met my grandmother, my great-grandmother. The wolf was nothing to them but a chore. They knew we should never have left the old house on Flora Avenue where they had been *maitresses chez elles."*

She seemed to clear her head, recall vaguely that there was a question and a questioner.

"You're right," she said. "The men are all buried out there in the north with nothing above them but sky."

"They buried Ben up there, too, didn't they?"

She rambled like a scattered animal. "Mama brought me down to the cage but I could never stand the smell. For her, everything about the wolf was pleasure. 'The smell of the naked earth,' she called it. It smelled like shit to me." Her eyes met mine, concentrated as diamond. "You want to know about his body in the snow, don't you?"

I started to answer but caught my breath in my throat, terrified that a word would thwart her answer.

"It was an act of love," she said. "He was born to go naked into the wild. I let him go. I let him out of the cage. That was my job. It wasn't my mother's. When I found him in the cage, how could I not let him be the wolf?"

She had released him into the wild and he had run all the way to his death—becoming the beast he had longed to be. I had misunderstood. The story of men who died was the story of women who lived. The Wylies are not men who come out of Abermarley, out of the broken-down stones and trees to find a land of opportunity. They are the women in quiet villages, the women looking up from their kitchen tables, their beaded prayers, to the dark fields on the edge of town. They won't be married properly by the church door. Instead, they run through the narrow, cruel forest, momentarily free. Then they wake up in a silent mansion where not even the servants gossip. The men remain in the basement, howling into themselves. The women are in the empty up-stairs, silent, scrutinizing their own desperations.

"I can't stand to talk about this anymore," she said, and walked away as she had always walked away before, the way she would eventually walk away from Leo, I knew. In the inconclusive life of Poppy Wylie, nobody lasted long.

She turned back for me. "I'm going to let you keep that," she said, nodding to the painting.

Generosity is what I never could have expected. Mercy. Or was it carelessness? The allure of Poppy's floating world, her easy life, her sumptuous declining beauty was that it could cancel little lives like mine, that it didn't need to bother with the mere stuff of the world any-more. Money is everything now. Poppy had been to the end of money and human wildness. She wandered the exhaustion of all possible desire.

I was so lost in my relieved and greedy reveries that I didn't even no-tice Leo leave the house. I just saw his Prada suit entering the car, then the car pulling away. Kate was standing beside me and I hadn't noticed her either. I wasn't noticing much apparently. "He's gone," she said.

"What did he want?"

"He wanted to feel guilty."

She knew her man. Leo's guilt was friction to grit himself against the grease of all the money. With his guilt emblazoned on his secret heart, he could betray his wife and abandon his child and catapult him-self into the stratosphere. So long as he felt bad about it.

Sigma joined us, her eyes heavy with suppression. She wanted to watch a Star Wars movie with me, she muttered. I asked her if we could see *The Empire Strikes Back*, my favorite, and she agreed, and then I knew she must be really down, so we put on *The Phantom Menace*, her favorite, and cuddled.

*   *   *

Things were starting to look up. The graphs were growing pleased with their human subjects once again. The stock market soared above its pre-crash mark, the unemployment rate tripped below eight percent, and even median incomes inflated the slightest little puff. Therefore restaurant front offices again giggled dismissively at apologetic requests for Friday night tables, glossy magazines thickened tumescently on the newsstand shelves, and I heard stories of friends leaving jobs of their own volition—exhausted Americans at least imitating hope. The delirious music that had stopped was starting up again, not quite out on the street but in small rooms off the alleys. The ancient dreads continued to rumble underneath it all: inequalities widening, food prices spiking, the natural world more threadbare with each season. But the apocalyptic mode has always nestled comfortably at the heart of American prosperity. The world has always been about to fall apart, which is fine so long as I can make a living.

There was more action, more fun, more stuff, more chances to get lucky. And nothing can compare with the blessed state of getting lucky. A big score succors the soul more than God or heroin or justice. One night at the party for a book about the crash on the rooftop of the Chamberlain, high above the city, I theorized to myself that the species was gathering money into fewer and neater piles so we could burn it in bigger and brighter conflagrations. The potlatch of the earth had begun. And there, in the crowd swaying without dancing, the tight suits in dark colors, the loose drapes of rich textured fabrics, lamés and laces, gold hoop earrings and sculpted bodies, I saw Jorn Pelledeau again. He had left *Vice* by then. He was with MSNBC, I think. Our gazes crossed each other's, recognition immediately swallowed by our mutual acknowledgment that we didn't matter to each other. I had won. I didn't need stories anymore. I already had the girl and the money. Media, in its petty Götterdämmerung, was of the least possible concern to me anymore. I loved the times I had been given to live in. I wanted to gamble more.

That night I learned about Lee Taggart's death in the poker room of the Borgata, where a bank of distracting screens conveniently flashed financial news alongside horse and dog races. He died in chains, lashed to a cage in 15 Central Park West. Apparently at Taggart's request, a rent boy had beat and choked him to unconsciousness, and then accidentally to death.

The police never even charged the hustler. After all, the victim owned the cages.

I was given my last look at the Wylies the day after Halloween. They were in the crowd I was struggling against on my way to the subway. A few stores were putting up Christmas decorations, and Christmas in SoHo is the ultimate proof, if proof were necessary, that love is not enough. There must be spending money, too. Anna Savarin, in the frosty glory of an ivory cashmere coat, radiated. Beside her, a bounding bright boy ran from window to window. She tried to rein him in as he scampered from her grip for glimpses of the world's magnificent stuff. His eyes glimmered with curiosity and defiance, his messy hair and his face dusty from already forgotten adventures—a fighter, a boy after my own heart, with a soul for any fate. I thought of my father as a boy. I thought of myself as a boy. If we could scrape away what time does to men, we would love every boy. If we could wash away the grime, the boy would be waiting at the beginning, full of greed indistinguishable from hope. Max's mother watched the tender futility of his animal self with sorrowful eyes. She knew: We get what we want and then it destroys us.

All in a moment, mother and son drifted into the keen consuming crowd. Their vision passed from me. I'm no Communist: It seemed perfectly logical that the profit from the labor of tens of thousands would fall to them.

It hadn't yet snowed by mid-November, so I flew up to visit my mother again. Who could say when a sudden storm would render the road from Edmonton impassable?

On the way up I stopped at the Legislature Building in Edmonton to see the floors my great-grandfather laid. The Cabots were originally the Cabottos, until Ellis Island, and Cabottos were marble workers for generations before my grandfather insisted his sons graduate from high school. They came from Lucca, a miraculously unbombed Italian town whose cathedral floors are a UNESCO World Heritage Site, today covered in Plexiglas for the tourists' inspection, far too beautiful to be walked on. I suppose I should be proud of this heritage. In the 1990s, while all my friends were discovering their ethnicities—the Jews upping their quotient of Yiddishisms, the Irish tattooing shamrocks on their asses—I could never be bothered with my Italianness. I figured that my ancestors came to the New World for good jobs and a chance at a family and an old age in which they could drink themselves comfortably to death, not so I could be proud of some shitheel village they'd abandoned. Patriotism is not a family trait: Our true tribe is the human dust blown from every continent—the Italians, the Chinese, the Jews, the Greeks, the peripatetic Russians and Indians. We belong to that mongrel messiness that has no name and no flag.

Perhaps the men and women who know how to make things are obsolete. Perhaps the whirlwind of numbers will sweep their skills away. Nonetheless, I was proud of the floor of the Legislature. If there had not been a janitor mopping, wondering what the hell I was looking at, I might well have lain down on its simple pattern of black-and-white squares, spread myself like some initiate.

When I drove out of Edmonton the fall light was distant and intense, the sun farther away yet its heat somehow closer, less muted. The air is so crisp in an Alberta autumn that to pass from light to shadow is to skip from midsummer to midwinter in an instant. Northern Alberta is my country but it is not my home. It is nobody's home. The original tribe that lived in this place was the Beaver. Before conquest, somewhere around two thousand of them hunted and fished the whole of the Peace River basin, and even they stuck to the water, hardly ever venturing onto the hard lands beyond. When the paleo-people arrived in the new world, a world new thirty thousand years ago, their hunger poured down the continent, past vista after vista of infinite dangerous promise, but they looked at this country and passed by. They knew that humanity would find no welcome here. What I see and what the Beaver saw are the same: A place of no habitation and no name. Two hours outside of town, I pulled up on a pair of black wolves as they feasted on the carcass of a roadkill doe. They looked up as I rolled down the window, kept feasting, but after a few minutes of glut, they jogged away, looking back and then running, looking back and then running. Wolves are wilder than other wild things. They have refused civilization. I remembered my father. His smiling assurance: Fathers shepherd their children away from the pointlessness, the basic irrelevance of life, and then they die, leaving their sons shivering in the emptiness, just when we most need the warm cover of their deceit.

Only when dinner was on the table—crispy lake trout and wild rice with sweet crusty black bread—did I remember the anniversary. My father had died in late November. We were eating his favorite meal. From the steam-cleaned earthiness of the smell, I was carried back to eating with my father at nine-thirty at night fresh from shooting a fourteen-point buck in Stellerton; I was once again at Nobu eating grilled maitake and a raft of tuna with an editor from the *Times*, bread and butter in a market in Berlin, and then back again at the orderly table of my mother.

"A simple meal feeds simple people," she said.

"I'm not sure how simple I am anymore, Mom. My divorce went through last week."

I hadn't told her about Kate and Sigma. I wasn't sure what I had to tell. She forked an asparagus tip with a few grains of rice and a bit of fish. She always ate things mushed together. "Where do you think you'll go now?" she asked. The pleasant thought that I was going nowhere suffused me. Before I could answer, the arrow of her gaze straightened to the window. For a moment I saw my mother the way she must have looked as a small child, my mother before duty. "The snow," she said.

Outside very fine, very small flakes were beginning to sweep grandly down through the orange cone of the front porch light. She stood up from the table and shuffled in her sock feet to the window.

"It's always like this at first," she said, wondering. "A few big flakes but when I see them I can already see the snow covering everything, can't you?"

"The snow's well overdue," I said.

She stared awhile, then looked away, which always meant more than anything she said. "It's a new start for everybody."

*   *   *

The wispy clouds, vague as suspicion, interrupted the huge silver moon that rose like a fin-de-siècle postcard as I strolled after dinner into its bland glare. Now that I was certain I wouldn't have to leave New York, I could cherish the childhood fear that the dark wild creates. There were still anxieties about the situation. I had seen in Kate's eyes before I left, the fluttering of a doubt, though about what I couldn't say. I was confident I could deal with the situation. Even if Kate turned against me, her daughter loved me too much. I was part of the family now. I belonged.

The Wylie cottage was neat, and the first sight of its massy stones lingered in the smooth vapor of evening. The stars were rising. I sat on a boulder near the edge of one of the Wylies' lakes. The cold was settling in, drifting from the north. Happiness, surprising and urgent, rose to my throat. Was it the certainty about New York? Was it the moon? My father's black bread? My mother's sighting of the first snow? Say I was happy by constellation. A constellation is the light of stars removed by hundreds of millions of light-years striking the eye at the same instant.

Beyond the Wylie's cottage, the wilderness sloped away in the darkness like mist.

If I were stronger, I would have headed out into that infinite cold, into the vastness where a man can howl properly. Instead I turned back to the quiet, well-lit house of my mother.

ACKNOWLEDGMENTS

Jofie Ferrari-Adler delivered this book to the world with Jonathan Karp and PJ Mark and Jennifer Lambert beside him, and I am grateful to all of them for their care and their concern and their intelligence and their skill and their judgment and their ability to deal with money. For other kinds of help: Julian Porter, Bob Fulford, John Honderich, James Frey, David Granger. For all of the above and everything else: Sarah Fulford.

ABOUT THE AUTHOR

Stephen Marche is a novelist and culture writer. For the past five years he has written a monthly column for *Esquire* magazine, "A Thousand Words About Our Culture," which in 2011 was a finalist for the ASME National Magazine Award for Commentary. He also writes regular features and opinion pieces for *The Atlantic*, *The New York Times*, *The Wall Street Journal*, *The New Republic*, and elsewhere. His books include two novels, *Raymond + Hannah* and *Shining at the Bottom of the Sea*, as well as a work of nonfiction, *How Shakespeare Changed Everything*. He lives in Toronto with his wife and children.